AN UNEXPECTED DEATH

A Caitlyn Jamison Mystery

Mary E. Maki

M. E. Maki

Copyright © 2015 by Mary E. Maki

Visit the author at www.CaitlynJamisonMysteries.blogspot.com

Published in the United States by Mary E. Maki

ISBN-13: 978-1518778155
ISBN-10: 1518778151

'

Cover photo by Richard Welch, Cayuga Images
Author photo by Raymond Maki

Printed in the United States of America

This book is dedicated to my friend and writing partner, Andrea Zimmermann, who encouraged me all the way to the finish line.

~ The Event ~

Friday Afternoon

Barn chores provided an escape from the confines of school, the forced discipline of team practice, and the pressure of parental expectations. It wasn't easy being a teenager. He wished time would rush by so he could be off to college. He was going to study urban planning at an Ivy League school after which he would create eye-pleasing environmentally sensitive landscapes.

And that is how he got involved in the environmental movement. The scars the oil drilling sites left upon the landscape were ruining towns all over the northeast. He had talked with some of his classmates and they had formed a group to be proactive in ridding these rigs from their backyard. They didn't want oil rigs in or around Riverview. He smiled as he thought about another evening out with his comrades in arms. Their cause was righteous and one day they would go down in history.

He rubbed his temples to relieve the beginning of a mild headache due to the coming storm. This was but a minor annoyance, because he enjoyed storms, especially when he was in the barn while Mother Nature spent her rage on the outside world. Maybe this would happen today.

The earthy smells of spring always awakened his senses, the green buds appearing on the trees, the colors of spring flowers, the creaking of barn boards warmed by the sun, and of course listening to the first harbinger of spring, peepers.

In the barn he was free to be himself and he enjoyed its particular effect on his senses. The perfectly dried hay was stacked in the loft above. No chance of fire in this barn from hay baled before it was ready. The oat bin's grainy scent welcomed him as he scooped up a handful.

Rudy heard him enter and uttered a soft whimper, awaiting the treat he knew was coming. Todd put out his hand so Rudy's warm moist nostril could search for every last grainy nugget. Todd buried his nose in the soft neck loving Rudy's smell of fur and leather. Spending time with Rudy was the best and Todd knew any confidences he shared with his horse would be kept. He stroked the Quarter Horse's soft neck and told Rudy about his day. Suddenly, Rudy's neck muscles tightened. Todd turned to see what was upsetting the horse.

"What're you doing here?" Todd asked. He could barely see the outline of the person through the shadows, but he suspected who it was and the reason for the visit. He didn't have the time or inclination to indulge this person in conversation. Todd turned his back and continued to stroke Rudy's neck.

"I want you to stop," a voice demanded.

"Ha. You must be kidding," Todd responded.

He turned his attention back to Rudy, then laughed again, just to make the point and bring Rudy into the conversation.

Except for Rudy's murmurs, there was silence. Todd wondered if his unwanted visitor had left.

As he started to turn to see if he was alone, a silver flash crossed his peripheral vision, striking his head with a deadly blow.

~ ONE ~

Sheriff Ethan Ewing was tired. It had been a long week and now the switchboard was swamped regarding the forecast for "Nor'easter Anna," yet another "storm of the century." How many of those could there be?

Why did weather people need to name storms?

This was the first major spring storm, so the naming pattern reverted back to the first letter of the alphabet.

Why did Riverview residents think the sheriff's office had all the answers?

All he knew was he was tired and ready for the weekend.

The storm was coming on the heels of one of the hardest winters in memory. There had been rain, ice, snow, and more ice. Homeowners had spent hours on ladders chipping away at ice dams only to be faced with thousands of dollars of damage to their homes. The record snow and the unusually warm spring weather caused a melt that swelled the river's level to an all time high; neither the land nor the river could absorb another drop.

A drenching April rain with high winds was predicted, producing fear of flooding and more power outages. Not knowing where else to go for information, everyone called the sheriff's office. Should they evacuate? What happens if the power goes out for long periods? Ethan knew if the authorities predicted the worse case scenario, people panicked. If the storm was played down and someone got hurt, lawsuits were guaranteed. It was a no-win situation.

To add to the stress, there were people in town who didn't think a thirty-five year old sheriff could do the job. They were used to a more "mature" presence, and someone from Upstate, and they weren't shy about letting him know. He had thought his experience as a New York City police officer would have gained him some stature here, but apparently not. He was getting tired of the comments and wondered if he was the right fit to be sheriff of Riverview, New York.

Ethan's experience had trained him to keep an ear to the switchboard, so the incoming call caught his attention and his instincts kicked in. He listened as Maddie, his dispatcher, asked the pertinent questions, and then turned and announced in her fast-clipped accent, "Sheriff, Myra Tilton's on the line; says Todd's hurt, but won't give details. She's called the Doc, wants you to come. Told 'er if her son was hurt, the sheriff don't need to drive out, but you know Myra, she don't listen."

"Not Myra again, not tonight," sighed Ethan. "We've a storm coming. We'll be going all weekend."

Deputy Tom Snow, who was working the counter, turned and said, "Boss, want me to drive out there? It'll probably take a few minutes, and you can get home and get some rest. We don't know how many calls we're going to get during the night. Might as well get some shuteye when you can."

Tom Snow was fresh out of police academy and was anxious to please. So far Ethan was impressed with Tom's work ethic. He was a handsome young man, just under six feet tall, brown wavy hair, and striking blue eyes. No wonder women's heads turned when he walked through town in his crisp blue uniform.

Ethan heaved a sigh and glanced at the clock. He gave himself a once over making sure that his uniform looked professional, belt straight, shirt tucked in tight. His hand hovered briefly over his car keys before he grabbed the keys to the patrol car.

"Thanks for the offer, Tom, but I'd better go. You stay here and help Maddie with the switchboard."

This was not the first time he had been summoned to the Tilton's for an "emergency." The last time was when Myra experienced an anxiety attack, probably caused by starting her cocktail hour a bit early. Who could blame her, married to banker Jerry Tilton?

Ethan thought about the first time he met Jerry Tilton. When Ethan arrived in town he didn't know if he should rent or buy. He had made an appointment with Jerry Tilton to talk about a loan.

Jerry's thin frame and pointed nose reminded Ethan of Ebenezer Scrooge, and maybe that was an appropriate persona for a banker. By the end of their conversation, it was evident Jerry, speaking for the bank, wasn't interested in securing a mortgage with such a small down payment. Jerry suggested Ethan rent something until he could get a feel for the area and build up some more savings. Ethan took that advice and found a small bungalow near the lake in which he was able to work a rent to own deal.

~

Within minutes Ethan was on Riverview Heights Road where the Tilton's home was located. He turned into the Tilton's driveway, and not seeing Myra or Doc Morse's car, he drove towards the barn. If there'd been an accident, most likely it occurred there. He peeked into the barn; everything was quiet.

He heard a dog barking in the house.

Could they be in the house?

He then heard Myra's voice coming from behind the barn. He hurried around the building.

Myra was kneeling in the high grass. The fading afternoon light accentuated the highlights in her medium length brown hair that now fell across her face, a face that now appeared older than her fifty-something years. Her perfectly manicured nails were covered with dirt and blood.

Myra was rocking back and forth holding the head of her sixteen-year-old son. She was talking softly and imploring him to respond. She held his head with one hand while stroking his face with the other.

Ethan knelt down next to her, noting the blood on her clothes. He took Todd from her and saw the deep cut on the side of the boy's head. As Todd was transferred from his mother to the sheriff, Ethan discreetly placed two fingers against the soft flesh of Todd's throat to check for a pulse. There was none.

"Myra, let me hold Todd while you wait for Doc. Send him right back. And then go to the house and call your husband. Oh, and don't let the dog out."

I can't have a dog running all over the crime scene and I don't want to be the person to tell Myra her son is dead. Let Doc Morse do that.

Mascara smudges trickled down Myra's cheeks as she numbly obeyed his instructions. Rounding the corner of the barn she collided with the doc. Unable to speak, she pointed to where Ethan was holding Todd.

Ethan looked down at the handsome young man who had met an untimely death. What evil had presented itself in this sleepy Upstate New York town? What happened here this afternoon? He had no answer.

Out of the corner of his eye he detected movement. Ethan froze, his breathing stopped. Speeders and shoplifters he could deal with, but what frightened him most were snakes, and there was one coming towards him from under the barn and through the tall grass.

Just then Doc Morse arrived, dropping his heavy black bag with a thump on the ground. The startled snake slithered back towards the barn. Ethan let out a sigh of relief. Doc Morse, nearing retirement, was still agile enough to kneel quickly so he could examine the body. He rose, a little more stiffly, and gave Ethan a nod to confirm what they both knew.

Sotto voce he said, "This was no accident."

~ TWO ~

Caitlyn Jamison tucked her shoulder length hair behind her ears as she watched the cursor blink on the computer screen. A quick glance at the top right corner of the same screen showed the digits turn to 5:00 P.M. Her workweek *should* be over, but the photos taken early this morning for The Outdoor Foundation's annual report, due Monday, remained to be downloaded. She ate another handful of potato chips, checked the phone and listened to the messages. Two clients needed to speak with her.

Nick had not called back.

Her morning's work had been successful. Hitting the road early, driving against the eastbound Route 66 commuter traffic, she reached Virginia's rural countryside by 8:00 A.M. She found a back road and drove until she found the perfect spot that provided a view of verdant rolling pastures with far off vistas of the Blue Ridge Mountains. They were perfect visuals to intersperse into the foundation's report. Her early arrival provided an opportunity for close-up shots of leaves still sparkling with early morning dew. An inner peace always settled over her on these photo shoots.

Halfway back to Washington her cell phone emitted the tune of Stevie Wonder's *I Just Called to Say I Love You*, the ring tone she assigned to Nick. Before she had started photographing this morning, Caitlyn had put the phone in her many-pocketed camera bag and forgot to take it out. She pulled over as fast as she could. By the time she dug the phone out of her bag, it stopped ringing. The call was identified as "missed."

~

Two years ago when Caitlyn was thirty years old, she left a lucrative position in a New York City graphics design firm to start her own graphic design business in Washington, DC. She felt the corporate environment and the claustrophobic cubicle assigned to her had stifled her creativity; she needed a change.

Caitlyn also needed a change to cover another failure in her life. Her breakup with Roger was nasty. He was controlling and wouldn't leave her alone. She thought about a restraining order to keep him from her doorstep, but the fact they worked in the same building made the situation difficult. Her best option was to escape.

Years of frugal living allowed her to escape, but she quickly realized she hadn't put away quite enough to cover the cost of living in Washington. When an affordable efficiency apartment in a renovated military base housing complex near Arlington Cemetery became available, Caitlyn grabbed it. The space served as her office while her plan of a downtown office was put on hold.

She worked hard to build a client base and now made enough to meet expenses with a little left over. The downside of running a business from home meant clients had 24/7 access through email and cell phone. She didn't mind now, but there would come a time when she would want time away from work.

And, Caitlyn hadn't planned on Nick Spaulding. They had met in December at a holiday party hosted by one of her clients. She had noticed him right away. He was handsome, about six feet tall, give or take an inch, with dark wavy hair, expensive cut, and from his taunt muscles and thin figure she knew he must work out regularly. She didn't want to be melodramatic, but all she could think of was his smooth complexion, set off by his dark hair made him look like a Roman god. Just thinking about him made her tingle inside.

It wasn't long before he was by her side, and during that evening she was happy to learn that he wasn't married, he had a great sense of humor, and before the evening was over, he asked if he could see her again.

Since then they hadn't had the opportunity to spend much time together. His travel schedule seemed to be unending.

On their first date Nick explained he worked for New York's Senator McConnell. The senator chaired several committees, which required Nick to travel, sometimes with the senator, and sometimes on his own. When Nick was on special assignment, they wouldn't have much contact so Caitlyn took advantage of the time working nights and weekends getting her business up and running.

Nick was an enigma. He never really talked *about* his work, the people he met, or the issues he covered. His information was always vague. She knew Washington was a town of secrets, but she didn't feel she was any kind of threat. She knew how to keep a confidence and she thought he would know that by now.

She sat back and continued to stare at the blinking cursor. How much did she *really* know about Nick Spaulding? Supposedly he was on assignment in China, but he hadn't contacted her, either by email or text since he left two weeks ago. And now the missed call.

Damn!

~

Caitlyn jumped at the sound of her cell phone. She didn't recognize the area code, but thinking it to be an anxious client, she thought, *might as well answer it. I have nothing else to do this weekend.*

Caitlyn gently touched the connect icon and said, "This is Caitlyn."

She heard a sob, then a whispered voice.

"Hello?" Caitlyn said again, this time louder.

"Caitlyn, it's . . . Aunt Myra. Caitlyn, Todd's been murdered."

~ THREE ~

Jerry Tilton was trying his best to focus on what Anna Jones was telling him about why she needed a business loan. Anna was what the locals called "born here," apparently a term that gave one a higher status in the community. Anna had come to the bank because she considered herself an entrepreneur and wanted to start a business selling notions. Jerry inquired what exactly were "notions," and Anna was only too happy to go into a lengthy description of her plans. She would sell bolts of cloth, needles, thread, yarns in all colors and textures, buttons, patterns, and before she could continue, Jerry held up his hand.

"Thank you, Anna. I understand now. Sewing items," Jerry said curtly.

"Oh, and much more," Anna said as she moved around in her seat. She took a breath to continue. She wanted to share the news with everyone.

"Thank you. I get the idea. What a nice addition to the town a store like this will make," Jerry said interrupting her once more and trying to keep the annoyance out of his voice.

The last thing we need is a notions store. There isn't enough population to support it. And isn't sewing a thing of the past?"

Jerry knew two things about Anna: She was hard working and would put her all into the business, and more importantly, she was part of the wealthy and influential Jones family.

Impeccably dressed in a dark blue suit offset by white blouse with a hint of a collar, Anna's hands remained in her lap through her explanation, which impressed Jerry. He hated that most people, especially women, motioned with their hands as they talked. But not Anna; she was most prim and proper, stating her financial status, budget, and projected earnings. She had explained she wanted this to be her own venture and not use her inheritance money.

Jerry went through the appropriate procedures and then watched Anna leave the bank with loan papers in hand. He would play the supportive role because every vote would count when election time came. He was destined for bigger and better things, and the support of the Jones family would help.

~

But right now Jerry's adrenalin was running high, and his mind wasn't on bank loans or a notions store. Prior to Anna's appointment he met with two men from a financial institution in New York City. The plan they presented was almost too good to be true. In ordinary circumstances he knew it would not be possible, but with the backing of the powerful political and financial figures they named, the plan was failsafe. In the meantime he would control his attitude toward the people in this town. His future as the next state senator was at stake and he would need their votes.

The plan the men proposed was for Jerry to be the next president of one of the largest Wall Street firms. After certain critical accounts were put in place, he would be nominated for Senator Smith's seat in November. Senator Smith had recently announced serious health issues were forcing him to step down. With the existing powerbase in Albany, Jerry didn't need to do a thing except follow orders given by the senior senators. His dreams were about to come true. The men told him he had two days to make a decision; he needed two seconds, long enough to inhale and exhale.

The answer was yes.

The shrill ring of his private line made him jump. He pulled a handkerchief from his suit coat pocket and wiped his brow. He picked up the phone. "Tilton here," was all he needed to say. He listened carefully to the voice on the other end of the line and the only words he uttered were, "yes" and "o.k." When the call from Albany ended, he carefully returned the handset to its cradle. He again wiped the sweat from his face and tried hard to control his breathing. His heart was racing.

He glanced at the clock across the room that told him the bank was closing for the day.

As he started to pack his briefcase his secretary buzzed him and said, "Mr. Tilton, your wife's on the phone."

~ FOUR ~

Friday Evening

Ethan watched as Doc Morse walked Myra to the house. She had come running back out after she called her husband. Doc met her before she could reach Todd and gave her the devastating news. He gently put his arm around her shoulders and pointed her back towards the house.

The wind was getting stronger and the storm's first raindrops hit Ethan's face. He needed to hurry if he was going to gather evidence.

He grabbed the evidence bag from the car and jogged back to the crime scene. He set up a secure perimeter, then took out his small notebook and quickly jotted down every detail from the time of the 911 call, a time he remembered well since he was about to leave for the day.

He noted his time of arrival, the position of the body, and the fact Myra was holding her son. The crime scene had been contaminated by her, as well as by him and Doc Morse, but it couldn't be helped. Obstructing evidence further was the tall grass and general untidiness inherent at the back of any barn.

Ethan pulled out his digital camera and took photos from every angle. Between the setting sun and the approaching storm, light was disappearing fast. He knew time was of the essence. He clicked away. Better to take too many photos than not enough. He stopped every so often to jot down more notes. He would need those when the culprit went to trial.

He reached down and searched Todd's pockets. He knew a teenager would carry a cell phone. Ethan found the phone in the front right pocket of Todd's jeans. He checked to see if it was on, and it was.

He grabbed a Faraday bag and slipped the phone inside. The Faraday would protect the phone and keep it from receiving any network signals. If Todd's killer was sophisticated, a delete data signal could be sent to the phone. Ethan did not want to risk it. He would grab the phone's power cord when he searched the house.

Ethan greeted the funeral director with a nod indicating the body could be removed. As the body was being wheeled away, Ethan cringed as a loud clash of thunder sounded right overhead.

~

Doc Morse came back to stand by Ethan's side.

"Myra's in the house. I got her a cup of tea. Jerry should arrive shortly. I can't imagine who would want to harm Todd."

Doc paused, looking around before continuing his report.

"I estimate the time of death between 3:00 and 4:30 p.m. The deep cut in Todd's skull probably caused immediate death, but I won't know for sure until I do the autopsy."

Ethan nodded as he jotted down the information the doc provided. This was going to be a difficult case given the young victim and the paucity of evidence. He checked his watch, 6:00. Maddie was still on duty. He pulled out his cell phone, touched "Favorites," then "Dispatcher." When she answered, Ethan said, "Maddie, Todd's been murdered."

"What? Can't be! He's a good kid. Sheriff, that's horrible," Maddie took a breath.

Maddie was always the professional, so her outburst surprised him. He knew she left unsaid the fact the Tiltons were an important family in town. Jerry played the hail fellow well met persona very well, but Ethan knew he could be obdurate in his business dealings. Jerry Tilton's powerful friends could make Ethan's life difficult if he was unable to bring Todd's murderer to justice, and quickly.

Justice was probably not the right term for this situation, he thought, *Jerry Tilton will demand revenge.*

"Maddie, notify the state police. They may need to get involved if our assailant has left the area. I'll have more information after I've had a chance to go over the crime scene."

14

While listening to Maddie, Ethan noticed two men quickly packing up their van parked alongside the road. They looked like surveyors. He wondered if they really were and if so what was Jerry Tilton planning for the property. It was a lovely piece of land, half field and half forest. He knew the town residents wished it would stay as it was, preserved as a recreation and wildlife area. Ethan suspected Jerry Tilton didn't care much for preservation.

Holding the phone to his ear, he started walking towards the surveyors, hoping to catch them before they drove off, but he was only able to capture the license number as they sped away.

"Sheriff, storm warnings are dire." Maddie continued. "Counties south of us have power lines down. Jeff's here to relieve me at the consol. Tom said he would stick around a while longer. They're telling everyone to get home."

As Maddie talked, wind-driven raindrops, like small chards of glass, slashed the side of Ethan's face. The rain was destroying the crime scene. He had to finish his work fast.

"Got to go if I'm to collect evidence. Fill Jeff and Tom in on what happened. And remember, nothing to the press," Ethan warned.

He ran back to the car for his spotlight. The tall grass behind the barn would make the search difficult, but it had to be done and quickly. Assuming the position of someone looking for a contact lens he combed the area with his fingers.

The grass behind the barn was about six inches high and showed foot traffic patterns. He couldn't tell which were Todd's, which were the killer's, Myra's, Doc Morse's, or the two men from the funeral home. He wondered if the murder was committed where the body was found or did it take place inside the barn and the body ended up outside as Todd tried to escape his attacker.

The patterns on the grass near the back door indicated two people had exited. Did someone surprise Todd while he was working in the barn? Had Todd lunged for the door, or did the killer drag him out? Was the weapon in the barn or did the killer bring it?

And what possible motive?

15

He systematically worked on his hands and knees from where the body was found. He combed the tall grass and fought his fear of the snake as he went about his search. His fingers touched an object. Carefully picking it up, he sat back and studied what he'd found. It was a pin with some sort of symbol on it; a symbol he didn't recognize. Was this pin something the killer dropped or was it here for a long time? He needed to examine it closer, in better light.

Along with the blood swabs, he secured the rest of what he had collected. The rain became steadier and streamed down into his eyes. There was no time for an evidence ruler photo, so he turned and raced back to the car just as torrential rain fell soaking him to the bone.

Ethan placed the evidence bag in the car, putting the Faraday bag holding the pin into his pocket.

Torrential rain or not, before he headed to the house to talk with the parents, he had to search the barn. He pushed the heavy door aside and entered the area. He heard the horse moving around, the storm was probably upsetting the animal. With flashlight in hand, Ethan surveyed the layout. He noticed the back door wasn't far from the horse's stall.

What was the sequence of events, and is the murder weapon still here?

Scanning the light along the wall he saw a number of items that fit. Those items had to be gathered this evening. He made another call to the office, this time Jeff was at the dispatch consol.

"Jeff, ask Tom to come to the Tilton's barn and secure anything that could be used as a weapon. He'll need a number of large evidence bags."

"Right, sheriff," Jeff said. "I'll let him know."

When he was through in the barn, Ethan drove as close to the house as possible. He had to talk with the Tiltons, as painful as it might be. He rushed onto their covered porch and softly knocked.

Jerry Tilton, his face pale, eyes red, answered the door. A little white dog barked at his heels. Jerry seemed annoyed by the animal as he let Ethan in, and motioned him to follow. Jerry quickly returned to his wife and held her tight as she sobbed into his shoulder. Ethan knew what a hard-hitting businessman Jerry Tilton was, but here at home, at least tonight, he presented a different persona.

How many of us do that when the demands of professional life force us to adopt a certain personality in order to do our jobs? Sometimes the professional personality is not who we really are, and if the switch back in the home environment doesn't happen when the office door is closed, relationships suffer; families suffer.

"I know this is a difficult time, and I apologize, but I have to show you something." Ethan held up the Farraday bag containing the pin.

Jerry and Myra looked at the bag with a questioning expression.

"Sorry, Sheriff, but we've never seen it before," Jerry Tilton responded after getting affirmation from his wife. "Do you think it has something to do with Todd's murder?"

"I can't say, sir, but I'm going to consider it a lead for now. We're calling in the state police and are doing whatever it takes to find this person. Anything you can remember might be the clue we need."

When the couple didn't respond, Ethan continued, "I'll leave you for now, but I'll need to talk with you again tomorrow. Would afternoon be convenient?"

Jerry nodded.

"Is there anyone we can contact for you?"

Ethan knew it was an unnecessary question as the Tiltons were capable of contacting whomever they wanted without assistance, but it was the right thing to say in the circumstances.

"No, no one, thank you Sheriff. Now if you don't mind, I need to get Myra some tea. Doc Morse left a sedative that will allow her to sleep. I doubt I'll get any."

~ FIVE~

Saturday Morning

Ethan woke early Saturday morning to a dripping sound.

That can't be good, he thought as he lay in his warm bed.

He fought the temptation to roll over and go back to sleep since he didn't get much during the night. The wind and rain pounding against the house didn't allow for much rest, and neither did his worry about the murder of Todd Tilton.

He should get up and check out the drip. He hoped it wasn't the roof since he didn't have time to deal with repairs. Although he was renting for now, he had the option to buy, but what he hadn't factored in was the fact he was responsible for any upkeep. That took time and money, and on a policeman's salary, he had little of each.

He did have a murder to investigate. With hands behind his head he thought about what they knew so far. Not much. The doc should be able to tell him more about the cause and time of death. He found the pin, took blood swabs, and Tom had collected the items from the barn. He prayed at least one of those items would prove fruitful.

In spite of the seriousness of the situation he chuckled. He had thought being the sheriff of Riverview was going to be a cushy assignment. He had a nice office in a small rural town populated with good country folks and a few minor infractions during the week. Now a murder investigation and the circumstances couldn't be worse—a popular kid whose father was president of the local bank. He couldn't screw this up and become a laughing stock. With that thought, he quickly threw the warm comforter aside and faced the day.

After a long hot shower he passed the full-length mirror hanging on the bedroom door. He couldn't help to notice that at thirty-five, and without much opportunity for regular exercise, he still had good muscle tone. He wished he could do something about the scar on his upper right forehead, but unless he decided to go the plastic surgery route, it would have to remain. He rubbed his hands through the blond strands of hair. Was it thinning? Something else to worry about. His stomach was still tight, but he noticed a bit of flab around his waistline. He needed to fit weight lifting into his day. That would start . . . tomorrow.

To finish his morning routine, he made coffee and spread his toast liberally with farm fresh butter.

He always waited until the last minute before putting on his uniform. He only had three and couldn't chance dripping butter on it.

In his previous job, when he worked the streets of New York, Jennie would kid him that his brown eyes didn't match the "police blue" of his uniform.

One of his Riverview uniforms was a tan shirt with dark brown pants. He wondered what she would say now about his eyes matching his outfit.

As comforting as his morning routine was, it brought back memories of mornings together with Jennie. For five years she was part of his life. Would he ever be able to move on from their marriage? The answer, so far, was no. He had not been in touch with her after she walked out four years ago. Her announcement that morning had shocked him to the core. It was at the end of the school year when she stated she was moving to Wisconsin with a friend, name withheld.

Apparently her friend had a job offer and she was sure she could find a teaching job as well. And that was it. She left and Ethan was unsuccessful in attempts to connect with her, though he admitted he didn't try very hard. He was deeply hurt by her betrayal, and his ego wouldn't allow him to go after his wife.

His life was in limbo wondering if some day she would come back, or was she gone forever. He knew she had been unhappy living in the city. She was a country girl who couldn't acclimate to city life. His job kept him away from the house for too many hours, and so he didn't appreciate the extent of her unhappiness. He knew she hated his job. She starting talking about finding herself, but he never thought she would act on it.

~

Ethan located a large pot in the kitchen pantry to catch the drips coming from the ceiling in the corner of his bedroom. With the pot in place, he pushed the curtains aside. The rain had stopped, but the sky was overcast and gloomy, and tree limbs littered his yard. He was thankful he wasn't called during the night with emergencies.

He went back to the kitchen and was finishing the last of his coffee when the phone rang. Maddie filled him in on the road conditions.

"Sheriff, a couple bridges washed out in town, but the highway crew has the roads blocked and are making arrangements for repairs. Some of the businesses in town have water damage. Shop owners are out and about surveying the damage. The fire company is going around seeing if they can be of help, pumping out basements and stuff like that. It was a bad storm, but people are saying it's not near as bad as in '35 or '72."

"Thanks, Maddie. I'll be in shortly."

Ethan climbed the stairs to his bedroom, opened his closet door and decided the blue uniform was appropriate for what he faced today.

As he locked the door to his house he stopped and thought, *what if Jennie comes back?*

~ SIX ~

When the commuter plane tipped to position itself for landing on the east side of the lake, Caitlyn caught a glimpse of the landscape that had been part of her childhood. She never intended to return to this small Upstate New York town, but her aunt's tearful phone call changed that. She was about to land back in the Finger Lakes Region for the first time since she was in high school.

Getting a flight to New York after the nor'easter pounded the east coast all Friday night and into early Saturday was almost impossible. But by late Saturday morning a seat became available on a commuter plane, and so here she was about to land.

Caitlyn had spent just four years in Riverview before her father accepted a vice president position with a large oil company. Funny, she almost forgot where they went next. There were so many moves, one faded into another. But she liked Riverview and during her time there she made good friends. Although a small town, Caitlyn appreciated that fact that Riverview had the right amount of stores, churches and social organizations. Renwick, just fifteen miles south had two colleges, which kept the county economically solvent and provided the area high school kids with various athletic events and social options.

The town was situated in the middle of the state, if an exact middle could be determined within the boundaries of a state shaped like a backward L.

Caitlyn liked Riverview because it sat along a tributary that fed into the lake below. The town fathers had had enough foresight to restrict development along the river, thereby keeping water from destroying properties built there. Instead, a park was built that featured walking paths, benches, trees and picnic tables.

The entire area was blessed with spectacular vistas created by the hills, valleys, and lakes. Residents enjoyed the rural farm community lifestyle. Tourists came for the seasonal experiences, and a certain number returned and settled in the area. All these people had one thing in common: they loved and protected Riverview's ambiance.

As the plane tipped, readying itself for landing, Caitlyn saw the lake she loved so much. It had remained in her heart no matter where she lived.

The flight attendant's announcement brought her back to reality. Her cousin had been murdered, and she was about to join her estranged family.

"Please remain in your seats until the plane is fully stopped," came the announcement.

In the "that doesn't mean me" mode seatbelts were unbuckled and belongings gathered. Everyone seemed to be in a hurry to depart the plane.

Everyone, that is, except Caitlyn.

~ SEVEN ~

The sheriff's office was bustling when Ethan arrived. Maddie was talking with the highway superintendent, while managing calls coming into the switchboard.

Madeleine Smith, or Maddie as she wanted to be called, was nothing like her birth name implied. Her short stature, curly out-of-control red hair and the most beautiful green eyes he had ever seen belied the fact she was a powerhouse.

Ethan had appreciated Maddie from the first day he met her, and he didn't know what he would do without her. She managed the front desk, the dispatch center, and handled all clerical duties. She was hardworking and dedicated, and she didn't seem to mind when she was asked to put in extra hours.

Then she started dropping hints that it might be nice to get together with him outside the office. He didn't want to destroy their good working relationship, so he made excuses as to why he couldn't. He couldn't get entangled in a relationship with someone he worked with, and Maddie didn't know he was married.

Tom was already on duty, at the counter talking to several residents who were reporting storm related problems. Ethan knew the roads were bad just from his drive into the office, but he couldn't get involved with storm related issues. There was a murder to solve.

~

Maddie waved phone messages at Ethan as he made his way to this office. He grabbed the bunch and gave her an inquiring look, which she ignored since the highway superintendent continued talking to her through the exchange.

Ethan went into his office, sat down at his desk and ignored the red blinking light on his phone. He looked at the three phone messages Maddie had given him. All were from a man named Robbie Robinson, *News5*.

Ethan wondered if this reporter was after storm damage news or if somehow he found out about Todd Tilton's murder? If it was storm damage, he could have gotten the information from Maddie or the highway superintendent. He threw two of the messages in his wastebasket and put the third message aside. He would deal with the reporter later. He got up and went to the door, motioning to get his deputy's attention.

"Tom, here are the items I collected at the Tilton crime scene. I swabbed some blood samples. They are probably Todd's, but just in case his assailant was scratched, these might be helpful. Also, there are samples the doc gathered from Todd's body. Ship these items priority overnight to Bode Cellmark Forensics in Lorton, VA. This is top priority. Then, I want you to go back through the Tilton's barn looking for possible murder weapons. Anything we might have missed last night."

"Yes, Sir," Tom replied as he shifted his weight from one side to the other, uncomfortable with the command.

"Sir, on the samples, I was told by the state police that they're to be sent to the forensics lab in Albany."

Ethan took a breath. He didn't want to lose his temper with Tom, for the young deputy was only doing what he was told.

"I don't need to remind you this isn't an ordinary case. A young man with a very influential father has been murdered. Ship off the items using my name in the 'From' line along with Riverview Sheriff's Office. I worked with Bode when I was in the city, so although they might not have a file on Riverview, my name will be in their computer," Ethan said.

"Sir, I don't mean to argue, but I don't think a private lab like Bode is in our budget," Tom said.

"Let me worry about that," Ethan replied with impatience. "Now get these things properly sent off so they have them first thing Monday."

~

Ethan arrived at the Tilton's late Saturday afternoon. He was sensitive to the family's need to make funeral arrangements, but he needed to search Todd's room and collect any evidence there. He should have done it last night, but under the circumstances, he decided the search could wait another day. Ethan knew better than to push too hard or the family will resist questioning.

He stood at their front door collecting his thoughts. The first thing learned in police academy was the family was always the first suspect in a murder investigation, a fact almost as tragic as the crime itself. Ethan took a deep breath and pushed the white rectangular button adjacent to the door, ringing a chime inside the house.

The door opened immediately, and before him stood a lovely young woman. A woman he guessed to be in her early thirties. Not who he expected to answer the door. The woman's smooth creamy skin, highlighted with a few freckles, was offset by wavy red hair.

Not red really, more mahogany, he thought. He wasn't into colors, but for some reason it was important to describe what he saw.

"Hello, Sheriff. I'm Myra's niece, Caitlyn. Please come in. Aunt Myra and Uncle Jerry are in the living room. They're expecting you."

"Caitlyn, glad to meet you. I'm Sheriff Ethan Ewing. And, yes, I'm here to talk with Mr. and Mrs. Tilton."

Why was he so tongue-tied?

Caitlyn smiled, noting his awkwardness, and said, "Let me lead the way."

The Tiltons sat next to each other on a brown leather couch, which faced the fireplace. The side chairs were arranged for easy conversation. The windows were beautifully draped, while sheer curtains allowed a subtle light to filter in.

I wonder if Myra did the decorating or was it done by a professional?

"Please sit down," Caitlyn said, pointing to one of the side chairs.

Ethan sat, but remained at the edge of his chair.

Myra and Jerry Tilton remained silent, staring into space.

"This is going to be difficult," Sheriff Ewing began, "but I have to ask where you were on Friday afternoon."

Jerry Tilton acted shocked by the question.

"What the hell does that mean? Are we suspects?"

"Mr. Tilton, this is as unpleasant for me as it is for you. I have to establish a timeline for the family in order to figure out what happened to Todd." Ethan explained.

While they gathered their thoughts, Ethan asked another question.

"Do you have any hired help? If so, I'll need to talk with them as well."

"We have a cleaning lady, Rosita. She was here on Friday. I don't know what time she left. It could have been before Todd arrived home from school. She told me she was going out of town for a few days. I don't know when she planned to return, but she promised to make up her time. I didn't pay attention to when that would be. Sorry," Myra stated as she brought a handkerchief to her face to wipe the tears.

"Does this woman have a phone?" Ethan asked.

"She does, but it isn't working right now. She dropped it and hasn't had it repaired or replaced yet. It really wasn't any of my business, since she's very punctual and I don't ever have the need to call her," Myra stated as her hands twisted the handkerchief in her lap.

"It's imperative you call me as soon as you hear from her," Ethan said.

Myra nodded indicating she understood.

Jerry stood up and paced. "I find this line of questioning outrageous. You're here bothering us when you should be out combing the neighborhood and setting up roadblocks."

Myra put her hand out to stop her husband from pacing. Ethan noted Caitlyn stood back, not wanting to insert herself into the conversation. Smart move. Jerry nodded assent to his wife's gesture and sat down in the seat he recently vacated.

26

"I was at the bank all day. My employees can verify that."

"Did you go out for lunch?"

"No. I had an unscheduled appointment. My secretary brought me a sandwich."

"Thank you, Mr. Tilton. Now, Mrs. Tilton, where were you on Friday afternoon?"

Myra hesitated, "I had a 1:00 meeting in Renwick. I picked up a few groceries and arrived home around 4:30. I put things away and went looking for Todd." Her voice broke and she sobbed. Jerry put his arm around her shoulders.

"What meeting what that, Mrs. Tilton?"

"A women's group."

Ethan sensed by her vague response and body language that there was more. He sensed Myra didn't want to explain in front of her husband so he let it go for the time being.

"Any more hired help?"

"Well, Clyde Jones. He helps with the farm work. The locals have a term for people like me, 'gentleman farmer.'" Jerry said with disgust. "I know they mean it to be derogatory, but I don't care. I like having land around me. Since I can't work the land myself, I hire a local to do it. You would think it would be a good thing in this rural community."

"Can you tell me where I can find Mr. Jones?" Ethan asked.

"He lives in the house about a mile north of here," Jerry replied.

"One more question. Can you tell me if Todd had any enemies?"

"He was a kid; of course he didn't have enemies," yelled Jerry. Up pacing again, Jerry was working himself into a rage. He turned to face the sheriff with as much control as he could muster from his trembling body.

Ethan saw Jerry's anger boiling up. He had seen this type of reaction before in other victim's family members.

This guy is used to being in control and is now facing a situation completely out of his control, thought Ethan. *At least he doesn't seem to be taking it out on his wife.*

Ethan's thoughts were interrupted by Jerry's cold measured tone, "*Sheriff,* you will find whoever did this and see that they are punished to the full extent of the law."

Ethan made no response to Jerry's demand. Realizing more information wouldn't be forthcoming, he said, "I need to see Todd's room, his computer and any other electronic equipment he owned."

Jerry Tilton rose and headed for the stairs.

Ethan nodded to the women as he followed Jerry.

At the top of the staircase they turned right and went to the end of the hall. Jerry Tilton paused with his hand on the door handle. Ethan waited. Jerry slowly turned the handle and the door opened letting muted light filter into the dark hallway.

The room's windows faced three directions and under different circumstances it would be a delightful space. Ethan took a quick look around. It was not what he thought an average teenage boy's room should look like, but then he didn't know Todd. He expected posters of rock bands to fill the walls, clothes strewn everywhere, closet doors open. Instead there was a disquieting neatness to the space.

Making mental note of his impressions, Ethan's eyes went to the desk that held Todd's laptop. He unplugged the device and carefully wrapped the cord.

At that moment he realized in his haste to leave the office, he had forgotten to refill his stock of evidence bags. He noticed an empty duffle bag near the desk.

"May I use the duffle for the computer and power cords?" Ethan asked.

"Make sure we get everything back," Jerry said stiffly.

Ethan packed the electronic equipment into the duffle. He opened each desk drawer, gently moving papers around. There didn't seem to be any other electronics, and no other items of interest. He opened the right hand drawer and found an iPad, which he tucked carefully into the duffle. He pulled out the other drawers, but didn't see anything of interest.

Ethan got down on his knees and glanced under the bed. Again he was surprised it was not filled with paraphernalia or the odd dirty sock. He checked the closet. He gave the room one more glance and decided there wasn't anything more there.

When they returned downstairs, Jerry Tilton was even more upset. More of what represented his son was being taken away.

Caitlyn came forward and suggested Ethan return another time when her aunt and uncle weren't under so much stress.

He agreed, touched the rim of his hat and said, "Ma'am, I really am sorry for your loss."

"They are devastated, as you can imagine," Caitlyn whispered.

"Yes, it's a difficult situation," said Ethan. "Will you be here long?"

"I'll need to get back to DC, but I'll stay a day or two after the funeral."

"Then we shall see each other again," stated Ethan.

"Yes," replied Caitlyn.

~ EIGHT ~

Saturday Afternoon

Caitlyn watched Ethan get into his car and drive away. It was unsettling that she had felt an immediate attraction to him. He was about her age, mid-thirties, about six feet, brown hair and brown eyes. He wasn't wearing a wedding ring, but that didn't mean anything. She noticed the small scar on his forehead and wondered where it came from. *Maybe breaking up a fight,* she thought letting her imagination roam.

She was embarrassed to feel flustered around him and the fact she had noticed some of his more intimate details. She gently closed the door and shaking off those thoughts, she went in search of her aunt.

Myra was in the kitchen pouring a gin and tonic. Caitlyn watched her aunt, noticing her features and movements. Myra was nothing like Ann, Caitlyn's mother. In fact, no family resemblance at all. While her mother was tall and slim, Myra was shorter, maybe about 5'4" and a bit on the heavy side.

I wonder what happened to cause the riff between Mom and Myra, Caitlyn thought. *Sisters should be close.*

Caitlyn wished she had a sibling, especially a sister, someone to grow up with, and someone with a shared history. Her mother never talked about her relationship with Myra and what went so terribly wrong. When Caitlyn called Ann to tell her about Todd's death, her mother said they wouldn't be able to come north for the funeral. They would send flowers. Caitlyn was devastated that her mother was not going to make the effort to come to New York.

~

Sensing someone behind her, Myra turned, "Want a G&T?"

30

"No thanks," replied Caitlyn, "maybe a glass of wine later."

Myra remained at the counter looking out into the back yard. Caitlyn approached her aunt, hesitated a bit about the intimacy, but then put her arms around her.

"Oh Caitlyn, I'm so glad you're here," sobbed Myra.

Caitlyn held her aunt and let her cry, carefully wiping away her own tears. She wondered how long she could stay to help Myra get back on her feet. She'd planned ahead and brought her laptop. She could work from anywhere, at least for a short while.

~

As Myra sobbed, Caitlyn dealt with her own grief, something she had been too embarrassed to share. Maybe it was best to get it out in the open, and maybe if she did it would stop haunting her.

"Aunt Myra, I have something to tell you," Caitlyn whispered.

Myra tensed. She couldn't handle any more bad news, but she sensed something was bothering her niece, and it was best to get it out and over with.

"Let's go sit down," Myra suggested, grabbing her drink.

Myra led Caitlyn to a small sitting room that lent itself to intimate conversation.

Caitlyn sat next to her aunt, took her hand and explained, "Todd called me several weeks ago and left a message. He said something about a project he was involved with and wanted input. At the time I was facing several work deadlines, and since Todd and I weren't close, I didn't think it necessary to return his call right away. I was very busy." It was no excuse, and it didn't make her feel any better.

She remembered thinking, *if he was trying to get last minute help on some school project he had put off, then let him pay the price of procrastination.*

Myra listened and sighed, "We all have our regrets, don't we?"

Caitlyn continued. "Later, curiosity got the better of me and I checked him out on Facebook. I enjoyed seeing the family photos Todd had put on his page, and reading the blurbs he wrote. Through Facebook I finally felt a connection to him. Just as I was going to give him a call, I had a client emergency and then just forgot."

If I had talked with Todd, could I have, in some way, prevented his death? Whatever "project" he was involved in, could it mean others might still be in danger? How was she going to deal with this guilt?

Caitlyn pulled herself back to the job at hand.

"Let's go out to the sun porch and make a list of what needs to be done."

She believed working through the details of what needed to be done over the next few days would help them both with their grieving.

Caitlyn stood up, took her aunt's hand and led her to the small glass enclosed porch.

Sitting next to Myra brought the reality of their family's dysfunction to her. She was the absent cousin. She'd never tried to get to know Todd. The estrangement of Myra and her sister had put a wall between the two families. The next generation, Caitlyn and Todd, didn't have the time or opportunity to make amends, and she was not there for him when he needed her.

Caitlyn decided she would not sit still. She would find Todd's killer, and in the process she would correct the dysfunction this family had lived with for so long. Although it was years since she was last in Riverview, she thought she knew this town better than the sheriff. She would develop a plan, one in which she hoped the sheriff would not interfere. She would find out who killed her cousin.

Lost in her thoughts she did not hear her uncle enter the sitting room.

"What are you two doing?" asked Jerry.

Caitlyn heard the impatience in his voice so she was careful with her response. He was a difficult man to deal with in the best of times and this was not the best of times.

"We're just taking a break, Uncle Jerry. Want to join us?" Caitlyn replied before Myra could tell her husband anything different.

"Absolutely not! I'll be in my study. I have a number of calls to make and I don't want to be disturbed."

As soon as he left the room, Todd's little white Shih Tzu, Summit, jumped up and plopped down next to Caitlyn. It was comforting to have a warm fuzzy body next to her. She suspected it was a comfort to Summit as well. He needed to find another person in which to be alpha, and he picked Caitlyn. She didn't mind. She reached down and stroked the soft floppy ears. She suspected this little furry ball would become her best friend.

Myra looked at the dog, now snuggled next to Caitlyn.

"I think he has finally found his soul mate," Myra said.

"What do you mean? I thought he was Todd's dog."

"Actually, he's a rescue I brought home one day. Not exactly a teenage boy's sort of dog, now, is he?" Myra said. "Todd was an animal lover, so of course he was good to Summit. But I didn't sense a real connection between the two of them. Not like I feel now."

Caitlyn looked down at the dog sleeping peacefully beside her with new appreciation, now knowing his history.

"I know Shih Tzu means 'lion,'" whispered Caitlyn, "but I know you are a lamb."

The dog answered with a light snore.

"Okay, Myra, I know this won't be easy for you, but let's start with the obituary."

~ NINE ~

The first time Ethan Ewing saw the white Victorian building that housed the Riverview sheriff's office he knew this was the place for him. Inside, the polished pine counters, oak desks, and requisite gray metal filing cabinets lining the back wall provided all the essential items. His office had probably been used as a walk-in pantry when the house was built. He didn't mind the small space. All he really needed was a desk, chair and filing cabinet. Two additional small chairs for guests sat opposite, which made the space seem even smaller, but Ethan didn't plan to spend a lot of time in his office. He would be a man about town, just like he was in the city.

He liked the way Riverview's main street was lined with mature maple trees. A few evergreens were strategically placed into the landscape to give year round color.

Main Street ran perpendicular to Riverview Park. A number of Victorian style houses lined the street, some of which had been restored and utilized as town offices. The combination of quaint storefronts and municipal reuse of the houses kept Riverview's Main Street attractive and vibrant.

Ethan thought about his career that began on foot patrol in the Borough of Queens. Shop owners along his beat had welcomed him into their stores where they proudly displayed new merchandise or asked him to sample a new concoction. He didn't mind tasting all the good food to his and their delight. He knew his presence in the neighborhood was appreciated, helping to provide a safe environment for them in which to work and live. Crime was ever present in the city and his neighborhood beat wasn't immune. He had longed to be a detective in major crimes, but he had no appetite for the political games that were requisite in climbing that particular ladder.

After Jennie left he had a lot of time to think. It was then that he made the decision to leave the city, where, because of his refusal to "play the game," he knew his career was at a dead end. He would try something different, and when the position opened in Riverview he applied and got the job.

He knew working in a small town meant long and irregular hours, and that is what he faced today. A murder investigation didn't wait.

~

Ethan stopped by the morgue on his way back from the Tilton's. He knew Doc Morse, who also served as medical examiner, would be hard at work, even on a Saturday afternoon.

"Hi Doc," Ethan said as he entered the cool autopsy room.

Doc Morse had been Riverview's town doctor for over forty years, and was their only medical examiner. Ethan wondered how much longer this man would hold up under his grueling schedule.

"Oh, hi, Ethan. I didn't think I'd see you today."

"Well, you know what they say, 'no rest for the weary,'" laughed Ethan. "I've just been out to see the Tiltons."

"And how did that go?" asked Doc with a hint of sarcasm.

"Did you know they have a niece? She came up from DC when she learned of Todd's death."

Doc Morse put down his scalpel and thought.

"Yes, I do remember now. Myra's sister and husband lived here years ago. There was a daughter, and this must be the one. Kate, Catherine, something like that."

"Caitlyn," stated Ethan.

"Ah, yes. What a pretty name for a pretty girl." Doc thought some more. "You know, something happened while Caitlyn was here. I heard rumors, but then her father was hired by one of the big oil companies and they left. Whatever it was got pushed under the rug. To my knowledge the family never returned to Riverview."

Doc Morse turned back to the autopsy table where Todd was laid out.

"The lad has a deep cut on the side of his head, looks like it was made with a heavy object, which I realize isn't much help to you. Then he was hit again on the back of the head. Since he was in or near the barn your murder weapon could be any number of things. A shovel, iron rod, probably not a pitchfork."

"Could this have been done by a woman?"

"Yes, if the woman had enough strength."

"And the time of death?"

"I would say between three and four Friday afternoon. I wish I could be more accurate on the time, but I can't."

"I understand. So Todd came home from school, went to the barn to feed his horse, do whatever chores needed to be done, and either interrupted someone, or someone came into the barn and he turned to see who it was."

"The person was right handed. The wound is on the left side of the head, with an additional blow on the back. He was hit twice," added Doc.

"Thanks, Doc. Not much to go on, and I suspect evidence was lost with the storm. Our switchboard was lit up all afternoon with calls about trees down and flooded roads. The road crew has things under control, so I can concentrate on the case. I'd better get busy visiting the neighbors to see what they might know about what happened at the Tilton's on Friday afternoon."

~ TEN ~

Ethan gave the weathermen credit, though he doubted the recent Nor'easter could be considered the storm of the century. It was a powerful wind and rainstorm, powerful enough that it hindered his investigation, and he was under intense pressure to make up for lost time.

While Deputy Snow called all the survey companies in the area to find the one working on Riverview Heights Road Friday afternoon, Ethan would interview neighbors.

As he reached for his keys, Maddie was at the door.

"Sheriff, Robbie Robinson, *News5*, is here to see you."

"Not now, Maddie. I have to get on the road."

"Sorry, sheriff. He's very insistent, and I think you should give him a few minutes and a few morsels of information to get him off your back."

"You're right. Send him in," Ethan said with a sigh. He put his keys back in the top drawer and waited for the reporter to enter.

"Thanks for seeing me, Sheriff. I know you're busy with the destruction done by the storm, and then a murder on top of that. What can you tell me about your investigation?" Robbie asked.

How did this guy find out about the murder? Small town, people talk. Get used to it.

"There isn't much I can tell you at the moment," Ethan said. He paused, "Evidence has been collected, and we're coordinating with the state police. I'm sure the culprit will be caught soon. If you check in with Maddie occasionally, she'll have updated information. Now, if you excuse me, I have a murderer to catch," Ethan stated, picking up his hat, not hiding his impatience.

~

Ethan decided to talk with the Tilton's neighbor, Clyde Jones first. The highway crew had done a good job of clearing the streets of the storm's debris, but as Ethan drove out of town, the roads became more treacherous.

He was careful so as not to damage his car by driving over fallen tree branches. As he drove he radioed back a report of what he saw so the highway crew could plan their work.

He finally arrived at the house where Clyde Jones lived. As he drove into the driveway Ethan was surprised at the condition of the house. He had passed this way many times, but never paid much attention, and never thought a member of the Jones family lived there. The wood siding needed a fresh coat of paint, and some panels had green algae stains. The windows were dirty, paint was peeling on the window trim, and the house looked like a tear down.

Before he left the office he had asked Maddie to fill him in on the family.

"The Jones family is prominent in the area. Considered 'born here,'" Maddie explained. "Unfortunately, this rural town still has a caste system of sorts favoring folks with descendants here a hundred years or more. The rest of the people are 'new comers' and aren't immediately welcome into the social circles."

Maddie thought the town was changing because of the number of people moving in, but the sheriff should keep the history in mind when talking with Clyde. On the other hand, she mentioned Clyde was in trouble with the law a few times, though nothing bad. A night or two in jail for drunk and disorderly was about the worst offence.

Although he came from a well to do family, he was disavowed, or more accurately, he had distanced himself from the family. Clyde marched to a different drummer.

"I think he might have a job somewhere, besides doing hired hand work for the Tiltons."

As an afterthought, Maddie added, "Oh, and probably the most important piece of information you need to know is Clyde spent time in the Army. He was in Vietnam, came back with a bunch of strange tattoos. And he just wasn't the same person. He was always somewhat of a loner, but it got worse."

"What do you mean?" Ethan asked.

"Well, it's just hearsay, but supposedly he has nightmares and flashbacks that sometimes makes his behavior a little erratic. That's why the previous sheriff gave him a lot of slack."

Armed with Clyde's background information, Ethan took a deep breath and knocked on the door.

The door opened immediately and before him stood a tall man, over six feet, but thin. The tattoos running down his arm told Ethan this was probably Clyde Jones. Clyde was a man in his mid-sixties, graying hair in need of a cut, and from his appearance Ethan suspected Clyde probably suffered from post-traumatic stress. Though thin, Ethan noted Clyde's muscle tone and strong looking hands.

"Saw ya drive in, sheriff. What ch'ya want?" Clyde asked.

"It's nice to meet you, Mr. Jones. It is Mr. Jones?" Ethan said.

"Yea, what do ya want?" Clyde responded with more than a hint of impatience.

Ethan was not going to let Clyde take the lead. "You may have heard Todd Tilton was murdered yesterday. I'm checking with the neighbors about what they saw that afternoon."

"I ain't seen nothin'," Clyde said as he started to close the door.

Ethan placed his foot across the threshold. "I'm not done talking with you Mr. Jones. We can finish this conversation here or down at the station. I believe you are familiar with the facility?" Ethan knew this was a low blow, but his patience was already wearing thin.

Clyde remained silent, arms crossed, his expression blank as he considered his options. "O.k. what d' ya want to know?"

"I already told you what I want to know. I want to know what you saw Friday afternoon. Vehicles passing by, people walking, anything out of the ordinary," Ethan explained.

Clyde thought a minute. "I don't pay no attention to what goes on around here. Got a lot of things on my mind. And I work, you know . . . but I seen surveyors down across from the Tilton's place late Friday afternoon," Clyde said. "And I saw the tenant lady walking around her yard. It ain't unusual though. She's outside a lot. Besides, I didn't get home from work until after three."

"Where do you work?"

"I work on the oil drill, over the border in the next county."

"And your hours are?"

"I work the seven-to-three shift. If traffic ain't too bad, it takes only twenty minutes to get home."

"Thank you, Mr. Jones. Now, did you know Todd?" Ethan asked.

"Tilton hires me to do yard work and stuff around the barn, things his son should've been doing if he wants to keep that horse. And Tilton don't pay me shit if you want to know."

"Then why do you keep working for him?" Ethan asked.

Clyde hesitated, wondering how much he should tell this newcomer sheriff.

"The extra money comes in handy. My other job don't pay nuthin' either. Have to work two jobs to make a go. Otherwise, I don't have nuthin' to do with them rich people. They aren't worth my time. In fact, I wish they were all d . . ." Clyde stopped midsentence.

Ethan waited to see if Clyde had anything else to offer. Clyde's silence told Ethan all he needed to know.

"Don't plan on going anywhere. I want you right here the next time I decide to have a chat with you," Ethan instructed.

Clyde scowled. "I've been keeping myself clean lately. Don't want no more trouble with you coppers."

"Have a nice day, Mr. Jones," Ethan said as he turned to go.

~ ELEVEN ~

Ethan stood by the car to observe the house Clyde referred to as the tenant house, and if it had a clear view of the Tilton house and barn.

Before he left the office, he had asked Maddie to do some research on the people who lived there. She did her usual efficient job and handed him a slim folder of the information she had gathered.

Apparently, the Risley's had arrived a couple years ago from somewhere in the south. They were renting the old Taylor place, now belonging to the Tiltons, and the property was referred to as their tenant house. The husband, Mac Risley, farmed the land on the north side of the road. The wife, Darcy, stayed home raising the couple's son, a teenage boy named Teddy.

Ethan noticed the house was a bit run down. He thought it curious Jerry Tilton allowed a house in this condition on his property. In contrast, Ethan noticed the front door was painted a bright blue. What was that about?

Turning to capture a panoramic view of the property, he noticed except for a large blue spruce at the end of the drive, the house had a clear view down the road to the Tilton's driveway. Maybe he would catch a break here.

The blue door opened after his third knock. Before him stood a woman with mousy brown hair streaked with gray. Her expression exhibited signs of stress. Her mouth was turned down into a frown that Ethan didn't know if it was her normal look, or was it displayed just for him. The woman's dark darting eyes told him he wasn't a welcome sight. Well, he should be used to that by now.

He would question her gently until he could figure out what was going on.

She could be suffering from something as critical as abuse, or just being in the presence of a police officer, he thought. *People talked about the white coat syndrome when visiting their doctors. The same could be said about blue coat syndrome when police showed up at the door.*

"Hello Mrs. Risley, Darcy, isn't it? Sorry to bother you. I'm Sheriff Ethan Ewing. I don't believe we've met. I'm relatively new to the position."

"Hello, sheriff," said Darcy. "I suppose this is about Todd Tilton? I heard he had an accident. Is he o.k.?"

"I'm afraid not," responded Ethan. "Todd was murdered Friday afternoon."

"Oh, my, I didn't ... I didn't realize," Darcy said. Her complexion paled and she grabbed the back of a chair to steady herself.

"Are you okay?" He asked.

"Yes, fine. It's just such a shock," Darcy said.

Ethan followed Darcy into the house where he helped her to a chair.

"Please sit down Mrs. Risley. I didn't mean to break this news so abruptly. I thought everyone knew."

"We keep to ourselves, sheriff. My husband, Mac, is a farmer. He's out in the fields for long hours. I stay here and care for the house and gardens, and of course our son, Teddy. Teddy isn't well. He has a number of medical issues I have to monitor. But I take good care of him," Darcy stated with pride.

"And where is Teddy now?" asked Ethan.

"Ah, he's out with his dad. They've driven into town to pick up tractor parts," Darcy said.

"I'll need to speak with both of them as soon as possible," said Ethan. "I need to know where each of you were on Friday afternoon and what you observed. I noticed you have a good view of the Tilton's barn."

"Why, sheriff, we don't spy on our neighbors," said Darcy, with a coyness she hadn't displayed before now.

"I'm not saying you do. But in our daily activities sometimes we observe things going on around us we don't really know we've seen until someone asks us," explained Ethan. "Someone came onto the Tilton's property Friday afternoon, either before or after Todd arrived home from school. You or your husband may have seen a car or someone walking the road."

Darcy held onto the arms of the chair to keep her hands from shaking. "I don't remember seeing anything, sheriff. I spend most afternoons in the gardens behind the house and in the kitchen preparing meals and putting food by."

Ethan could tell she was nervous and wondered why. He didn't know what "putting food by" meant, but determined it must be a cooking thing.

He was presenting his kindest persona, but decided he wouldn't get much more information from her. Maybe her husband or son would be more helpful.

"Okay, thank you Mrs. Risley. Here's my card. If you think of anything about that afternoon that might be helpful, please give me a call. And ask your husband to give me a call when he returns so we can find a convenient time to talk."

Darcy took the card and nodded.

"I can see my way out," said Ethan.

As he approached his car, his thoughts wandered to Myra Tilton's niece.

~

The 1890s tenant house the Risleys rented from Jerry and Myra Tilton was small, but adequate. In fact, Darcy felt it was more than adequate. Better than the second hand trailer they had in Arkansas. She loved how the bow window summoned light into the living room and how the floor to ceiling windows defined the personality of the white two-story building. The two upstairs bedrooms were small and shared the one bath. But the rent was what they could afford and Darcy had made the house cozy. Her sewing skills weren't the best, but she was able to make simple curtains and valances, bringing warmth to the old house.

Out the kitchen door to the back of the house was a cottage garden where generations before her grew vegetables and flowers. Tending crops on twenty-five acres didn't leave her husband, Mac, time for personal gardening, so Darcy happily took on the responsibility. She grew tomatoes, peppers, squash, turnips, lettuce, parsley and, of course, her herbs. She expanded the space in order to accommodate her growing herb garden, and produced a collection of dried herbs for potions. Since it was important for Teddy to have chores, he helped with pruning and weeding. They had a special relationship and she made sure he was always close by as she taught him about the various herbs and their healing properties. It was important to pass on her knowledge. Not everyone appreciated the use of herbs. She called those people "the ignorants," and she was sure the new sheriff was one. She was careful about the information she shared and was always prepared for backlash.

What made her most afraid right now was they might be evicted. When they arrived in Riverview they didn't have enough for a down payment for their own farm, so they rented. At first Mr. Tilton seemed nice. He gave them a good deal on the rent and even let Mac use some of his machinery. But lately Mr. Tilton's tone was curt and he kept asking when they might have enough for a down payment. Today she noticed surveyors working on the adjacent property. Were the Tiltons selling the land on this side of the road? She wondered if the surveyors knew of the old graveyard at the very back of the property? So when a policeman showed up at the door, what was she to think?

It was going to be difficult keeping Teddy from telling the sheriff too much. She had to figure out what to do.

~ TWELVE ~

Caitlyn had teased enough pertinent information from her aunt in order to draft an obituary. The strain was too much for Myra, so she excused herself and went upstairs to rest.

Caitlyn was so engrossed in developing an obituary for Todd she forgot about her phone until it started to vibrate against her hip.

She placed the laptop on the cushioned seat next to her and reached in her pocket.

"This is Caitlyn," she automatically responded.

"Cait, it's Nick."

"Oh my god, Nick, where are you? I've been frantic not hearing from you."

"Cait, can't talk long. I'm in Beijing covering meetings and the current leader, Xi Jinping. He's becoming very powerful and his regime could go either way. The senator is getting worried about China's economic health. Everything hinges on how Xi uses his power."

Before Nick would continue, Caitlyn jumped in, not taking a breath. She felt her news was more important than what was happening halfway across the world.

"Nick, I'm in Riverview. Riverview, New York. My cousin, Todd, was murdered yesterday. I'm going to stay here a while to help my aunt and uncle. When will you come home?"

"I'm so sorry, Cait. Wish I could be there, but there's no way I can break away from what's happening here. Got to go. Will call when I can."

Caitlyn stared at the silent phone in her hand. She wished she knew exactly what Nick did and where he was. He was always so vague. Before he left he told her about the Chinese leader, Xi Jinping. Apparently he was a charismatic fellow that was forging a different path from the one created by Mao Zedong, and the "collective leadership" of the despot Deng Xiaoping. She had read an article about the leader and his wife. Xi was tall, about six feet, his wife was described as "lovely," and Xi was described as a "Statesman of Vision." But there was always the pull of power and greed, and Nick told her he was worried about how Xi had reduced the number of decision-makers in his government and took on those responsibilities, including domestic security.

With a sigh, Caitlyn returned the phone to her pocket and picked up her laptop, typing the last few sentences, "Funeral services will be held Tuesday, April 29, 11:00 a.m. at St. Paul's Episcopal Church. Donations can be made to the charity of one's choice."

What was Nick really doing in China?

~ THIRTEEN ~

Sunday

Caitlyn didn't want to attend church services with her aunt and uncle. She'd rather sleep in. She'd had a busy workweek, and then the call from Myra meant quickly packing and arranging a flight to New York. During the flight all the emotional issues from her time in Riverview surfaced. It was time she dealt with them one way or another.

She pulled the covers back over her head until the soft knock on her door was followed by her aunt's voice reminding her they were leaving in forty-five minutes. Myra's hopeful tone told Caitlyn there was no choice.

She got up, showered quickly and put on an appropriate outfit. She hadn't packed a lot of clothes, so choices were limited. She dressed up her black slacks and hunter green knit top with a colorful scarf. Good enough.

She thought it strange that Jerry and Myra wanted to attend church services so soon after their son's murder. On the one hand, the religious community provided them the support they needed right now. Her cynical side said her uncle was first and foremost a politician. He would need a public appearance to attract the sympathy vote, and her aunt wouldn't make waves. It was not Caitlyn's place to make waves either, so she bit her tongue, sat back, and tolerated the ride.

The minister did a good job with the service. Caitlyn thought him a bit young to be a pastor, but she appreciated how he worked into his sermon the need for love, understanding and forgiveness.

After the service while the congregation consoled her aunt and uncle, Caitlyn stood back and people watched. It was intriguing to see how members of the congregation reacted to the Tilton's presence. And then one person approached her.

"Caitlyn? It's Abbie, Abbie Sullivan, from high school. I married Tim Hetherington. You might remember him?"

"Oh my gosh, Abbie. I didn't recognize you. I guess it's your hair style. You used to wear your hair long in school. I like the shorter look a lot. So, how are you?"

"I'm okay. I'm really sorry about your cousin. The community's in shock, and no one feels safe right now. We have a new sheriff in town, and I don't know if he's up to the job."

"I met the sheriff yesterday when he came to talk to Uncle Jerry and Aunt Myra. He's young, well, our age, but he seems to know what he's doing. He's already got the state police on the case, and he collected forensic evidence at the scene even though the storm was bearing down. In fact, Aunt Myra said he brought some sort of item in to show them."

"Oh, how could I forget about the storm? That must have made it even more difficult. We lost power for eight hours," Abbie said. "Won't keep you, Caitlyn, but wondered if we could have a chat. My husband and I own a winery up the road and there's something quite important I wish to discuss with you. Can you come out this afternoon? I know it's last minute and you must have a lot to do helping your aunt and uncle, but it's important."

Caitlyn couldn't believe Abbie was asking her to give up her afternoon to visit their winery when there indeed was so much to do to get ready for the funeral, reception after, then burial. There were thank you notes to write, envelopes to address, to say nothing of receiving the never-ending delivery of casseroles and flowers. The expectant look on Abbie's face and the appeal in her voice tore at Caitlyn's heart. There was a real need there and the answer couldn't be anything but yes.

"O.k. I'll be there. Is three okay?"

"Wonderful. Thank you, Caitlyn, and again, I apologize for the awkward timing."

"Don't think anything of it. By that time I may need to get away for a few hours."

~

The view from the winery's drive was breathtaking. Caitlyn stopped the car midway up so she could gaze out at the sparkling blue lake below. The glaciers of long ago left this land incredibly beautiful. She remembered the Indian legend stating when the Great Spirit rose from this land, his hands made impressions that became the ten Finger Lakes. Of course scientists presented an alternate theory about receding glaciers, but Caitlyn preferred to think it was the Great Spirit who had an impact on this beautiful area.

She continued the drive through the vineyards. Cresting the hill, she arrived at the building housing the wine tasting room and sales center. The building was designed to provide a panoramic view of the vineyards and lake beyond. As Caitlyn put her car in park, she saw Abbie at the door waving her in.

"This is lovely, Abbie," Caitlyn said. "Actually, incredible."

"We like it," said Abbie. "It's a lot of work, but Tim and I think of it as a labor of love. We found this property by accident. The real estate agent was showing us properties on another lake when this land came up for sale. We wanted vines that produced the best Pinot Noir wine, so we needed limestone soil. The real estate agent thought we were crazy, but we can actually taste a difference in the wines produced from grapes grown in that particular soil base. So, long story short as they say, this property came on the market. It's off the beaten track so our agent didn't think we would be interested, but Tim took a soil sample and we had it! We couldn't believe our luck."

"I didn't realize vines were so particular, and there is so much science in making wine," stated Caitlyn.

"Oh, you don't know the half of it," said Abbie. "Tim has degrees in both oenology and viticulture or we never would have tried. You need a solid science background and a strong constitution to tackle agriculture in this variable climate. Our vines have done well for us and we have developed a faithful clientele. In fact, Finger Lakes wineries have been around for a long time. Before Prohibition Finger Lakes wines were served at important social functions right along with California wines. But it wasn't until the mid-1970s that the small wineries were allowed to thrive. Until that time New York State's fees were exorbitant and there was so much bureaucratic red tape people like us didn't have a chance. But conditions changed when the Farm Winery Act went into effect, and now this region is full of successful wineries."

Caitlyn was fascinated with this part of New York State history, something she didn't learn as a teenage docent. She wondered what it had to do with her.

"I had an ulterior motive for asking you here, Caitlyn. I hope you don't mind," Abbie explained.

"Of course not, Abbie. What's the problem?" asked Caitlyn.

"Before I start it's only fair you sample our wine," said Abbie as she poured a glass of their Pinot Noir. "Swirl it gently, sniff, and then take a sip."

Caitlyn followed Abbie's directions. "Oh my god. This smells and tastes amazing. I've never had anything like it."

Abbie smiled at Caitlyn's reaction. "I've explained a little about the critical role soil composition plays in growing strong vines to produce grapes from which we make our wine. I'll now tell you how our livelihood is threatened."

Abbie took a deep breath. "Have you heard of fracking? The term is actually hydraulic fracturing, because it pushes fluids, water and chemicals, at a very high pressure into the ground to fracture the shale to release the oil or natural gas. The practice has been going on in states like Pennsylvania and Ohio for a few years. But right now in New York State each county decides whether or not to allow fracking. So far our county has said no, but the county a few miles north of us allows it."

Abbie took a breath to compose her thoughts. Caitlyn needed to know the essential information while not being overwhelmed.

"The fact our county is saying no upsets a number of our neighbors. On the plus side, the oil companies pay a small rental stipend and a royalty to the property owners. In this economy it is so tempting, and in some cases, the only income residents have. The companies provide tax revenues and create jobs. We recently heard a story about a small New York town near the Pennsylvania border where residents wanted to secede from New York. They watched as their Pennsylvania neighbors drove new cars, and renovated their homes, while the New Yorkers were struggling to make car payments and mortgages."

"There's more to this story isn't there," said Caitlyn as she poured herself another glass of wine.

"As I mentioned, the county north of us allows fracking and the oil companies were in there fast. The tankers loaded with millions of gallons of water roll up our road, resulting in wear and tear, and safety issues. We call them 'fracking outlaws' because we see them going too fast and passing cars on the solid yellow lines. We read it takes 400 tankers to carry enough water to one fracking site."

Abbie swirled the wine left in her glass. The wine trails ran down the glass giving off a golden glow. She took another deep breath and continued.

"Worst of all, the water is mixed with sand and chemicals. Those chemicals are radium, methanol, hydrochloric acid, formaldehyde, and god knows what else. Most states don't require the oil companies to disclose what they are injecting into the earth. There is a major loophole in the law, known as the 'Halliburton loophole,' allowing petroleum based products to be injected into the earth."

Abbie paused, trying unsuccessfully to get her anger under control.

"Bottom line, we don't know what is being injected and what impact those chemicals are having on the soil, the environment and in our bodies."

Caitlyn watched Abbie's face get red. This situation was having a hell of an effect on her friend.

Abbie took another breath, rubbing her hands together, and continued, "We keep close watch on our vines and are starting to notice some vines in the north fields are getting distressed, or are withering for no reason. We wonder if the toxic chemicals that are being pumped into the earth north of us are negatively affecting our soil composition."

"What about scientific studies?" Caitlyn asked. "Hasn't any of the universities around here done studies on this?"

"There are studies stating the combination of soil acidification and deoxygenation disrupts plant cell growth, which makes it difficult to grow even the hardiest crops. Some of the vines we are growing are extremely finicky about their soil conditions. It's an uphill battle since every fact about degradation of soil is offset by challenges from the oil companies. And money talks."

"This is all very interesting, and tragic, but what can I do about it?" Caitlyn asked.

"Caitlyn, we heard your uncle is involved in pushing through legislation to override a county government's decision regarding fracking. He is working closely with the oil companies so they'd have free rein in New York," Abbie said.

"Are you sure?" Caitlyn asked.

"I'm sorry, Caitlyn, but yes. I hate to hit you with this now. My timing is terrible, but I wanted to talk to you in person. This was not something to be discussed over the phone. I know you're leaving soon, so I needed to bring this to your attention, because we suspect your dad is involved as well."

"You must be kidding," Caitlyn said, sitting back in her chair. "My dad's in Florida and I don't think he and Mom have any contact with Uncle Jerry and Aunt Myra. Mom and Myra had a falling out years ago."

"Caitlyn, one of the unique features of the Finger Lakes wine industry is the owners and their winemakers get together regularly. They socialize, do blind taste tests of new wines, and are organized as a political group. From the minute we started planting vines, the winery community welcomed us with open arms. From those gatherings we learn what is going on, and that's where I heard your dad's name mentioned. I, too, didn't believe it, but on further inquiries, I was able to verify the information."

"This is quite a shock. It's going to take me a while to assimilate, but I'll find out for you, Abbie. I would hate for New York's wine industry as well as overall agriculture to be devastated for years to come," Caitlyn said. "One of my clients is The Outdoor

Foundation, so I'm aware of the environmental issues our planet faces. I know we need to find alternate energy sources. We can't continue to rely on foreign oil, especially from the Middle East. It's too unstable."

"We understand and it's why the winery community is supporting other ways of producing environmentally sound energy. Some wineries have put in solar panels, others are allowing windmills to be erected on our properties. At first there was a lot of discussion about this. Some thought our customers wouldn't like to sit and sip their wine while listening to the whir of a windmill. But the more we talked about it and surveyed our customers, the more we found they'd enjoy both the sound and the fact we were helping the environment. The industry even developed a fund to assist with installation of solar panels on homes and businesses. But there is a troublesome side to this, Caitlyn, one worrying us a lot. The environmental fervor has infected some, many are teenagers, and they are vandalizing drilling equipment. If they get caught, they could get arrested or even shot. The drilling companies are posting armed guards now. We've tried to stop this, but you know the passions of youth."

Caitlyn put her hand over Abbie's. "I sense there's something else?"

Abbie looked at her friend. A friend who miraculously appeared at just the right time. With a moment's hesitation she said, "I'm fighting cancer, Caitlyn. I didn't want to tell you right now. I wanted to separate my illness from the fracking issue. But I can see that we are still on the same wavelength and I can't hide anything from you."

"I'm so, so sorry, Abbie. I had a suspicion there was something, but I didn't want to be right. You have every right to fight for what you believe in, and apparently you feel fracking had something to do with your cancer?"

Abbie was not ready to reveal any more about her illness.

"Let's take a tour of the winery," Abbie said.

~ FOURTEEN ~

Ethan wasn't sure whether the Risleys attended regular church services, but he bet Mac Risley would be taking advantage of this sunny day following the storm to catch up on farm work. Ethan pulled into the barn adjacent to their rental property and knew he was in luck. Mac Risley's truck was there and the barn door open.

"Mr. Risley, Sheriff Ewing here. Can we talk?"

A figure appeared haltingly from the back of the barn, "Oh, hi, Sheriff. I wasn't expecting anyone, and after what happened over at the Tilton's I guess everyone's a bit nervous these days."

Ethan noticed Mac carried a metal crowbar in his right hand.

"That's what I wanted to talk with you about. I talked with your wife yesterday."

"Yes, I know. She was quite nervous about your visit. Nuthin' personal, uniforms does it to her."

"Did she mention I needed to talk with you as soon as you returned?"

"No, she didn't. I went straight to the barn with the parts, and by the time I went to the house it was dinnertime. She was busy getting dinner on the table. She's got a lot on her mind, and she doesn't always tell me everything. With the murder so close by and all, I think she's a little frightened. So, what do'ya want to know? I got to get back to fixin' this tractor if I'm going to finish spring plowing."

"I want to know what you might have seen Friday afternoon. Someone came onto the Tilton property and killed their son. The killer had to get on the property somehow, either by vehicle or on foot, and since you had the best opportunity of seeing something, being in the fields, I hope you have something to tell me."

Mac thought a minute, "Well, there were them surveyors. Darcy and I are quite worried about that. We're afraid Mr. Tilton is going

54

to sell the property we're renting. If he does, I don't know what we'll do."

"I understand, but back to what you might have seen on Friday."

"Well, to be honest, Sheriff, when I'm out plowing, I'm concentrating on where I'm going to make sure there aren't any big rocks or ruts in the way to break my equipment. I'm not just sitting up in the cab enjoying the scenery. I did stop for about an hour and rushed to the tractor store in town to get a part. Around 3:30 I think."

Just at the crucial time, thought Ethan.

"O.k. Thanks, Mr. Risley. If you think of anything, a car passing through, anything out of the ordinary, give me a call."

"Will do sheriff. You take care now."

Ethan watched Mac Risley turn and walk back into the darkness from which he came.

~ FIFTEEN ~

Monday

Caitlyn couldn't get Abbie's comments out of her head. They haunted her through the night. She tossed and turned trying to think of some resolution to this volcanic problem. Finally giving up on sleep, she turned towards the clock. The white digits told her it was only five a.m. *Oh, god,* she thought. *I can't get up this early. I'll be useless all day.* She turned her back to the offensive clock, pulled the covers tight under her chin, and successfully achieved the deep sleep that eluded her during the night.

Caitlyn rose at a more respectable 7:30 a.m., showered, dressed, and hoped her aunt and uncle were already about their day. She didn't feel like talking to anyone this morning, especially her uncle Jerry. She needed to get on with her plan. She didn't know when the sheriff's office opened, but she guessed the sheriff would be in by 8:30.

~

Caitlyn parked her rental car on Riverview's main street, a short walk to the sheriff's office. She noted the village was quiet this morning, and suspected residents were home cleaning up after the weekend storm. She thought about the townspeople going about their chores, and how the world goes on when her world and that of her aunt and uncle had suffered such a debilitating loss. Todd's murder was foremost on her mind, but bothering her was the disturbing information Abbie shared about Caitlyn's father. It couldn't be true. Caitlyn would know if her father was into something like that. Or would she? She and her parents were not especially close these past few years. She'd have to find out the truth, and it wouldn't be easy. Not only was there little contact lately, she and her dad didn't have the best relationship. In fact, their relationship was like oil and water – they didn't mix.

She put the issue aside for now and concentrated on Todd. The feeling of guilt and her strong sense of justice was driving her to action. She was going to meet with the sheriff and find out *exactly* what was being done and insist she help. She wondered how her offer would be received.

The first thing she noticed when she entered the sheriff's office was the number of blinking lights on the console. A middle-aged woman with curly red hair sat at the console, headphones on, talking with someone. Caitlyn waited until the woman finished before she approached her. The station appeared to be empty.

Maddie turned to greet the visitor.

"How can I help you, miss?" Maddie said.

"I'm Caitlyn Jamison. I'd like a word with the sheriff if he's in."

"Oh, yea, you're the Tilton's niece from DC," Maddie replied. "I heard about you. Please accept my condolences on the death of your cousin."

"Thank you, and yes, I came up from DC," Caitlyn responded. She wasn't sure how to take this woman. Her tone was curt, but her round face and sparkling green eyes couldn't help but to appear welcoming.

"I'll tell the sheriff you're here," Maddie said as she walked to the back of the office and opened a door.

"Sheriff, there's a Caitlyn Jamison here to see you."

"Show her in, please, Maddie," said Ethan, immediately standing.

"I'm sorry to bother you, Sheriff. I know how busy you must be with Todd's murder, the storm, everything," Caitlyn said.

"Please sit down and tell me what brings you to the office."

Maybe she has inside information to help solve this case quickly. Always look at the family first, kept rolling through his mind.

Caitlyn sat, but then quickly shifted to the edge of her seat to emphasize the point she was going to make.

"I'm here to offer my help. Before you tell me how kind my offer is, but you really don't need help, or can't have a civilian and certainly not a family member involved, allow me to make my case."

"I'm all ears," stated Ethan with a smile. It was refreshing to have a conversation with someone who didn't have a complaint, and Caitlyn's enthusiasm was a pleasant respite from recent events. He figured he could give her a few minutes of his time.

"I lived in this town for a few years and know some of the old timers; they might trust me. I suspect they don't trust you, being a newcomer. I could gather information quicker because people would be willing to talk to me. I've been gone a number of years, but I still have friends here and I need to do *something* to help my aunt and uncle. I can't stay in the house listening to them grieve and argue."

"Do they argue a lot?" Ethan asked.

"I was talking out of turn. Every married couple has their disagreements and with the added stress ..." said Caitlyn.

Ethan sat back in his chair and rubbed his chin, his favorite thinking position. He did need extra help with this investigation. His office staff was stretched thin meeting the demands of the storm. He had put out an APB and the state police were on the case, but so far not a hint of a suspect. He was getting frustrated. Caitlyn made a great offer, but it was not something he could legally consider.

"You know I can't do that. They would have my head on a platter if I allowed not only a civilian, but a civilian related to the victim to work the case," Ethan said.

"Then I'll do my own investigation," Caitlyn stated. She stood to go.

"You can't do that. I can have you arrested if you interfere," Ethan said, also standing, arms crossed.

Caitlyn's mulish expression told Ethan she was not going to budge. Her brow furrowed, her mouth was set. He thought she was cute even when mad. He knew if she left, he might not see her again. He didn't want her walking out of his life. He had to make a decision, and fast. Oh, the hell with it. He was sheriff. He could run this investigation any way he wanted. It may be the last investigation he would have here in Riverview, but he had to follow his instincts. Those instincts told him she would be an asset. And if that turned out to not be the case, then he would deal with it then. After a few moments of silence, Caitlyn gathered her purse and prepared to leave.

"Wait. I'm willing to take a chance," Ethan stated. "I may get in a lot of trouble for this, but I'm going to 'appoint' you as my assistant so you can accompany me on interview assignments. We will talk to people at the school, students, teachers, and administrators, finding out what we can about Todd, his friends, any possible enemies. It's important to keep careful notes and I'm going to count on you as my scribe. You know those little notebooks you see the TV cops carry? Well, I want you to carry a steno size notebook to capture more complete notes so there won't be any question about what people said. Do you understand?"

Caitlyn swallowed hard. When she offered to help, she never thought she would have to interview anyone at the school. She wondered if *he* was still there. She put her hands in her lap so the sheriff would not see them twisting. She had offered to help; she was given an assignment. She couldn't back out now.

"Yes, I understand. I'll get a steno pad and take thorough notes," Caitlyn said.

"Good, let's get started" stated Ethan.

~ SIXTEEN ~

Caitlyn had never been in a police car before. She was amazed at all the technology available to law enforcement today.

"What's the computer for?" She asked.

"I can pull up license plate numbers, run searches on names, just about anything in the law enforcement database is available to me on the spot," Ethan responded.

What he really wanted was to get to know her, so he took advantage of the segue.

"So, if I stopped you for speeding, I could immediately access any information on you that might be in the system. Would I find anything?" Ethan asked with a slight smile.

"I'm afraid you'd be very disappointed," Caitlyn responded. She didn't know exactly how to take him.

"Do you like living in the DC area?" Ethan asked as he approached the school grounds.

"I've only been there a short time, but yes, so far it's nice for my business. I'm a graphic artist, and am in the process of building a client base, so it's good for that. Washington is actually a beautiful city. The buildings are low, there are many parks and wide tree lined streets. Very visitor friendly. But now that I'm back here I had forgotten how nice it is with the rolling hills, lakes, and much less traffic," Caitlyn responded as they came to a stop in front of the high school office.

They walked to the building's entrance, noting the recently installed metal detectors on each side of the door.

After being buzzed in, they went directly to the office where they signed the guest book and asked to speak with the superintendent. Caitlyn knew it was politic to start at the top. As with every workplace there was a certain pecking order, even in schools.

Ethan knew that Superintendent Robert Boynton was new to the community. He came from a small district somewhere in the Adirondacks taking the typical track of an administrator. When educators wanted to advance, the way to do that was by taking administration courses, and then climbing the administrative ladder from principal to superintendent, first in the small schools and then every couple of years working their way up to the larger schools and more money. Since Riverview was considered a school of intermediate size, Caitlyn figured Mr. Boynton might be around for three or four years max. The frequent change in administration was not helpful for the local school and the continuity needed. For the administrator it was considered a step up the ladder.

"May I help you?" a male voice asked.

Caitlyn looked up at the imposing figure of the superintendent. He was well over 6'5" and probably weighed 200 pounds. His dark hair and heavy eyebrows made him appear like someone out of a horror movie. Caitlyn squelched a giggle as this thought floated through her head.

Ethan took command of the conversation. "I'm Sheriff Ewing and this is Caitlyn Jamison. I believe my office alerted you to our visit. We need to talk with teachers and staff, and then to the students who knew Todd Tilton."

"Come into my office first," Superintendent Boynton commanded.

The man clearly was asserting his authority. Caitlyn watched the power struggle between the sheriff and the superintendent with amusement, both men asserting their dominance with each trying to better the other.

Ethan hesitated in his attempt to keep control. He understood the power game and decided it wasn't worth his time and effort.

"Come into my office and we can discuss it," Boynton repeated as he looked Caitlyn up and down and then ushered them into the spacious corner office.

The superintendent's office was not what Ethan expected. The artwork on the walls was interesting. He didn't quite know how to describe it—a combination of shapes and colors one might interpret as erotic. The wooden carvings on the bookcases were suggestive. He didn't think the décor was appropriate for a school official, but decided to leave that for the board of education. He wondered what Caitlyn thought. He would have to ask her later.

"Mr. Boynton, as you know Todd Tilton was murdered late Friday afternoon. We need a list of Todd's classes and activities. Did he have a girlfriend? Who did he hang out with?" Ethan asked.

Boynton listened and then replied, "I'm sorry to say I didn't know Todd well. Of course everyone knew *of* him. He was one of our best athletes. You couldn't attend a basketball game without seeing Todd Tilton in the starting lineup and he often scored the highest points of the game. But for actually *knowing* him, knowing what he thought, what his likes and dislikes were, no, I didn't know him that well. But I'll let you talk with the teachers and staff. They'll be able to fill you in on Todd's personality, who he hung around with. We have grief counselors in the building today to help the students cope with his death, so I only ask you to respect their presence. And, it goes without saying you are not to disturb any of the classes."

Superintendent Boynton rose, ending the conversation, and walked to the door. He held the door for them and then walked them to the guidance office.

"Ms. Lowe, this is Sheriff Ewing and Caitlyn Jamison. They are here because of Todd Tilton's murder. Please give them any information you can about Todd."

Caitlyn and Ethan walked into the office and shook the offered hand, before turning to thank Superintendent Boynton as he closed the door.

"Thanks for seeing us on such short notice," Ethan said.

"I'm happy to help you in any way I can," Ms. Lowe responded. "We're all shocked. Todd is about the last person any of us thought something like this would happen to. He was admired by the students and the teaching staff. He is, or was, a very popular boy."

"Is there anyone you can think of who might have been jealous of him? Did he have a girlfriend?"

"Susan Doyle. She's a nice girl, average student, but, if I could speak in confidence, I don't think Todd's parents were too pleased. Mr. Doyle works for the parks commission, groundskeeper or something. I got the impression the Tilton's didn't consider the Doyles in the same class. I know it doesn't seem right in these times, especially in a small town, but that's just my observation. And you know, of course the Tilton's are newcomers here."

Caitlyn made notes while Ms. Lowe talked. She thought how foolish it was people weren't accepted into the community unless they were born here. The community was still divided by the "born here" and the "come here." She wondered if and when society would ever change the perception. Caitlyn wondered if her uncle, a "come here" was headed towards greener pastures. Riverview might be just a stopping off point on his career ladder. And with the death of his only child, what he would do now?

"Who else did Todd hang around with?" Ethan asked.

Ms. Lowe put her hands together and closed her eyes.

"Let me think. Denny Mathews seemed to be Todd's closest friend. They were quite competitive. Sometimes it worried me. I thought they might get into a fight the competition was so fierce, but to my knowledge that never happened. Oh, and I probably should mention the new boy, Teddy Risley. I was surprised to see Todd take a liking to him. You see, Teddy is a different kind of student. He's not slow or anything, he's just sick a lot. He has some sort of inherited disease or something. I haven't quite figured it out. I noticed him sitting by himself in the cafeteria looking longingly at the group of kids Todd hung around with. You know, the athletes and cheerleaders, the ones you might consider the popular kids and everyone wants to be in their circle. Always lots of laughter and joking around. I felt bad for Teddy, because I knew he wouldn't have a chance of getting in with that group of students. And then I noticed he and Todd talking quietly in the back of the library. I felt good about how things work out sometimes, but now I'm not so sure. You should talk with Teddy as well as the school nurse."

"I will, and thank you for all the information."

"You should talk with C.K. He's close with the boys and might have more information," said Ms. Lowe.

"C.K.?" asked Caitlyn. She couldn't believe the coach was still working.

"Sorry. That's what we call Coach Kollner. He's the athletic director here, coaches the basketball team, and some of the girl's teams. We call him C.K. for short."

"Thanks, we certainly will talk with . . . C.K," Ethan said.

Ethan rose to leave, shaking Ms. Lowe's hand.

"The nurse's office is right next door."

They walked to the next office and lightly knocked on the door before entering.

"Come in," a large matronly woman answered, putting out her hand. "I'm Mrs. Nelson, and this is Mrs. Richland, one of Todd's teachers. And your names?"

"Sheriff Ethan Ewing and Caitlyn Jamison. We're investigating Todd Tilton's murder and wondered if we could ask you a few questions?"

"Oh, yes, of course. We'll do anything to help. What a horrible thing. The students are very upset. We have counselors here today. Are you sure it was murder? Who would want to harm that sweet boy?"

Ethan waited patiently until Mrs. Nelson took a breath between her multiple questions and then jumped in fearing he wouldn't get another chance.

"We're still waiting for the coroner's report, but yes, all indications point to the fact it was murder. What can you tell me about Todd? Did he have any medical conditions we should be aware of? Did you know of any enemies? And, what can you tell us about the new boy, Teddy Risley?"

"My, you certainly do have a lot of questions. Now, let's see. To my knowledge Todd didn't have any serious medical problems. A little asthma now and then, but nothing so serious it stopped him from playing ball. He was a star athlete, you know."

"So we've been told," Ethan said.

Caitlyn was taking notes as fast as she could. Mrs. Nelson was a fast talker.

Is it nerves or is she always this hyper?

"We heard a couple of basketball players from another school were upset with Todd because he was high scorer at the game against them, which knocked them out of the sectionals. They threatened to 'get even,' but you know how words are thrown around sometimes," Mrs. Nelson said.

"What are those boys' names?" Ethan asked.

"I don't know who they were; there was a rumor going around about some players who were out to get him. I didn't take it seriously. But you could ask the coach."

"And what about Teddy Risley?"

"Now he's a handful, both physically and emotionally. He can have a violent temper. Don't know what sets it off, but the principal was called a couple of times to take him out of the classroom. The family has been here for several years. Southerners, you know. The mother is very protective. In fact, I think she doesn't let the father have much to do with the boy. Very strange family dynamics, I say. Let the boy grow up, I say. She's always hovering, and getting in trouble sending in her herbal recipes. We aren't allowed by law, you know, to administer anything not prescribed by a physician. We can't make her understand. She even threatened the school with a lawsuit, don't cha know."

Ethan turned to the teacher.

"And your observations, Mrs. Richland?" Ethan said.

"Very much the same. I teach math courses here and Todd was an exceptional student. He was looking forward to furthering his education. He was quite creative, too. I was just talking with the art teacher, and she said he was one of her better students. He loved to do sketches, and she thought he was destined to be an architect or urban planner."

"Did he get along with the other students?" Ethan asked.

"Oh yes. Todd was a serious student, so when he was in the classroom, it was all work. He kept his playtime to the athletic field or basketball court," Mrs. Richland said.

Ethan thanked the women for their time and headed to the conference room where he and Caitlyn were scheduled to meet with the students.

~

Ms. Lowe provided them with class schedules for Susan Doyle, Denny Mathews and Teddy Risley. As luck would have it, Susan's study hall was this hour, and then Denny and Theodore were in the same study hall the next hour. Ethan asked Ms. Lowe to bring Susan to the room designated for the interviews.

Susan Doyle's long blond hair fell halfway down her back, the highlights making a halo-like appearance. Susan was sixteen years old, but she looked and acted much older. Her mid-calf length skirt and peasant top told Caitlyn that Susan revered the 60s look.

Ethan started with small talk, a technique to help the interviewee relax. He asked Susan about school, her favorite subjects, and girl friends. Once he sensed Susan was more at ease, he turned to questions about her relationship with Todd Tilton.

"We were going out," Susan replied to Ethan's question regarding their relationship.

"And what exactly does that mean?"

"I don't know," Susan thought a minute, then responded, "I guess it means we were going steady; you know; we didn't date anyone else."

"Did you attend his games?"

"Of course. I'm a cheerleader," Susan responded.

Ethan could tell she was about to break down, so he softened his tone, as he watched Caitlyn slide a box of tissues towards Susan.

"So you were able to witness Todd's relationship with the other players."

"Everyone liked Todd. Well, some of the guys were jealous of him. He was good at almost every sport. Denny can tell you more. You know, locker room talk. Denny was Todd's best friend. At least until the new kid showed up. We couldn't figure out why Todd befriended him. He's weird."

"You mean Teddy Risley?"

66

"Yea."

"What's weird about him?"

"I don't know. He is. He's sick a lot, and he has tempter tantrums. And he's from the South. He complains about the cold. He talks funny; he doesn't fit in."

Ethan thought Susan's favorite phrase was "I don't know" or, "you know," but he was thankful it wasn't "like." He still hoped he could get some useful information from her.

"We heard Todd was threatened by players on the neighboring team. Do you know anything about that?" Ethan asked.

"Yea, Todd mentioned it. He didn't think it was anything serious. Guys blowing off steam."

Susan, one more question. Can you tell me where you were Friday afternoon?"

"Yea, that's easy. I was home with my mom. My grandparents were coming and we had to tidy up."

"Thanks, Susan. I see your study hall period is almost up. I hope I didn't take too much time away from your homework. I appreciate your talking with me, and if you think of anything helpful in finding Todd's killer, even if you don't think it's relevant, please give me a call," Ethan handed Susan his card.

Susan got up, wiped her eyes, and turned to go. Swishing her silky hair as she turned, she walked out the door.

~ SEVENTEEN ~

While waiting for the next student, Caitlyn finished writing her notes from Susan's interview. She wanted to capture every bit of their conversation as well as the body language. Her training as a graphic artist provided her a good eye for detail. She could tell when a person is telling the truth, or not, and Caitlyn detected a few times when Susan was uncomfortable, not making eye contact as she answered.

Caitlyn's phone vibrated against her hip. Thinking she should let it go to voice mail, curiosity won out and she pulled it from her pocket. Nick! She looked at Ethan, nodding an apology, and said she really needed to take the call. She cupped her hands around the phone in an attempt to provide better audio as she quickly walked towards the front door of the school. She needed to get outside the concrete walls to get better reception.

"Where are you?"

"Hold on. I've only a minute and I shouldn't be talking to you at all," Nick explained. "Things are heating up here and I won't be able to call you for a while, I'll try to text, but don't worry. I should be home in a couple of days."

Caitlyn ended the call by saying, "Be careful, Nick. Come home soon."

The line was breaking up and she could barely make out what he was saying. That would work in her favor when she explained her involvement with a murder investigation. She walked back into the school still wondering what Nick was really doing in China and how safe he was.

When she arrived back in the interview room she found Ethan talking with Todd's friend Denny Mathews.

"Sorry. It was an important phone call," Caitlyn explained.

Ethan's annoyed expression told her that he wasn't happy with her abrupt departure. This was a murder investigation, and not any murder investigation, but one of her own cousin. She realized she had made the wrong decision to leave the room when interviews were in progress and when Ethan depended on her to take notes.

Denny, the cool teenager he thought he was, responded to Ethan's statement. "No problem, man. Anything to get out of class."

Ethan didn't think it was funny.

"I thought this was your study hall time," stated Caitlyn.

"Yea, but who wants to spend free time reading textbooks," stated Denny. "I'd rather be in the gym shooting baskets. Now that's the best use of my time."

Caitlyn did not respond. She was already in enough trouble. She shouldn't get into a discussion about the value of education and how so few are picked for sport careers.

Ethan turned to her and frowned before he continued his questions.

"Denny, do you have any idea who may have wanted Todd harmed?" Ethan asked.

"Nope. Todd was real well liked."

"Did you know about the threat Todd received from the boys in the neighboring town?"

"Yea. We talked about it a lot. Todd said it wasn't a big deal, but I knew he was concerned. One night we were down at Reilly's playing pool and we saw a bunch of guys drive by real slow."

"What's Reilly's?" Caitlyn asked.

"It's the teen hangout in this hick town," stated Denny.

Ethan gave her another warning look. It was his job to ask questions. She was to observe, take careful notes, and not interrupt.

"Did Todd have any other enemies? He was popular and a good athlete. Sometimes that can create jealousy that gets out of control," Ethan asked.

"I think people liked Todd enough and if they were jealous of him, it wouldn't be to the point where they would go and kill him. Man, that's drastic."

"What else can you tell me about Todd?" Ethan asked.

"Well, he did get into an altercation with the coach," Denny said.

"When was this?" Ethan asked.

"I don't know, 'bout a month or so ago. I don't think it had anything to do with the team, but I asked Todd about it. He said to never mind. It wasn't any of my business. So I dropped it," Denny said.

"One more question and then you can get back to your study hall. Tell me where you were on Friday afternoon."

"I was where I always am on Friday afternoons. I work at Dean's Drug Store, stocking shelves," Denny replied.

"Okay, thanks, Denny." Ethan said as he handed him a card.

Next on the list was Teddy Risley.

This ought to be an interesting discussion. Susan had a good point. Why would a popular teenage boy like Todd Tilton all of a sudden befriend a new kid who showed no athletic ability and therefore didn't fit in with Todd's crowd?

~

"You wanted to see me?" Teddy asked as he stood tentatively in the doorway.

Teddy Risley was a fifteen year old boy who appeared small for his age. He acted timid and would need a lot of coaching to get him to open up.

"Yes, Teddy, please, come in. Or do you prefer to be called Theodore?" Ethan replied.

"Teddy is fine."

"Thank you for taking your study hall time to speak with me. As your teacher may have told you, I'm investigating the death of your friend and neighbor, Todd Tilton. I'm talking with students who were friends of Todd, and your name came up. I'm hoping you can tell me about Todd and if you know of anyone who might have wanted to hurt him. So, tell me a little bit about yourself."

It didn't get past Caitlyn the fact Ethan was using the personal pronoun for the interviews. It was no longer "we," but "I." She'd really screwed up.

Teddy stared at the floor. He didn't make eye contact.

"Todd told me how it felt to be popular. It wasn't all good you know, to be popular, to be the top athlete. He worked to keep his grades up and be the top scorer on the team. His parents demanded it. It really bothered him. And he couldn't talk to his friends about those things. That's why, I guess, he hung out with me. No one else in this lousy school was interested in getting to know me, so I guess he felt secure he could talk to me and I wouldn't tell anyone else."

Ethan felt sorry for this young man. He was tall, gangly, and almost gaunt looking. The cowlick at the back of his head didn't enhance his looks.

"What did you share with Todd? Or was your relationship one-sided?" Ethan asked.

Teddy was silent again. Maybe he didn't understand the question. Ethan suspected this young person had much on his mind, and he was not about to reveal it for fear of . . .*fear of what?* This was going to be one hard nut to crack. He was a troubled young man, and they'd needed to tread carefully.

"So, Teddy, can you tell me where you were on Friday afternoon?" Ethan asked.

"I stayed after for some math help with Mrs. Richland. I took the late bus home," Teddy responded.

Teddy didn't want to tell this policeman any more about how he felt, so he remained silent, and studied his shoes.

Ethan decided not to push. He would try another time to reach Teddy.

"Thanks Teddy for coming in to talk with me."

As Ethan handed him a card, Caitlyn watched to see if Teddy made eye contact. He didn't.

"Teddy, contact me if you think of anything else that might help us catch Todd's killer," Ethan said.

~

Glancing at her watch, Caitlyn knew the coach was next on their schedule. She was hoping they'd run out of time.

"You know, not everyone has good memories of high school," Caitlyn said.

"No, I suppose not," Ethan replied. He completely missed the fact that Caitlyn was trying to open a dialogue about herself. Instead, his mind was on the current situation and thinking about the three students they had just interviewed.

Before she could explain more they arrived at the gym doors. Upon opening, they noticed an adult female was putting a group of young women through warm-up drills. Caitlyn watched a moment before she figured out they must be getting ready for field hockey practice. That was something not offered in her day. In fact, not many athletic choices were offered when she went through school.

Times sure have changed.

~

"Excuse us," Ethan said as he poked his head into Coach Kollner's closet-size office.

"Come in folks," responded an older man with a balding head and a hint of a wheat belly.

Caitlyn observed this old man. He was nothing like she remembered. *Apparently C.K. didn't exercise with his team. Or at least not often enough. Would he remember her, and more importantly would he remember what he tried? Or was she only one of many young female students?*

She steadied herself by holding on the back of a chair as she stated her name while carefully watching his expression. No change; he was oblivious. Another right she would wrong while in Riverview.

"I was hoping you could tell me about Todd Tilton. Tell us about his personality on and off the court. And if you put any credence into the threats by his neighboring school rivals," Ethan asked.

C.K. leaned back in his chair and thought a moment.

"You know, I've been thinking of nothing else since I heard about Todd's death. He was a great kid, a real loss to the team. It's going to be hard to replace him. Over the years I've found the school environment is a microcosm of society. You might say it's a place where kids take on adult behaviors, and with that comes the good and the bad."

C.K. paused a moment collecting his thoughts. He was thinking about the lovely woman in front of him. If only she had come without the sheriff, he might have been more willing to share ... but he continued.

"So, yes, we have our share of friction between students, between players. A team should work as one. Unfortunately that is not always the case. Even though Denny and Todd were good friends, I knew there was a lot of tension between them. They are both juniors, both popular boys, but Todd always seemed to win out. He scored higher each game, and was elected captain of the team this year. I could tell this grated on Denny.

And then there were the threats from the other team. I know the guys were joking about it, but I sensed they were a little scared. I certainly was taking it seriously, and have been on the phone with their coach several times. We're watching these kids closely."

"Do you think Denny or these other kids could have taken the sport seriously enough to harm Todd?" Ethan asked.

"I certainly hope not," replied C.K. with a sigh. "It would destroy our basketball program, as well as damage morale in the entire school. Like I said, I've been keeping a close eye on the kids. Even hired an assistant coach this year. I'm getting on in years."

"Thanks, Coach. Oh, I heard you and Todd had words a few days ago. Can you tell me what that was about?"

Coach Kollner's back stiffened.

"I don't know what you're talking about. We had a conversation, but I was only correcting some of his plays. Nothing more than that."

Ethan didn't believe the coach. There was more to their "conversation" than the coach was saying. Something else he would have to dig into.

"I appreciate your candor and know we will be talking again. In the meantime, if you think of anything, do contact me." Ethan stated.

The coach nodded, lost in his own thoughts of Todd and of the woman who was now leaving his office.

~ EIGHTEEN ~

Ethan and Caitlyn walked down the hall towards the front doors.

"That guy gives me the creeps," Caitlyn said, referring to their talk with the coach. After that came out she wasn't sure whether or not she wanted Ethan to take the bait and continue the conversation.

"He's just an old man who has been *the coach* all his life and is desperately trying to keep that status. It's hard to let go. Coaches carry a special aura, if you want to call it that. They're placed on a higher plane and I suspect it's because of our society's fascination with sports and sports figures," Ethan explained

Caitlyn was half listening. Her attention was caught by what she noticed as they passed the cafeteria.

"Wait! Let's talk to the woman over there."

Ethan had walked on, but noting Caitlyn was no longer by his side, he stopped and turned to see what she was looking at. He surveyed the cafeteria and noticed the woman Caitlyn pointed out.

"Why?"

"Because if you want to know what's really going on in the school, you ask the cafeteria ladies. Those are the people kids relate to. They're the motherly types. They're not teaching them, testing them, or disciplining them. What they do to the best of their ability and budget is feed them," Caitlyn responded.

When Ethan and Caitlyn approached, the woman stopped wiping down the table she was clearing. They introduced themselves and explained why they were there.

"May we have a minute of your time?" Ethan asked.

The woman looked around as if she would be reprimanded for interrupting her work.

"I guess. My name is Harriett Wilford. What can I do for you?"

"Did you know Todd Tilton?"

"I know all the kids who go to school here; some better'n others, mind you. Of course I knew Todd. He was very popular. Everybody knew 'im."

"And what can you tell me about him?" Ethan asked.

"Well, I don't like to gossip, ya know."

"I'm conducting a murder investigation, Harriett, so anything you can tell me about Todd or anyone he hung out with is not gossip."

"Well, he was popular, as I said, but recently he was getting friendly with Teddy," Harriett replied.

"What can you tell me about Teddy Risley?" Ethan asked.

Harriett started wiping down the table again with fast hard swipes. Caitlyn noticed the woman's face muscles tense as she chose her words carefully.

"I don't like to gossip, ya' know," Harriett repeated.

Ethan was losing his patience.

"Harriett, this is a murder investigation. Anything you can tell me about Todd's activities at school will be helpful. It may provide us with an important piece of information to find the killer and bring justice for Todd and his family."

Harriett thought about what Ethan said while continuing to wipe down the table and stealing glances over her shoulder.

"It was a strange combination at first," she stated in a whisper. "Popular boy and a kid who didn't seem to have much personality. But I seen 'em together quite a lot lately. Not always at lunch, but sometimes during free time they would be sitting together talking. I couldn't figure out what they might be talking about until one day I was wiping down a table nearby and I heard Todd telling Ted something like he felt the same way. I think he used the word crushed. Yea, that's right, crushed. They both felt smothered. And then the next minute I hear 'em talking soil and water. Now what d'ya think that means?"

Caitlyn knew what some of it meant. She wished she could give this woman a hug. Harriett the cafeteria worker may have provided them with a break.

~ NINETEEN ~

On their way back to the office, Ethan had to swerve around several downed tree branches. He made a note to alert the highway department about the debris in the road. It should be cleaned up before the school buses rolled this afternoon.

"So, what did you think about the interviews?" Ethan asked.

"I always note whether there is eye contact," Caitlyn responded. "Both Susan and Teddy had trouble keeping eye contact when they were responding."

"Does that necessarily mean they are hiding something?" Ethan asked. "Or could it be their youth and lack of self esteem?"

"Possibly both. We'll have to find out." Caitlyn said, hesitated, and then asked, "What did you think about the coach?"

"As I said before, he's just an old man past his prime. Probably living in the past. But I didn't like the way he was eyeballing you. I hope that isn't an indication of something deeper."

Caitlyn started to say something when Ethan interrupted as he stopped the car and opened his door.

"Here we are. Let's find out what problems Maddie has had to deal with this morning."

~

When they entered the sheriff's office Maddie was making a fresh pot of coffee.

Caitlyn watched her and thought, *Maddie could be so attractive if she only did something with her curly mop of hair and applied a little makeup. Her facial features are nicely proportioned even if she is a bit on the stocky side. With the proper clothing, her figure would be accentuated in just the right places.*

"So how'd you make out at the school?" Maddie asked.

Caitlyn walked over to the row of metal chairs and chose one closest to Ethan's office door. While Ethan filled Maddie in, Caitlyn watched the two of them while she sipped the welcome cup of coffee.

Maddie has a crush on her boss and she doesn't like competition. I wonder if it bothers Maddie that I'm assisting Ethan with the interviews.

Ethan gathered the mail from the inbox and said, "Let's go into my office and compare notes."

Once seated in the cramped office, Caitlyn pulled out her steno pad and started reading her notes.

"They each agreed Todd was a good student and good athlete. The students on the other hand hinted at Todd's unhappiness with the pressure put on him to succeed by his parents, and even some peers. His friends wonder why he befriended Teddy Risley. I think you met the mother. Teddy seems to be a bit strange. He is quiet, shy, has a temper, and doesn't make eye contact. To me it's a sign of some sort of emotional state. But I detected something else, some other intimacy Teddy could not or would not share."

"I agree, but there's something about Denny that bothers me," Ethan said.

"Like what?" Caitlyn responded.

"His good friend is murdered and he seems calm and flippant with his answers. I expected a very different reaction from him," Ethan explained.

"Could it be his defense mechanism? Maybe he's still trying to process the event. It's normal for teenagers to think they're invincible," Caitlyn said.

"My hunch is it goes beyond that. Kids can get pretty worked up over their place on athletic teams. I've seen it before. What seems like a tiff ends up being much more. Tempers flare and before they know it, things get out of control. I'll ask Maddie to do a little background check on Denny and his family. Just to satisfy my curiosity," Ethan said.

"In the meantime I'd like to visit the Risley's to get a feel for the family dynamics. I've a good excuse since they're neighbors and rent from Uncle Jerry. Would it be a problem?" Caitlyn asked, though her mind was made up. She was going to visit the Risley's whether Ethan approved or not.

"I guess it'd be okay for just a friendly visit. The mother's name is Darcy. I talked with her the other day. Just make sure your visit is only that. We can't do anything to jeopardize the investigation."

"I understand," said Caitlyn. "And I'm really sorry I left to take the phone call."

"Never mind. I just wanted to make sure we captured complete and accurate notes of all the interviews." Ethan said.

As he responded, he fought his rising emotions. He couldn't, wouldn't, let himself become too fond of her.

"It won't happen again," said Caitlyn, crossing her fingers she would be included in future interviews. It felt good to be part of a team in the search of her cousin's killer, and part of a team with Ethan.

"Deputy Snow followed up on the surveyors working on Friday. It appears they're on the up and up. Jerry Tilton is having his land surveyed. The surveyors didn't know why, they were just hired to do it. They didn't see anything out of place either, though they admitted when they're working they're intent on getting accurate measurements. I checked the company's record and it appears to be a legitimate business. The items I found at the scene were sent to forensics, and it might take a while to get the results. They always have a backlog, but I cashed in some chips and was told our case would be put on a higher priority," Ethan said, steadying his voice.

Caitlyn didn't want the discussion, the intimacy of working closely together to end, but knew it had to. She closed her steno pad and handed it to Ethan.

"Thanks for letting me ride along today. It helped me feel like I'm doing something for Todd."

Ethan shook off his emotions and tried his best to be professional.

"I appreciate your help. With Tom working on storm related issues, I appreciated the backup. Your notes look complete and will be helpful."

Caitlyn stood to leave.

"I need to head back to help Aunt Myra. I'll let you know if I learn anything more at the Risley's," Caitlyn said.

~ TWENTY ~

Before she visited the Risley's, Caitlyn went back to the house to check on her aunt. She hadn't told Myra what she was doing today, only that she was going "out." Myra deserved an explanation, and Caitlyn knew Summit would miss her. She was growing fond of the little bundle of fur, and wondered if they would allow Summit to go home with her.

Summit, who fancied himself the official greeter, met Caitlyn at the door. He sniffed her, ran in circles, and then picked up his favorite toy of the moment. He raced back and forth expressing joy at her arrival.

"Hello?" Caitlyn called. There was no response. Myra must have gone out, so Caitlyn decided this was a good time to call her parents.

She walked to the sun porch, her favorite room in this large farmhouse and pulled out her cell phone. As Summit jumped up and snuggled down next to her she scrolled through her contacts for their number. When her mother answered Caitlyn was at a loss for words. How does one describe the range of emotions she had experienced since arriving in Riverview?

"Mom, it's Caitlyn. I'm still in Riverview. The funeral is tomorrow. I think everything is set. Aunt Myra and Uncle Jerry appear to be handling things okay. Sometimes I don't know what to say to them. I plan to stay a few more days to help." Caitlyn spilled everything out before her mother could say a word.

"I'm so relieved you are able to help, Caitlyn. And Myra must so appreciate you being there. I'm glad everything is going as well as can be expected in these horrible circumstances. I wish I could come up, but, well, I didn't want to tell you because I know how you worry so, but I fell last week. Stupid really. I broke my leg and am in a full leg cast. Slows me down, and there was no way I could comfortably fly, switching planes, and all that."

"My god, Mom. Why didn't you tell me? I could have come down to help you for the first few days."

"That's exactly why I didn't tell you," her mother replied. "I know how busy you are getting your business up and running. And, I really didn't need any help. What I do need to do is slow down, read a lot, and stay off the leg until it heals."

That was so much like her mother that Caitlyn decided to switch the subject.

"Okay, so, Mom, is Dad there?" Caitlyn asked.

"Why, no, dear. He's traveling on business. I know, he's supposed to be retired, but the oil business seems to need his expertise, and to tell the truth, he loves it. Retirement was difficult for him. He got tired of playing golf every day, and he missed his colleagues. So this works. He travels several times a month. He won't tell me where. Says it is 'need to know.' Like old times, wouldn't you say?" Her mother chuckled.

"Mom, you mean you have no idea where he is?" Caitlyn asked.

"Dear, he calls me almost every day so there's no need to worry. And you know we live in this supportive community so if I ever need anything ..." Ann said.

"Mom, do you think he has contact with Uncle Jerry?" Caitlyn asked.

"Now why would you say that, dear? You know we haven't had the best of relationship with them. So sad of course, but sometimes it's how families are," Ann explained.

"I met one of my school friends and they said they thought Dad and Uncle Jerry were working together. Do you think dad would give me a call? And since you brought it up, what did happen between you and Myra?" Caitlyn asked.

The silence lasted so long Caitlyn thought the connection was lost.

"It's all water under the bridge as they say. Have to go now dear, time for my Bridge game, and my ride is here," Ann replied in a rush.

The dial tone told Caitlyn her mother had hung up without answering her questions. And although she said she needed to rest, her social activities seemed to continue on schedule.

There had to be another way to find out if her father and uncle were involved in a scheme to allow oil companies unlimited access to Upstate New York land.

~ TWENTY-ONE ~

Monday Afternoon

The Risley tenant house was a quarter mile from the Tilton's so Caitlyn decided to walk over. On the way she planned her conversation with Darcy. Ethan warned her: No questions, just conversation and observe the family dynamics. She would stick to the script. Maybe.

She noticed the house was in need of a coat of paint. The lawn needed attention as well. The recent rain was going to do some good, but there was a large amount of crabgrass. One large oak tree in the front yard would provide summer shade, and two scraggly boxwoods flanked the front steps. This yard needed some serious TLC.

There was no garage so their vehicle was parked on the dirt driveway near the front entrance. The only striking thing on the house was the bright blue door. Caitlyn approached and knocked.

The door was opened by a woman in her mid-forties. Her brown hair, streaked with gray was pulled back and wrapped in a loose bun. Caitlyn noticed a family resemblance between mother and son. A flowered apron protected the woman's flannel shirt and jeans. She wore clogs on her feet.

"Yes? What do you want?" Darcy Risley asked.

"I'm Caitlyn Jamison, the Tilton's niece. I've come for Todd's funeral, and am staying a few extra days to help. Since my aunt and uncle are out, I was lonely, so I thought, why not visit the neighbors?" Caitlyn said.

Darcy thought this young woman a bit forward knocking on people's doors.

"I'm kinda busy right now," Darcy replied. "But I guess you can come in for a minute or two."

"That's very kind. Thank you. I don't mean to intrude," Caitlyn said.

"I'm drying herbs, so come into the kitchen. We can talk while I work," Darcy said.

"I'd like that," Caitlyn replied.

For the next thirty minutes Caitlyn learned more than she ever needed to know about herbs and their medicinal properties. She learned Darcy intended to market her herbs and take Teddy on as a partner.

"You have a fine collection and an exciting business plan," Caitlyn said. "When are you planning to set up your business?" Caitlyn knew immediately it was the wrong thing to say. Darcy's face turned red.

"I haven't decided yet," Darcy replied angrily.

Caitlyn didn't know what she said that upset Darcy, so she changed the subject.

"What herb is best for sadness?" Caitlyn asked.

Before Darcy could answer, the door opened and Teddy entered the kitchen. When he saw Caitlyn he stopped and started to back out.

Darcy on the other hand glowed at the sight of her son, all hint of anger vanished.

"Teddy, this is the Tilton's niece, Caitlyn. Say hello."

"Hi," Teddy said.

"Actually, we met at school this morning. I was talking with some of the students and teachers about my cousin. I'm sad I didn't get to know him better, and now it's too late. I guess I was trying to make up for those lost years," Caitlyn explained. She hoped Teddy wouldn't betray her white lie. He would know she was doing more than trying to get to know her cousin's friends. Caitlyn continued to look from mother to son to see what unspoken conversation might be going on between them.

"Well, then, Teddy, dear, come sit down and have your milk and cookie. I have it all ready for you," Darcy said.

Teddy looked from Caitlyn to his mother. "No thanks, Mom. I think I'll go up and do some homework," Teddy replied.

When he was out of earshot, Darcy sat down at the table across from Caitlyn.

She sighed, "I don't know what has gotten into him lately. We always sat with milk and cookies when he got home from school, but lately he wants to go to his room."

"Don't you think it's normal teenage behavior?" Caitlyn said.

"Not my Teddy. We're close; we do everything together. His health hasn't been the best, you know, and I'm the one who cares for him," Darcy said. "It's why I started my herb garden. To make sure he has the best natural care."

"Is Teddy close with his dad as well?" Caitlyn asked.

"I should say not," Darcy was quick to respond. "Mac's role is to provide for us. I'm the one who cares for Teddy."

Darcy's change of tone made the atmosphere tense and claustrophobic, and the herbal formulas Darcy was mixing was giving Caitlyn a headache. She thanked Darcy for the visit and said she better get back.

"So much to do, you know," Caitlyn explained.

~ TWENTY-TWO ~

Monday Late Afternoon
The grandfather clock in the front hall was finishing its fifth and final chime when Caitlyn let herself in the front door. Otherwise the house was quiet.

"Anyone home?"

The only answer was Summit racing down the stairs barking with joy. As he jumped up on her legs, she stroked his soft curly head.

"You must have been so sound asleep you didn't hear me come in," Caitlyn said.

After Ethan had left the house on Saturday afternoon, her uncle had made it clear no one was to enter Todd's room. As Caitlyn reached the second floor, she looked down the long hall. With Todd's door closed, the hall appeared dark and sinister, an appropriate setting for what she was going to do.

She needed to find out what Todd was involved in that got him killed, because her instincts said this was not a random act. The sheriff could be right. It might have been a teenage squabble gone wrong. But with whom? Unlike the sheriff, she didn't think Denny was capable of killing his friend. She didn't have more information on the boys from the neighboring school who had threatened Todd, so no judgment there. Could it be someone in Todd's circle was jealous of his relationship with Teddy? There were too many options, and therefore, she had to search his room for any clue the sheriff might have overlooked.

Caitlyn listened carefully for sounds within or outside the house. No one home yet. She didn't know where her aunt was or when she might return. The bank closed at five so her uncle could arrive at any time. This was her only window of opportunity.

"Come on Summit. You'll be my partner in crime."

Summit wagged his tail in anticipation and followed Caitlyn down the dark hallway.

She took a deep breath and turned the knob. Stuck.

Damn! Did Uncle Jerry lock the door?

She tried again, this time putting weight on the door with her shoulder. It opened and light flooded the hallway. Caitlyn was surprised at what she saw. The room was not what she expected. No posters of sports heroes, cars, or movies. Instead, the walls were painted a pale blue decorated by a lovely poster of the Adirondacks. There was a framed oil painting of a local landscape, lush green trees of varying colors, cascading down to a sparkling blue lake. She hurried over to the desk where she was somewhat relieved to find a typical teenage mess. She rifled through the papers, mostly schoolwork. She opened the top desk drawer and looked through. Nothing but pens, pencils, small pads, receipts for various items. Todd's junk drawer. The top right side drawer was much the same, though with an empty spot where his laptop had been stored, and now in the hands of the sheriff.

She opened the middle drawer and found Pendaflex files. None were labeled, so she walked her fingers through them. When she got to the very last one, it flopped forward from the weight of a 6 x 9 black leather book. She wondered how the sheriff missed it. At the moment she opened it she detected a noise downstairs. She quickly closed the book and slipped it into her pocket. She headed for the door and stepped out with Summit at her heels when she became face to face with her uncle.

"What the hell are you doing in there, Caitlyn? I thought I made it clear that room is completely off limits," Jerry roared, his face beet red.

With pounding heart Caitlyn did her best to remain calm.

She smiled and said, "Oh, Uncle Jerry, I wasn't in Todd's room. Summit got shut in there somehow. I arrived home and heard him whimpering. I looked all over the house before I found him up here. I was letting him out. I know he must be hungry and thirsty, so I'll take him to the kitchen and get him some dinner."

She hoped her uncle believed the white lie.

"I don't know how that could have happened, but thank you for letting him out. He's a pesky dog. We should get rid of him," Jerry stated. His grim expression spoke volumes.

Caitlyn cringed. How could her uncle be so cold hearted as to "get rid" of his son's pet? This made her even more determined to take Summit with her when she left. Caitlyn took Summit to the kitchen and scooped some food into his dish. She whispered a thank you as she made a hurried retreat to her room to read what was in the black book Todd carefully hid behind his files.

~

Ethan pulled on protective gloves and carefully picked up the pin found at the crime scene. He had not yet sent it to the forensics lab. He wanted to do his own research on it first. He returned the pin to its protective bag and turned to his computer.

What did people do before Google?

He typed in "Pin with Eagle head." His screen populated with results. He scrolled down to see the most likely and settled on the Fraternal Order of Eagles. A photo near the end of the article showed a pin similar to the one in his hand. He read each order was assigned a specific aerie number, and if he could clean this pin off enough, he might be able to read the number imprinted on it.

Reaching the end of the article, Ethan knew the FOE supported a number of causes, such as heart disease, cancer, and handicapped children. He would have to find out if Jerry Tilton was a member of this organization, even though he disavowed recognizing the pin. If not, then it was likely this pin came off during the struggle with Todd. And if he could figure out the aerie number, he'd be able to narrow down the list of suspects due to their specific geographic location.

Ethan smiled as he pushed back in his chair. This small pin might provide him with an important break in the case.

~ TWENTY-THREE ~

Tuesday

The Riverview St. Paul's Episcopal Church, built of stone in the early 1800s, was an historical landmark. The sidewalk from the parking lot to the impressive wooden front door was designed to bring parishioners alongside the church so the stained glass windows could be viewed and appreciated prior to entering. It was a nice way to set the tone for worship.

Attending funeral services was part of Ethan's job, at least the funerals of crime victims. He had been taught there was a chance the killer might attend, though Ethan was not convinced of that line of thinking. But he had to cover all the bases, do everything by the book, so here he was sitting in the back pew of St. Paul's Episcopal Church.

Ethan nodded to residents as he walked into the church, which by the time he arrived, was packed. He expected as much.

Jerry Tilton was an important person in the community. Not well liked, but important in the fact he was feared more than revered. People needed the bank; they needed loans. It meant keeping on the good side of Jerry Tilton.

The family arrived and Ethan couldn't help keeping his eyes on Caitlyn Jamison. She was as striking dressed in black as she was in sweater and jeans when he first met her on Saturday.

The service was well done. The minister knew he was to perform his best if his congregation continued to be a beneficiary of the Tilton's. Myra Tilton looked a wreck. She walked in supported by her husband and Caitlyn. Jerry stood tall and no emotion touched his face. Ethan wondered what was going on inside his head at this moment. Tilton had showed a softer side on Friday evening, but now public persona was displayed.

Following the service the family received their guests in the recently built church hall. It was a lovely setting with large floor to ceiling arched windows looking out onto the church garden, a space tended by the St. Paul Garden Ladies who were always raising money for one thing or another. The food was plenty and people were enjoying the repast provided by the Tiltons.

Ethan mingled among the guests, introducing himself to those he didn't know. It was important for the community to know he was concerned and doing his best to find Todd's killer.

He noticed Caitlyn talking with another woman. They seemed quite animated, and so he pondered the connection. Before he could pose the question, Caitlyn broke free and approached him.

"Hi, Sheriff," said Caitlyn.

"Oh, hi. I see your aunt and uncle are holding up pretty well," Ethan replied.

"We've gotten through the funeral and now face the burial. We'll go to the cemetery after everyone leaves."

Ethan nodded, understanding the burial was to be private.

"Any more news on the investigation?" Caitlyn asked.

"The state police are working with us. I've been covering a number of bases, but nothing much has come of them. And then there are things I can't talk about. I think you understand," Ethan said. "By the way, who is the woman you were talking with a moment ago?"

"Abbie Sullivan Hetherington. We were friends when I lived here. She is one of those people who is a friend for life, even though we haven't been in touch. Abbie and her husband, Tim, run a winery up the lake. I met her after the church service on Sunday. She asked that I visit to show me their winery and catch up a bit. I thought it strange when she asked me to come Sunday afternoon, since she knew there were many details to attend to, but there was something in her voice and face I couldn't turn her down. I figured it would be good to get out of the house for a few hours, so I drove up."

Caitlyn paused, wondering whether this was an appropriate time for this conversation. She had to control her impulsive nature.

"She told me something disturbing. This isn't the time or place to share the information with you, but I'd like to get your opinion. It may or may not have anything to do with Todd's murder."

Before Ethan could respond, Caitlyn noticed her aunt waving to her.

"I see Aunt Myra is looking for me. I'd better go. Maybe we can talk tomorrow?" Caitlyn said.

"Sounds like we need to," Ethan said.

~ TWENTY-FOUR ~

With the funeral, reception and burial behind them, Jerry, Myra and Caitlyn returned to the house in silence. There was nothing left to say to each other or to anyone else. They each had to deal with grief in their own way. Jerry stomped off to his office and closed the door. Myra headed to her room, also closing her door.

Caitlyn was left alone. She was emotionally spent. She wandered through the house wondering if this broken family could ever be fixed.

The three of them had lived on adrenaline the past few days, each busy with their own duties, each trying to keep an emotional balance.

At some point the balance will tip, and she suspected as the reality set in and the condolences stopped, the devastation would hit. How would they each react?

Caitlyn struggled with what she should do. She should get back to Washington, back to her business, back to her life. But as she watched her aunt, knowing how fragile she was at this moment, and knowing Jerry was not capable of providing the emotional support Myra needed, Caitlyn decided she had better stay a few more days.

Besides, Ethan seemed to welcome her help with the investigation. And then there was Abbie's situation. Caitlyn couldn't leave until she got to the bottom of it. She knew she couldn't make a big difference in how the oil companies operate, but there was a chance she could make a small one. She had to try.

When they arrived home from the funeral, she fed the dog, but Summit had sniffed at his dinner and walked away. It was apparent he, too, felt the loss, and with head hanging, the little dog followed Caitlyn as she went to her room.

When they were securely locked in she retrieved Todd's black book out of her pants pocket and she settled back against the big pillows as Summit snuggled close. She had just begun to read it the day before when her aunt had knocked at the door needing Caitlyn's help. So, now, as Summit snored away beside her, she opened the first page again. Her phone rang.

"Caitlyn speaking."

"Caitlyn, it's Doris at The Outdoor Foundation. We were expecting a draft of our annual report on Monday, and we still haven't received it. Is there anything wrong?"

"Oh, Doris, I'm so sorry. No, I mean yes. I was finishing your report on Friday when my aunt called to tell me of a death in the family. I hopped a plane and went to her. I'm there now, in Upstate New York. I have my computer with me and will send off the draft immediately," Caitlyn said.

"I'm so sorry to hear about your family emergency, Caitlyn. Will you be able to continue work on the report?"

"Yes, Doris. Of course."

"You know I love working with you, but Mr. Peterson is getting upset about the lateness of the report. I heard him talking about trying out another agency. You do realize we have to review the draft, make additions and corrections, get it back to you, and then to the printer. The printer's deadline is next Monday, and that's cutting it close. Our board of directors meeting starts that Thursday," Doris said.

"O.k. You'll have it shortly. Send it back as soon as you can and I'll make the revisions and get it back to you well before Monday," Caitlyn promised.

"All right. I'll look for it in my email within the next few minutes," Doris said. "Bye, Caitlyn, and again, I am sorry for your loss."

Caitlyn hit "end" and rushed to her laptop. How could she forget her most important client? If she lost The Outdoor Foundation account, she wouldn't have enough money to pay her rent. What a mess.

~

After finishing the final touches to The Outdoor Foundation's annual report and sending it off, Caitlyn spent the next hour tending to her other clients. She sent off emails updating them on their projects. She told them where she was and why. After hitting send on the last one, she noticed there was still enough daylight left for a brief walk.

She needed to get out of the house, clear her head and decide how to get information out of her father about what his oil company, or any others for that matter, planned for New York State. She was sure he was still working for them in that capacity. Why else would they need a consultant with his background? He claimed he was retired, but she never believed it. Every time she called, her father was "traveling." Her mother claimed to know nothing, but Caitlyn thought she was lying, or at least not telling the whole truth.

Caitlyn decided to head to the barn and visit with Rudy. She was sure the horse missed Todd and his daily visits. Her uncle had arranged for a farm hand to care for the horse, letting Rudy out to pasture during the day, bringing him in at night, feeding, grooming, arranging for the farrier, but that wasn't the same as having a soul mate. She instinctively knew Todd and Rudy were soul mates. The least she could do was spend time talking with Rudy before he was sold to the next owner, which she was sure her uncle would do.

It wasn't easy to slide the heavy wooden barn door open. As she pushed, red flakes fell and clung to her fleece jacket. She whisked them away while acclimating herself to the dark interior. She stepped over the threshold and stopped to let her eyes adjust. She heard something, something different than the horse. It was a creaking sound, probably the barn boards cooling as the sun went down. At least that is what she told herself.

"Hello," Caitlyn called out. She was probably being silly about hearing sounds, but if the farm hand was in the building doing chores, she didn't want to startle him. There was no response to her call, and the noise ceased.

Was her imagination getting the best of her? Was the place of Todd's murder giving her the creeps?

She took a deep breath - *get a grip*. She was here to get away from stress, not add to it. And she was here to visit Rudy, to stroke his long neck, and to let him know he was still loved.

Once her eyes adjusted to the darkness she searched for a light switch or pull down cord. Nothing. She chided herself for not checking out the location of the switches in the daylight. She would make do, walking carefully so she wouldn't trip over anything. She saw the dark outline of Rudy's head leaning out of his stall, happily munching on hay he had scrounged from the floor. She stopped to watch him. Every so often he would raise his head, mouth full of hay, look at her, then continue his munching.

The life of a horse, she thought.

A scraping noise came from overhead. Rudy stomped his hoof. Something was making the horse nervous. A chill went down her spine. Was her imagination in overdrive, or was there someone here and not responding to her call?

"Hello?" Caitlyn called out again. "Is there someone here?"

She thought she detected a rustling overhead. It was probably mice scurrying away as a result of her voice. She prayed, *let it be mice and not rats*. She hated rats and mice weren't far behind. She failed to factor that in when she planned to visit the barn, which was prime real estate for the rodent population. Maybe she should reconsider her visit with Rudy.

Curiosity got the better of her and she looked up to see what was making the sound. As her head began to tilt upward, a heavy weight hit, knocking her down and taking her breath away. The next thing she knew she was flat on the floor and no idea what happened until she felt the weight of hay bales on her chest.

She must have blacked out, but for how long? She pushed the heavy hay bales away, coughing away the hay dust in her throat. Her strength was spent. At some point she thought she heard the door at the back of the barn slam shut. Caitlyn sat up carefully, stunned, and with the start of a wicked headache. She hoped she didn't have a concussion.

Did someone intentionally try to hurt her? Or were the hay bales precariously perched so they fell by accident? If so, how come she heard the barn door slam?

She tried to put the chain of events into perspective.

If Rudy could talk.

Without thinking she pulled the phone from her pocket and touched Ethan's cell number.

"Caitlyn, I'm in a meeting now, can I call you back?" Ethan whispered.

"Ethan! I think someone just tried to kill me."

~

When Ethan arrived at the Tilton's, Caitlyn was in the house cleaning up. Myra was bustling around with peroxide, bandages, and a bottle of aspirin.

Caitlyn explained the series of events, stating the fact she was not sure whether there was anyone in the barn. The bales could have been piled too close to the edge, and the rear door could have blown shut. There could be a reasonable explanation for her accident.

"I'm sorry you came all the way out here. I should have thought things through more clearly. It was . . . well, . . . I was scared."

"You did the right thing. We can't discount this simply as an accident. I'm going out to the barn to see if there is any evidence you interrupted someone," Ethan said. "Stay in the house tonight. I'll call you tomorrow morning."

~ TWENTY-FIVE ~

Wednesday, Riverview, NY

It was still early, but Ethan needed to check on Caitlyn. He called her cell to avoid the Tiltons, since Jerry Tilton called him every day grilling him on the progress of the investigation. Ethan didn't tell him what was learned at the school, especially the relationship Todd developed with Teddy Risley. There were things he didn't want the public to know, even the father of the victim, especially the father of the victim. The more he learned about Jerry Tilton the less respect he had for the man.

Ethan picked up the phone and dialed.

"Caitlyn here," A sleepy voice answered.

"It's Ethan. Did I wake you?"

"No, well, yes, I guess so," as she rolled over to look at the clock. "What's up?" Caitlyn said.

"I wanted to check in to make sure you're all right from yesterday's adventure."

"I'm a bit sore, but I'm fine. A few scratches on my face and a bump on my head where I hit the floor, but those will soon disappear. And thank god the headache is gone. Did you find anything in the barn to explain what happened?" Caitlyn asked.

"Not much. But from what I observed of how the hay is stacked in the loft, I think someone was up there and intentionally threw the bales on you."

"Oh my god! Why would someone do that? I don't pose a threat to anyone," Caitlyn said.

"I don't have the answer to that, but I plan to find out," Ethan responded. "I found something at Todd's murder scene and want your input," Ethan explained.

Caitlyn sat up in bed untangling her legs from the still sleeping Summit, before she continued.

"Oh, and there is something else I wanted to mention before I forget. There's a property up the road. It looks run down, but it also looks like someone lives there. Do you know anything about it? I haven't had time or opportunity to ask Uncle Jerry or Aunt Myra about it," Caitlyn said.

"Yes, I know it and I visited the man who lives there. His name is Clyde Jones, a recluse. I don't have a good feeling about the guy. There is definitely something going on with him. I have my deputy doing a background check," Ethan said.

"I should have figured you were on top of that. I plan to see Abbie this morning. I want to learn a little more about the environmental issue they're facing. She told me my father and uncle might be involved, but I haven't been able to verify that fact. I asked my mother to tell Dad to give me a call; he hasn't. That tells me he's up to no good," Caitlyn said.

Ethan didn't respond. He knew better than to pass judgment on relatives not his own. He didn't want to get into Caitlyn's family dynamics.

"What did you want to talk with me about?" Caitlyn asked.

"Nothing in particular. Enjoy your visit with Abbie," Ethan said as he hung up.

~

Caitlyn gingerly climbed out of bed, rubbing her hip that was bruised from hitting the barn floor yesterday. She felt the small bump on her head. Thankfully, the swelling had gone down during the night. She felt guilty about leaving the rumpled sheets, blankets and comforter, but they would have to stay rumpled until Summit decided to rise and shine.

Refreshed from her shower, Caitlyn grabbed her phone and headed for the door.

Summit woke and raced after her not wanting to be alone. As he jumped from the bed, Todd's black book slid onto the floor from its hiding place within the comforter's folds. And as Summit launched himself out the door, his back legs sent the little book sliding under the bed.

~

The kitchen was quiet when Caitlyn and Summit appeared. She thought her uncle would be up getting ready for work.

Must be nice to be a banker.

Caitlyn found ground coffee in a container in the right hand cupboard. She poured water into the coffeemaker and waited impatiently. In the cupboard just above the coffeemaker were Wedgewood china cups, the kind with the narrow lip that Caitlyn preferred. While her coffee was brewing she went to the pantry where Summit's dry food was stored. She poured a bit in his bowl and freshened his water.

With fresh brewed coffee in hand she made her way to the sun porch. The early morning April sun had not yet warmed the room and the night's chill prevailed. Caitlyn didn't mind. She loved the light coming through the glass and pulled a throw around her to keep warm.

Because of Doris's call last night, Caitlyn turned her attention to her clients. She turned her laptop on and began working on pending projects.

Her thoughts then went to Nick. Since her conversation with Abbie, something was nagging at her, but she couldn't quite put her finger on it. And she wondered what was going on with her father. She pulled out her cell and punched in his number. If he wasn't going to call her, she would call him. The phone rang, and then went to voicemail.

"This is Herb Jamison. Leave me a message," was all she heard.

"Dad, it's Caitlyn. I need to talk with you. Please call me as soon as you can." She clicked "End" and sighed.

What exactly were the men in her life up to?

~ TWENTY-SIX ~

Jerry Tilton left for the office earlier than usual. He was expecting two gentlemen from Albany to be there before the bank opened for business. They wanted to meet yesterday until Jerry told them he needed the day for his son's funeral. Funeral or not, some things couldn't wait, and Jerry Tilton knew it as well as the next.

Jerry had told his secretary he was expecting some banking colleagues and asked her to arrive earlier than usual and get coffee ready.

He was seated primly at his desk when his secretary showed the two men into his office.

The men were non-descript. Black suits, white shirts, ties with a subtle diamond pattern. Colors barely discernable. Their height, weight and crew cuts gave them a similar appearance. Jerry knew these men would be seen, but not noticed. There was nothing that stood out and there was a good reason for that.

Maybe they're twins, Jerry thought with amusement.

"I've asked Laura to bring us coffee. She should be back in a few minutes," Jerry said. He wanted his guests to be as comfortable as possible.

"Thanks, much appreciated. We know you have a plane to catch later this morning to make the meeting with the oil company board, so we'll be brief. First, introductions. All you need to know is first names. We assume you are aware of the secrecy surrounding this project."

"Yes, I am," Jerry stated.

"You can call me Jack; this fellow is John," Jack said with a smile. "As you know, Senator Smith is failing and will not be able to fill out his term. That forces us to adjust our timetable. We won't have time to put you in as CEO of the bank in the city. You'll be appointed to fill out the senator's term."

Jerry was astounded. He had no idea the plan would escalate so quickly. He thought he could ease into the senate post after getting to know the players on Wall Street. Developing relationships was an important first step. Without that he wondered if he would be up to the task.

"Of course, whatever you think is best," was all he was able to say.

"Our research vehicles are scouting out the Catskills, and fanning out from there. We located several rich veins and our rigs are on the way to those areas. So far no one's the wiser. Bulldozers are preparing land, and nobody has noticed," Jack said.

Jerry was confused. What was Jack talking about? The oil drilling was occurring in the middle of the state. He would play along and hope it would all become evident.

"You need to be ready to travel to Albany at a moment's notice. You've been versed on how to vote, correct?" John asked.

"Yes, of course. Last Friday's meeting brought me up to date," Jerry replied.

"Good. We can't have a misstep," Jack said. "We need to get back and you have a plane to catch. Good talking with you, Mr. Tilton. We look forward to seeing you in Albany."

Jerry stood as his guests took their leave. The meeting was over so quickly Laura hadn't had a chance to serve coffee. This whole thing was like a whirlwind. As the men shook hands, and took their leave, a niggling doubt entered Jerry's mind.

The money and power inherent with the position was so enticing. But was he doing the right thing? Damn Todd for raising the environmental questions; questions that now nagged at him.

~

Caitlyn drove the country roads to the Winding Creek Winery. On the way she passed a number of small Amish farms. She slowed in anticipation of coming upon a horse drawn carriage or Amish youngsters biking their way to school.

She pulled into the now familiar driveway leading up the hill to Winding Creek's tasting room. This time Abbie wasn't at the door waving her in. She looked in the window to see if anyone was around, then knocked. A man dressed in work clothes appeared and approached the door.

"Sorry. We don't open until eleven today."

"I'm Caitlyn Jamison, Abbie's friend," Caitlyn responded.

The door opened though Caitlyn wasn't asked to enter.

"I'm Tim Hetherington, Abbie's husband. Nice to meet you. Is there something I can do for you?" Tim said.

Tim stood in the doorway. His expression cold. Not the welcome Caitlyn experienced the last time she was here.

"I sent her a text last night saying I was coming today. I thought she was expecting me," Caitlyn said apologetically.

"Did she respond?" Tim asked, tone still curt.

"Well, no, I guess she didn't," Caitlyn replied.

Tim continued to glare at her, then his expression suddenly softened.

Caitlyn wondered what the hell was going on here.

"Okay, come in. You shouldn't be standing out in the cold," Tim said.

"What's wrong?" Caitlyn asked. Tim's body language and lack of hospitality told her something dreadful happened.

"Have a seat," Tim instructed without answering her question.

Caitlyn did as she was told, and waited.

"Abbie's down today from her latest chemo treatment. She mentioned that she told you about her cancer. She doesn't tell many people, so you must be someone she considers a close friend," Tim said.

Caitlyn nodded, not sure what was coming.

"The reason she insisted on seeing you the other day, even though it wasn't the best time for you and your family, was she *just* had had her chemo treatment. They give a steroid with the treatments so for the next few days she's flying high. She has a lot of energy and gets everything done within those few days. Then she crashes. And that's what happened today. She can barely get out of bed. I just took her some broth, which seems to be the only thing she can keep down," Tim explained.

"I'm so sorry. Is there anything I can do?"

"No, thanks. Abbie plans her time well, and when she's down, most people don't notice. They think she is in the back doing paperwork," Tim said. "Her 5E doctor is coming this afternoon. Acupuncture, plus weekly massage with essential oils, helps," Tim said.

"What's 5E?" Caitlyn asked.

"Oh, sorry. It's Five Element Acupuncture. It corrects the imbalance of energy in the body by keeping the body's meridians open. Abbie feels much better after a treatment, and then a few days after she has a massage that includes reflexology with essential oils."

Caitlyn leaned forward as Tim talked. She was interested to learn about these natural medicines and what her friend was doing to help herself.

"These professionals keep Abbie's organs working as well as strengthening her immune system, which is being destroyed by the chemo. Seems like a Catch-22. The essential oils help with the healing process. It's a multifaceted approach to bringing her immune system back."

Tim stopped to see if Caitlyn was ready to hear more. Once he got going he tended to mind dump. Her body language gave him the answer.

"The most important factor though is diet, and we were surprised, no, shocked when her oncologist told her to eat whatever she wanted. The medical community has come so far, but they still don't seem to understand the *basics* of health. Abbie took a blood test to see what foods her body could handle right now while the chemo is pumping poisons into her body. We eliminated the foods on her 'red' list, and she only eats foods listed on the 'green' list. It hasn't been an easy road for us, but we are doing the best we can to fight this disease. Abbie knows a positive mental attitude is as important if not more so than the chemo. It's why she stays involved in the day-to-day operation of the winery. I wish this fracking issue hadn't come to the forefront. She doesn't need that kind of negative energy."

"I know we all have cancer cells in our body. What do you think Abbie's trigger was?" Caitlyn asked.

Tim's voice wavered with emotion.

"Abbie believes her cancer came from contaminated ground water due to the fracking in the next county. After she graduated from high school, her family moved to Dimock, Pennsylvania. Abbie went with them and worked in the area for a number of years. You may remember the 2009 news story about the well blowing up on New Year's Day. It was a neighbor of Abbie's parents.

Consequently, Abbie's parents' well was declared contaminated, and they were forced to move. By that time Abbie was living elsewhere so she didn't think much about it, except for worrying about her parents. They seem to be o.k. It turns out they were juice and soda drinkers, whereas Abbie, the more health conscious one, drank lots of water. Recent reports show high fructose juices and sodas are not good for you, but in this case, they were better than the water.

Since we learned of the fracking in the next county, Abbie insists we ship our water in, and we have a purifying plant on site. It's a horrible expense, and it may break us, but Abbie's fanatical about it. There's no reasoning with her. Clean, safe water has become an important issue with us, obviously since our product is producing high quality wine. We wonder if the next world power struggle will be over water."

Tim hesitated and took a deep breath. Caitlyn sat in silence letting him gather his thoughts.

"Anyway, Abbie believes your father and uncle are involved somehow and are pushing for more drilling. She hopes you can do something to stop this practice before it destroys not only our livelihood, but all of New York State agriculture."

Caitlyn was devastated at the news. Abbie's health, their livelihood, all wasted because of oil company greed. And now she was angry.

"Okay. Tell Abbie I'll do whatever I can."

Caitlyn got up, turned to go, then turned back and gave Tim a hug.

"Take good care of her and yourself."

~ TWENTY-SEVEN ~

Caitlyn was in a rage when she arrived back at the Tiltons. Her friend had cancer, brought on by poisonous chemicals being pumped into the ground. She thought about the situation on the ride home and became madder by the minute.

She let herself in the front door, slamming it behind her, and went straight to the kitchen, barely acknowledging Summit who was barking his way down the stairs. As was his habit, he ran to find his favorite toy, squirrel, and came running back. Caitlyn didn't bother to acknowledge him.

Instead, she stormed into the kitchen. "*Aunt Myra,* what do you know about Uncle Jerry and Dad working together on behalf of the oil companies?"

Myra continued to dip her tea ball up and down into her fine china cup.

"I prefer the old fashion way of making tea, don't you dear?"

Myra didn't wait for Caitlyn to respond.

"I love to mix my own blend of tea leaves."

"Aunt Myra, answer me," Caitlyn demanded. "Are you drunk?"

Myra turned on Caitlyn with fire in her eyes, "How *dare* you ask me that? My son has been murdered. I'm numb. Don't you understand? I am *numb* and right now I don't care about much of anything."

Caitlyn took a step back, shocked by her aunt's angry retort. Both women were about to explode and nothing good was going to come from this. They stared each other down, both taking stock of the situation, until Myra broke the silence.

"I'm sorry, Caitlyn. You know I didn't mean that. I don't know anything about Jerry's business. I suspected they've been in contact, even though your mother and I aren't anymore. Sad state, isn't it?

Sisters who should be close aren't. I guess we've both made mistakes and neither of us can break the wall of silence," Myra said.

Myra leaned back onto the counter.

"To further answer your question, your uncle and I don't share much. He's driven by power and greed, two attributes that will eventually bring him down. My life revolved around Todd, supplemented by charity work. Now Todd is gone and my desire for volunteer work has waned. I'm floating aimlessly trying to figure out what the next stage of my life will be. I know I won't see my son graduate from high school, college, get married, and present me with grandchildren. When I think about those things I'm brought to despair. But where does despair bring you? No place I want to be. I have to reinvent myself. Figure out what to do next, and whether or not it will include Jerry."

Myra was quiet for a moment as she collected her thoughts.

Caitlyn let her own anger and frustration subside to be replaced by a feeling of compassion for her aunt's predicament. Families were never what they seemed. There was hidden turmoil, disappointments and despair in every family unit. Some kept it hidden better than others.

Occasionally Caitlyn played the mind game of wishing she was someone else. Sometimes a good looking and gifted movie star, sometimes someone she met who possessed beauty and poise. "*I wish I was her,*" she would say to herself. And then she brought herself back to reality knowing inside the façade was probably some turmoil, including self-doubt, low self-esteem, dysfunctional family situations, even abuse.

"I think your father and Jerry are working on something that has to do with energy, but as far as any details, I can't help you. Jerry is either at the bank or at some meeting. A man called here once and said he was with some oil company. I asked Jerry about the call and he brushed me off. I never asked again. He can keep his secrets. I have mine," Myra said.

"I understand, Aunt Myra, but I recently met with a friend from high school. She and her husband have invested their life savings in a winery north of here. They work hard and now are seeing some of their vines withering. There's fracking in the county a few miles north of them. Do you know what that is?"

Myra nodded.

"My friend, Abbie, has cancer she says is from soil and water contamination. She and Tim, her husband, are spending more than they can afford on purified water for their own use and for the winery," Caitlyn explained.

"I'm sorry to hear about your friend. And I know the news is full of controversial articles about fracking, the amount of water being trucked in, wear and tear on the roads, chemicals, known and unknown being forcefully injected into the earth."

Myra paused a moment before continuing.

"A lot of people want to lease their land. It's a gamble, really and I don't know what the answer is," Myra said.

Before she could respond, Caitlyn's phone vibrated against her hip. She pulled it out of her pocket and looked at the screen. "I have to take this, Myra. It's one of my clients. Let's talk again later," Caitlyn said as she ran from the room.

~ TWENTY-EIGHT ~

Caitlyn powered up the laptop. Doris had given her a heads-up that revisions were on their way and would need a quick turnaround. Caitlyn clicked into her email and waited for mail to load. As soon as she saw The Outdoor Foundation PDF, she printed the pages from her portable printer. Utilizing a split screen, she sat cross-legged on the bed frantically working the revisions into the foundation's annual report. A consistent scratching at the door broke her concentration.

Resigned, she got up and opened the door a crack, enough for Summit to enter.

"You are a pain, you know," Caitlyn said lovingly.

She scratched the little dog's furry head as they both jumped onto the bed. Summit snuggled down next to her for a few minutes but quickly became bored and starting nuzzling her, hoping for some playtime.

Caitlyn didn't have time to play. The turnaround time for this project was imminent and there was much more to do. She couldn't get this one graphic to line up correctly and was swearing under her breath at the software program designed to work flawlessly, but wasn't. To get Summit off her back, she grabbed a pen and threw it on the floor.

Summit jumped off the bed after the new toy. He moved this new object around the floor. It was very different from what he was used to, round and slippery. He inadvertently shoved it under the bed. *Uh oh, now what?*

The bed frame was low to the ground and he didn't want to get stuck under there, but the new object was such fun he had to try. Flattening himself against the carpet, and with an extended front paw Summit almost reached the pen. He wiggled and stretched. His paw grasped at the object. He finally hit something solid, extended his claws, and raked the object out from under the bed. But it wasn't the fun object that went under. This was bigger and flatter.

Darn.

With his little dog determination, he flattened himself even more, pushed a bit with his hind feet, and stretched his paw as far as he could until he reached the cylindrical object he wanted.

Caitlyn was aware of the battle on the floor under her bed. She tried not to be distracted, but as the little dog butt kept wiggling around, she couldn't help to peer over the side of the bed. It was then she saw the black book.

How could she forget about the book she found in Todd's room yesterday? In her defense she did get the call from Doris telling her she would lose the account if she didn't get the annual report done. And then there was Abbie to think about, and what her father and uncle were up to, and . . . she reached down to get the book. At that moment the pen came flying out from under the bed, and a happy little dog backed out from under there as well.

Caitlyn picked up the book. Todd's name was printed neatly in the front cover. It was a diary of sorts. Caitlyn scanned the entries. She didn't have time now to read it word for word. The annual report was due back to her client within minutes. But her curiosity couldn't be contained. She wanted to know some of what was in the book. She scanned through the pages and skipped to the last one, her eyes widened.

Oh my god.

~ TWENTY-NINE ~

Wednesday Afternoon, China

Nick Spaulding sipped the hot Starbucks coffee as he sat in the Economic Summit. The afternoon sessions featured Southeast Asia leaders discussing the problems of China's unprecedented growth over the last thirty years. The Chinese people were demanding a higher quality of life, wanting things from new appliances to high-end cosmetics. The delegates discussed the fact China was now the world's largest consumer of food, energy and industrial commodities. This was all interesting background information, but Nick was waiting for the more serious discussion on energy.

A reporter next to him was busy typing on the portable keyboard attached to his iPad. Nick thought it was a great idea since he found working off the iPad was tedious. He preferred his Mac laptop. The newest version was slim and light, similar in weight to carrying an iPad, but easier to use.

When his neighbor stopped typing, Nick hoped to start a conversation. He wanted to know what others were doing at the summit.

"Hi, I'm Nick. This is a great conference, isn't it?" Nick said to break the ice.

"Yea, pretty good stuff. I'm Andrew," his neighbor responded.

"You like working with the iPad?" Nick asked.

"Once you get used to it, it's okay." Andrew responded, turning his attention back to the iPad.

Nick had to act fast if he was going to get any relevant information from Andrew.

"So, what interests you most at the Summit?" Nick asked.

Andrew had started typing furiously again. He paused, and with an off-handed remark signaling that he was not giving up any information said, "the food."

~

Nick put his coffee down as the presentation he had been waiting for began. The speaker was introduced with a long round of applause. Nick looked around at the audience and made note of who was in attendance.

"China has come a long way raising the standard of living of its people. The challenge we face is the amount of energy needed to support this new quality of life as more and more Chinese move up the ladder. The United States is the highest user of energy in the world, but China is a close second. The transportation sector will continue to require the highest use of oil as car sales grow exponentially. The question, fellow delegates, is how will the battle for oil be resolved between these two behemoths?"

Nick typed furiously as statistics were thrown out from the podium. The senator needed this information as well as information gathered during networking time at receptions and dinners. And then there was Nick's side affair, one that was going to make him a lot of money, and he hoped would not put him in jail. He scrolled down to the figures he gathered from the presentation, copied and pasted them into the two Word documents already started.

He would be careful to keep the documents separate as one was for the senator, the other for his deal with the American oil company. He was taking a huge risk by doing this side "consulting," but the money was too good to pass up. There was enough oil to go around and if an American company could make a few bucks from this information, what was the harm? He didn't think it would impact the energy bill his boss was working on.

His rationalization didn't work as Nick had begun to regret this collaboration, but he was in too deep now to back out. From the outset this deal complicated his life. When he was approached by the oil company he didn't know part of the deal was to develop a relationship with the daughter of one of their consultants. He balked at first. Personal relationships were dangerous. He was not going to get involved with an ugly overweight girl with greasy hair. But since the money was good, he decided it was only fair to check her out.

He met the girl, Caitlyn Jamison, at a holiday party and was delighted, and relieved, to find she was lovely as well as an interesting person. He eagerly agreed to the terms set forth by the oil company, knowing in the end there would most likely be pain. The instructions were to gain her trust so he could gain access to documents of The Outdoor Foundation, one of her clients. This large powerful environmental group was beginning to threaten well drilling in the Northeast and it needed to be stopped.

The oil company learned a division of The Outdoor Foundation was focusing on halting the oil and gas recovery in New York State. It threatened the company's Marcellus shale operation expansion in which plans were underway. The foundation was pouring a lot of money into stopping hydraulic fracturing in the northeast and Canada. If Nick gained intelligence on the foundation's plans as well as provide information from the meetings in China, he would be well paid.

~

Nick was not brought up to operate in the fast lane. He was the product of a Midwest farm family in which a serious work ethic had been instilled. His father's retirement plans included turning the farm over to Nick and his brother. Nick wanted no part of the farm. Instead, he wanted some control over his life. With farming, a successful year only happened if Mother Nature treated you kindly. A farmer could do everything right, and then one bad storm could ruin an entire crop, and the family lost income for the year and beyond.

Nick had experienced enough of those bad years while growing up and he wanted out. He had watched his father struggle with their mid-size farm, trying to compete with the mega farms taking all their profits. A small farmer couldn't compete, but his father wouldn't give up the dream, the way of life. Nick's brother, however, was willing to work the land. His brother's wife had a good paying job with benefits, so they would be okay and so far they were.

Nick was brought out of his reverie as closing remarks were made.

"In conclusion, China has rising discontent among its residents. We are seeing more and more riots and anti-government protests. People are protesting poor working conditions and rising inflation. Government leaders are addressing these issues with inflation control and higher spending on housing, education, health care and job creation."

Nick joined the round of applause, and then turned to his computer to add the figures he gathered. He sent one of his Word documents to the senator's private e-mail in Washington, and the other to his oil company contact.

~ THIRTY ~

Wednesday, Pittsburg, PA

The meetings of oil company executives were always held at the Sheraton Pittsburgh Station Square Hotel. The hotel was situated so guest rooms as well as meeting rooms had a view of the river. The hotel's restaurant employed a five star chef who produced the most delicious and creatively prepared entrees. Oil company executives expected nothing less.

Included in the group were consultants Herb Jamison and Jerry Tilton. Jerry made it to the meeting just in time.

Following his meeting with the Albany politicos, Jerry stayed at his desk getting personal business in order, barely making his flight to Pittsburgh.

Before the meeting began, Jim Hughes, the company president came over to Jerry, put a hand on his shoulder, and offered his sincere condolences.

"Thank you. And the flowers the company sent for the funeral were much appreciated," said Jerry.

"Have the police found anything?" Jim asked.

"Nothing of note. I keep calling, pushing, but nothing seems to be happening. I'm getting frustrated," Jerry responded, unable to hide his anger.

"Well, we appreciate the fact you made the effort to be here today, Jerry," Jim said as he patted Jerry on the back, and walked back to the head of the conference table.

Herb leaned over to Jerry and whispered, "I notice we're next to last on the agenda."

"You would think they would want to hear from us first," Jerry replied. "And thanks for the call last week after Todd died. I understood why you couldn't make it to the funeral. Probably best the way Myra and Ann are with each other. Terrible shame. Women!"

Herb nodded in agreement, and then said, "By the way, I received a message from Caitlyn. Is she still with you and Myra? Do you know what she wants? Ann mentioned Caitlyn was asking whether you and I are working together. Of course Ann doesn't know anything, and I assume you haven't told Myra anything either. Caitlyn is on the trail of something and I know her well enough when she gets the bit in her mouth she doesn't stop until she's satisfied."

"Sounds like a chip off the old block," Jerry laughed. "I agree. I don't want to say anything against your daughter, but she is, shall we say, tenacious."

"I'll give her a call after this meeting to see what's on her mind. I'll try to get her off the trail of whatever issue she has taken on, and I suspect it has to do with the environment."

The meeting was called to order by president Jim Hughes. He was well dressed in a suit, Herb was sure, made on Savile Row. The man had a commanding presence, standing over six feet tall, with hair showing signs of grey at the temples.

A poster boy for American business, Herb thought.

"As you all know, our drilling of the Marcellus Shale has been successful. We have a number of productive wells in Pennsylvania and Ohio. The newly found Utica Shale layer is now in our sights. This black calcareous organic-rich Utica shale runs 7,000 feet below the Marcellus layer and is full of natural gas and oil. In 2002 the Marcellus Shale was estimated to yield 1.9 trillion cubic feet of gas, the estimate was revised in 2008 to more than 500 trillion cubic feet of natural gas. Estimates for Utica Shale are even higher. Our scientists are working on estimates as to the quantity and the profits it will bring in."

Jim Hughes looked around the table to see if there were any questions. Seeing none, he continued.

"We have to be there first. We are getting landowners to sign on the dotted line giving us the right of first home rule refusal for their property. To accomplish this the New York State legislature has to override the counties' jurisdiction. When that happens we can keep contract payments to the lowest level. Landowners are hungry. It all works to our benefit. Our Albany lobbyists are paying off legislators to make this happen. If we can corner the New York

market, we'll have a better foothold into the other northern states as well as Quebec. That, my friends, is our long-term plan."

Again he stopped, providing a chance for comments or questions. He didn't want to get into any kind of discussion about his last comments, so he was relieved when no hands were raised.

"Marketing will be putting a positive spin on the process. They will play down the fact it takes an average of 400 tanker trucks to carry water and supplies to each site. Each site requires 1.8 million gallons of water, 40,000 gallons of chemicals, and sand. So far we have been highly successful. Our marketing department is working on ways to convince people the trucks are not as damaging to the roads as they think. Marketing is busy developing ads promoting the drilling, making it appear environmentally friendly. It is amazing what people will believe if they see it on the Internet or television."

The group sitting around the table listened intently as facts and figures were given.

The group clapped at the conclusion of Jim Hughes's speech. It sounded like everything was going as planned. Herb and Jerry were successful doing their part—working the local scene and getting approvals pushed through.

A few more presentations were made stating the status of wells in Ohio, Pennsylvania, West Virginia and Kentucky. They were milking the Marcellus Shale for everything it could give, and there was still more. Payments to land owners were minimum, and when oil or gas was struck, the payments remained minimal, though seemed a lot to those who didn't know any better or were desperate for any kind of income. Oil company profits were off the charts, but it was to be a well-kept secret. Everyone in the room, including Herb and Jerry had signed a confidentiality agreement. Everyone knew if they talked their families would suffer. They were being well paid to keep their secrets.

By the time Herb and Jerry made their presentation, it was well past two o'clock.

"We'd better hurry if we're going to catch our flights," Jerry said.

"My plane back to Florida leaves in about an hour. It'll be nice to be back in the warmth again. These April nights are too cold for me," Herb stated.

~ THIRTY-ONE ~

Wednesday, Riverview, NY

Caitlyn put a retractable leash on Summit. The poor dog needed more exercise than running up and down stairs and in the small fenced yard provided for him when nature called. Since the temperature was mild, she decided to walk the half mile to the Risley's. The exercise would do them good.

She didn't know what kept drawing her to the Risley house. The family dynamics intrigued her, and she was drawn to Darcy and the folkways she practiced. Or maybe she was drawn out of concern for Teddy. Was something untoward going on with this family or was Teddy just an introverted young man who will grow out of that stage? Caitlyn decided to follow her instincts as she always did. Sometimes it got her in trouble; she hoped this wasn't one of them.

When she reached the Risley's driveway she noticed Darcy's car parked near the house. She hoped Teddy would be home as well. She'd like the opportunity to talk with both of them.

She continued carefully up the drive, avoiding the pot holes, and made her way to the front door. She knocked on the bright blue door and waited. Nothing. She knocked again, louder and longer. Nothing.

Maybe Darcy was around back tending her gardens. Caitlyn and Summit walked around to the back of the house with Caitlyn calling Darcy's name.

Darcy, with earphones on, was bent over tending her plants.

No wonder she couldn't hear anything.

Caitlyn spoke louder, not wanting to startle Darcy, but loud enough to get her attention. She did, both. Darcy stood up with a start and a look of fright crossed her face. She recovered and waved a hand as she pulled the earphones from her head.

"Sorry, didn't mean to startle you," Caitlyn said.

"When I have these things on I can't hear a thing," Darcy responded. "What can I do for you?"

"Is Teddy at home? I have something to discuss with him."

"Like what?" Darcy asked with an unsettling sweetness to her tone.

"I'm curious about his relationship with my cousin, Todd. They're both the same age, in some of the same classes, and live in close proximity. It would only be natural they connected and maybe even became friends."

Darcy's hand went to her hip, which jutted out in a defensive posture. Caitlyn was surprised at the attitude change, and knew she had touched on a sensitive subject.

"Actually, Teddy's in town. He has a tutor, some man from school. Since Teddy is sick a lot, this teacher volunteered to get him caught up on his studies. Teddy goes there once or twice a week. I didn't like it at first, but the offer seemed too good to be true. We can't afford to pay a tutor, but Teddy assures us everything is on the up and up. And he seems to be doing better in school. I don't like him out at night, ya know? But I guess a coupla nights a week is okay."

Caitlyn tried to put this information in context to what she read in Todd's journal. Made sense. Tutoring – a great cover story.

"Okay, thanks Mrs. Risley. I'll let you get back to your gardens."

Darcy didn't reply. She pulled her earphones back on her head and bent over the plants.

~

On her way back to the house, Caitlyn received a text from Doris. Revisions to the annual report were being emailed at that moment.

With her computer fired up, she again used a split screen to make the modifications sent to her via PDF. There had to be an immediate turnaround since the report was due at the printers first thing Monday.

She appreciated the fact Doris gave her a heads-up when changes were coming. Doris had her back and Caitlyn had to figure a way to show her appreciation. In the meantime, she searched her bag for staples. When she packed her stapler, she didn't realize it was empty. Her uncle probably had some in his desk. Since he was late getting home—must be another "meeting"—she'd take a chance and rummage through his desk. She didn't think he'd miss a few staples.

Caitlyn checked to be sure Myra was in her room, and then quietly descended the stairs. She stopped at the bottom, listening, making sure Jerry had not driven in, and then went to his office. The door was unlocked. Apparently he trusted that no one would enter this sacred sanctum during his absence, and for that she was grateful.

She opened the top drawer first as it was usually where people kept miscellaneous papers and sticky notes, as well as pens and pencils, so no surprise staples weren't there. The second drawer on the right held Pendaflex files, which aroused her curiosity. She couldn't take the time now to explore, and that would be a real invasion of privacy, an act even her curiosity would not justify. In the bottom right hand drawer she hit bonanza finding a narrow flip top box labeled "Swingline Premium Staples." She lifted out a few. Jerry was so anal he might notice if she took more. As she closed the drawer it hit something in the back preventing it from closing completely.

"Damn." She didn't have time to dislodge whatever it was. Jerry would arrive home any minute, and it was about the time Myra came downstairs to start dinner. Caitlyn couldn't leave the drawer partially open. She pushed as hard as she could, listening for the elusive click as the drawer snapped into place. Nothing. She pulled the drawer out as far as it would go to check the alignment. The drawer was on its rails, so something must have fallen down the back to jam the drawer. She reached as far back as she could, but the back of the drawer prevented her from reaching the offending object. Caitlyn changed position, lying on the floor making her arm and hand as small as she could. Her fingers touched something. It felt like rumpled paper. If only she could grab an edge.

Summit started barking and headed towards the door. That meant someone was here, probably her uncle. And Myra would surely be coming down the stairs. Caitlyn was in full view of the stairwell. What would her aunt think if she saw her niece sprawled out on the office floor with her hand in the bottom drawer of Jerry's desk? It would be a hilarious scene if it wasn't so serious.

Caitlyn had to get hold of the object quickly. As she heard the car door slam shut, her fingers grasped enough of the paper to pull it out. Some of it tore, but she was able to dislodge most of it, and the drawer easily closed. Caitlyn stood up, stuffed what turned out to be an envelope into her pocket, left the office, quietly closing the doors behind her. She was crossing the foyer when her uncle opened the door. He didn't seem pleased to see her, and his briefcase looked larger than the one he usually carried to the bank. Something was bothering him.

"Hi, Uncle Jerry. Have a nice day?" Caitlyn asked.

Jerry gave her a look, then headed to his office. "Good enough, thank you," he said as he closed the office door behind him.

~ THIRTY-TWO ~

On her way up the stairs, Caitlyn's phone vibrated with a text message: *Meet me at Tony's Tavern 7:00. South bef U get to Renwick. No one will bother us there. Ethan.*

Caitlyn was relieved to hear from Ethan. There was much she wanted to share with him, and besides, she really enjoyed his company. She missed Nick, but Ethan was different. She couldn't quite put her finger on it, though one thing she enjoyed was the teamwork. That was what she missed most about leaving her New York job. Although there were many things she didn't like about working for a large firm, it did provide the opportunity to work as a team in developing marketing materials for all kinds of businesses.

Caitlyn sent a text back: *See you then.*

She took the staples to her room and filled her stapler. She carefully stapled the annual report pages before heading downstairs to help her aunt with dinner preparations.

~

Caitlyn excused herself from the dinner table saying she was meeting a friend.

Jerry and Myra didn't have much to say to each other these days, and maybe they never did. At any rate Caitlyn was bored with the silence and her feeble attempts at conversation. Saying she was meeting a friend wasn't a lie since she thought of Ethan as her friend.

As she left the house, she checked her hair and make-up. She smoothed back some stray tendrils, and headed out.

She drove south toward Renwick and found the tavern a few miles before she hit the city line. When she entered the building she saw Ethan wave from a booth located at the back.

"This is a private table for a busy tavern," Caitlyn said as she sat down.

"What can I get you?" Ethan replied.

"A glass of German Riesling would do the trick if they have it here," Caitlyn responded.

"Since the tavern is a popular spot for the college communities, they carry quite an extensive beer and wine selection, so I'm sure they will have something you like."

After the waiter served Caitlyn her wine, she leaned across the table keeping her voice low.

"I found Todd's journal. It was in his desk, in his room, to which I was forbidden to enter. I was under a work deadline so I put it aside. It then slid under the bed, and Summit dug it out for me the next day. I haven't read through it, but I skimmed the last few pages.

"Slow down. You found what? Why didn't you tell me, like, immediately? It's important evidence. You know how important any information is," Ethan said, clearly frustrated.

He was angry and embarrassed that he didn't find the journal during his search of Todd's room.

"I know. I'm sorry. It's been, well, you know, one thing then another. I was going to call you right away, but then I have this annual report hanging over my head, and Myra is an emotional mess, and so... well, listen, okay?"

Ethan nodded.

"Finish what you were saying. Sorry I interrupted."

"Apparently, Todd and a bunch of his friends, including Teddy Risley are going off on nightly forays damaging any oil fracking equipment they can find. I now have names of some of the kids involved. Interesting that Susan is named, but not Denny. I tried to talk with Teddy this afternoon, but apparently he sees a tutor a couple days a week to help with his schoolwork, or at least that is what he tells his parents. His mother is overly attentive to him, almost to the point of smothering, but what would I know? My mother was on the aloof side of the scale. To complicate matters I believe my father and uncle are involved with one of the companies drilling for oil or natural gas. My aunt told me what she knows, which isn't much, but it confirms what my friend Abbie heard. Did I tell you Abbie has cancer? She believes it was from the fracking in Pennsylvania near where they lived. The fracking introduces quantities of unknown carcinogens into the ground water."

"Slow down! You are all over the lot," Ethan said.

Caitlyn took a breath and a sip of wine. "You're right. I just did a mind dump, didn't I?"

She continued, "The last journal entry is a plan for something big. Maybe even getting hold of some explosives. These are kids. I don't think they even know where to get explosives, but the fact they are talking about such things is . . .scary."

Caitlyn paused, thinking through the conundrum.

"And I guess you can find anything on the Internet these days. We have to stop them if they are carrying out their plan, even with Todd gone. It may be ego on Todd's part, but he seemed to view himself as their leader."

Ethan thought for a few minutes, taking in what Caitlyn told him.

"We have several possible motives for Todd's murder, and most are connected to the environmental issues. It could have been someone who knew about the vandalism. That list could include landowners who want to lease their land, or oil company thugs. I don't mean to say these companies are mafia-like, but there are always fringes who feel they need to clear the way for progress. And, to their credit, there is no conclusive evidence as yet the chemicals being injected into the earth are contaminating the water source."

"I disagree, Ethan. Didn't you see the report on the central California aquifers and farm irrigation aquifers after three billion gallons of fracturing water were injected? Those sites were full of toxic fluids. Those toxins were arsenic, which weakens the immune system, and thallium, a component of rat poison. We can't let these toxic chemicals destroy the groundwater of Upstate New York. It would destroy the state's agriculture, wine industry, tourism, as well as the quality of life of residents. If there is even a hint of a chance, it has to be stopped."

"That's not a problem for us to solve; Todd's murder is." Ethan said with more force than he intended. "We have to find a way to stop these youngsters. We have to contact the kids listed in Todd's book. They can do more good by going through proper channels for change rather than nighttime vandalizing."

"I agree," Caitlyn said. "And, Ethan, don't kill the messenger."

With the tension broken, they turned to small talk while munching on peanuts and pretzels, before Ethan decided to get down to business again.

"Maddie checked out Denny Mathews and found he, too, has a problem with his temper. According to her sources in the community, Denny is very strong willed and if he doesn't get his way, he tends to bring up his fists. She confirmed he has a competitive nature, and is not the easiest person to like. This doesn't mean he would do anything to hurt his best friend, but it's something we have to keep in mind," Ethan said.

"I'm sorry to hear that. My impression of him was just an uncertain young man trying to find his place. Working through those growing pains," Caitlyn said.

"That may be so, but we can't disregard his temperament and history," and I need to see Todd's journal."

Caitlyn handed over the black book with much regret. She wished she had had the time to read the rest before she mentioned it to Ethan. She wanted to know her cousin better, and she could have done that through his written words.

~ THIRTY-THREE ~

Thursday

The sun pushed its way in through the blinds; it was the dawn of a beautiful day and Mother Nature was making sure nothing, including blinds, was keeping it out. Caitlyn woke and checked the bedside clock. It read eight o'clock. She couldn't believe she had slept this late. She peered over the covers to where Summit was stretched out and snoring lightly. He, too, was a late sleeper this morning.

She lay back down and pulled the covers tight to her chin. The room felt cold, and the bed so warm. So warm, too, were her thoughts about last night's date, if you could call it that, with Ethan.

They had enjoyed drinks and light snacks at the tavern, and it was exciting to share notes and brainstorm on the next steps of the investigation. She was pleased he accepted her ideas and he had gotten over being mad about the journal. He treated her as a respected member of his team and it meant a lot. She told him a bit about her life, her career path, and goals. He shared very little.

It seemed like the men in her life were not willing to let her in. What was it about her that kept those doors closed?

They finished the evening with a walk by the lake. Caitlyn had been so preoccupied with family matters since her arrival she hadn't taken the time to visit her favorite place as a teenager. She used to come to the park and walk along the shore.

It was so peaceful. The pebbles dotting the shoreline were perfect for skipping, at least the small flat ones, and finding them was the challenge she enjoyed. She especially liked to come to water's edge in spring and fall when the summerfolk were not around. She felt it was her private place, and the feeling returned while she and Ethan stood gazing at the hills with moonlight reflecting off the still water.

128

The evening finished with an ice cream sundae at the diner in Riverview. The diner was known for serving Hershey's ice cream, a brand Caitlyn liked the best but couldn't always find in the DC area.

~

Her phone vibrated on the dresser where she had left it charging overnight. She watched it dance around the surface as it tried to attract her attention. She didn't want to get out of the warm bed. And who could it be, anyway? She didn't think Ethan would call her this early, and besides, she thought they covered most everything last night. The phone stopped its vibrating dance and lay silent, followed by a chirp. A voicemail. Whoever it was wanted to get her attention. Dreading it might be Doris with more last minute changes to the annual report, Caitlyn decided she'd better check to see who was the insistent caller. If Doris, changes had to be done quickly, or lose this client. She couldn't afford that.

Running quickly across the room, she grabbed the phone, pulling it from the charger. She ran back to the bed and jumped under the covers again. Summit never moved.

She immediately saw the missed call was from her father.

The mighty has finally surfaced, she thought sarcastically.

Ignoring the voicemail, she scrolled down her contacts to her parents and touched their number.

~ THIRTY-FOUR ~

Herb Jamison didn't check caller ID before answering his phone, so he was surprised to hear his daughter's voice. He had just called her and left a voicemail saying they were headed out to breakfast.

"Dad, it's Caitlyn."

"Hi, honey. Did you get my voicemail? I said your mother and I were heading out to breakfast and I would catch up with you later."

"Sorry, Dad, no. I was in the bathroom and came running out as the phone stopped ringing."

Another white lie. This is getting to be too much of a habit.

"I thought I would return your call."

"Okay, breakfast can wait. What's on your mind?"

Caitlyn held her tongue. Why couldn't she have a normal conversation with her parents? Why were they always treading on eggshells? His businesslike tone warned her to tread easily.

"Did Mom tell you I'm staying a few days with Uncle Jerry and Aunt Myra? I think I've been helpful as they go through the grieving process."

"That's very good of you, Caitlyn. I'm so sorry your mother and I couldn't be there to support them. We were much relieved to know that you're there," Herb replied, waiting for the real reason she wanted to talk.

"Dad, I told Aunt Myra that I heard from Todd a while back, and didn't respond to him. I got busy with my own life and didn't take the time. It is something I will regret forever," Caitlyn confessed as she wiped a tear forming in the corner of her eye.

"I didn't know that, Cait, but you can't blame yourself. We all get busy and don't take the time for the more important things, like family," Herb tried his best to console her, while eyeing the car keys. His stomach was growling and he wanted to be on his way.

"I know, Dad. I just had to tell you," Caitlyn said. She needed to get back to what was really on her mind.

I'm not mentioning the murder investigation. Dad would go completely ballistic, she thought.

"I've noticed some drilling rigs around here and learned some disturbing news about the effect those rigs have on the environment. Since your career was in the oil business, I thought you might know something about this," Caitlyn explained.

She paused to gauge his reaction to her last sentence. When none came, she continued cautiously. "I wonder if you're consulting for your old company."

There was silence on the line as Herb pondered what he should say to his daughter, and knowing her, she probably was in possession of a lot more information than what she was sharing.

"Well, dear, I am consulting, but not for that sector of the company. I don't really know much about what they're doing, but I assure you, with all my years in the oil business, the majority of companies are conscientious and protective of the environmental impacts. So you can rest assured …"

"Spare me the company line; I'm your daughter, remember? I've heard it all before. Dad, I've seen the trucks. They're tearing up the roadways…"

"Listen, Caitlyn. You and your environmental freak friends have got to get the message. Oil and gas provide a better quality of life. And if you don't mind the cliché, there's no progress without pain."

"I'm not an environmental 'freak' as you so aptly describe me."

"Then you need to grow up and understand there is more to life than tree hugging. You spend too much time with that Outdoor Foundation or whatever it's called."

Caitlyn was shocked. How did her father know who her clients were? She decided to think about his last statement before she had any further conversation with her father.

"Fine, Dad, I'll continue to hug the trees as you call it, and you continue to destroy the planet. I don't think we have anything more to talk about."

The heavy click then silence was the signal her father was no longer on the line.

Her father was bull headed. He thought he was always right, with never an "I'm sorry" to cross his lips. Was she becoming more like him? Not willing to listen to another side of the issue?

Before she could put too much thought into that, she thought about the several disturbing things that were said during their short conversation. He called her a tree hugger. She cared about the environment, but never attended demonstrations or even a meeting to suggest fanaticism. Her client list was confidential. How in the world did he know about The Outdoor Foundation?

Then it hit her. Nick. During one of their pillow talks, she mentioned exciting information about the foundation's new mission in environmental awareness. Could it mean her father and Nick were somehow connected? Or was her father getting information from another source?

And how did Uncle Jerry fit into the picture?

She was sure he was involved in some way. Was she looking at an unhealthy triangle? If so, what part was she unwittingly playing? She sent Ethan a text requesting a meeting. This whole oil drilling business could well be the reason for Todd's murder.

First, she needed a brisk walk to clear her head.

~ THIRTY-FIVE ~

The wooded area behind the tenant house provided Darcy the only escape from the stresses of the day. She stopped to catch her breath, her heart racing, from her jog across the field. As she slowed and took deep breaths, she detected a sound. Someone was walking through the fields on the other side of the woods. Darcy was late to perform her morning rituals. If someone was coming she would have to hurry.

It was imperative the spirits of nature be appeased through offerings of bread and cakes. If she didn't keep them appeased she would be subject to the haints, the angry ancestral spirits. Darcy found it difficult to keep up all the daily rites, and when she couldn't, especially during the harsh winter months, her family suffered. Teddy got sick; they would run low on firewood. Darcy would be unable to start the car, all sorts of difficulties.

Sometimes she felt so alone. If only she found someone else in the area who practiced Appalachian Folk Magick; someone who understood the ways.

To stave off the haints, Darcy used her meager funds to paint their front door a bright blue, a color known to repel the spirits. Then one day while out walking she came upon this small abandoned cemetery. It seemed the right place for nature spirit worship, a quiet place of her own, and where no one would find her. And now this stranger was about to invade that space.

Darcy's mother died when she was young leaving her with a father who was cold and distant when he was even there. When he was around he was physically and verbally abusive to her and her two brothers. Darcy wasn't sorry to see him leave the family for "work" out of state, because her grandmother stepped in and took over raising the children. They were dirt poor as the saying goes, but the grandmother gave them some stability, meals, and whatever love she could. Darcy understood at a young age everyone was a product of their own upbringing, and it applied to her grandmother as well.

Her grandmother taught her the folkway introduced by the Irish and Scottish colonists that settled in the Appalachian Mountain area. Over the years the newcomers adopted aspects of the native Cherokee Magick, as well as African traditions from plantation slaves to form a unique cultural tradition.

Darcy remembered the day she came upon her grandmother talking to herself and throwing bits of bread out the back door. Darcy wanted to cry out because food was so scarce. Why was her grandmother throwing it on the ground? Her grandmother must have sensed Darcy's presence, as she turned around, smiled and held out her hand. Darcy walked slowly toward her grandmother and fell under her spell. Her grandmother took her hand and they walked to the back of the yard where they could not be heard by anyone in the house. There are certain turning points in one's life and that day was one for Darcy.

"It's time, my dear, you learn the folkways of our people," her grandmother had said. "You may have wondered why our doors are painted bright blue, and why I always scrape the crumbs from the table. You may have noticed I have a little jar in the cupboard where I keep those crumbs."

Darcy did wonder about it, but as a child she didn't dare ask. If Darcy asked too many questions her grandmother might pile on more kitchen chores.

"Those crumbs are to feed the spirits of nature. The evil forces can bring about destruction. It's our job to worship and keep the spirits happy. It's our way of life, Darcy, and now you're old enough to start the practice. It's Appalachian Folk Magick. Some call it Green Magick or Kitchen Witchery. We're not quick to forgive those who hurt us, and we banish enemies from our lives. It's why your father was sent away. I saw how he was treating you and your brothers. I didn't need another family to raise, but I couldn't stand by and watch you suffer at his hands. On the other hand, those of us who practice Kitchen Witchery will go to any extent to help those in need, even a stranger. Think about what I've said and we'll talk again. In the meantime, watch what I do. Take time to worship at the altars in the house. You probably haven't even noticed them. They are simple objects. The table in the hallway made of twisted sticks, the braided rug in the living room, the quilt on your bed and even the dream catcher hanging in the kitchen window."

Darcy listened intently. She knew this was the culture she was inheriting and, even at her young age, she understood the importance.

"I will, Grandma," Darcy responded, though she didn't exactly know how to go about learning the folkway. She would have to watch her grandmother carefully.

"Don't worry, dear," her grandmother replied, sensing her hesitation, "You'll learn it soon enough."

And Darcy did learn. She learned how to keep control in her life and how to control Teddy. She gave him herbs grown in her own garden, adjusting the doses to keep him dependent on her. They shared every moment of his growing up years. Every moment that is until recently when he started to break away. She began to feed him additional sage to weaken his immune system. Just enough to keep him feeling ill. Everyone thought sage to be healthy, which it is, but in high doses, it's harmful. Not enough to kill the person, but weaken them, which is exactly how she wanted Teddy so he would always be dependent on her.

Darcy turned at the sudden appearance of Caitlyn and a little dog.

"Hi Darcy, it's Caitlyn. I've been trying to find you. I saw you enter the woods, but didn't know exactly where you were going. Is this a cemetery? Oh, my gosh, I didn't realize there was an old cemetery on Uncle Jerry's land. I wonder if he knows." Caitlyn rattled on trying to get Darcy calmed down so she wouldn't run.

"What are you doing here?"

"Like I said, I was out for a walk and saw you enter the woods. I was curious as to what was here, that's all."

"Well, you might as well know, I come here to practice Folk Magick. It's something my grandmother passed down to me. It's comforting."

"I'm intrigued. Tell me more."

Darcy shared her story with Caitlyn, watching carefully to see when disbelief showed in Caitlyn's expression. Darcy was used to being ridiculed. But Caitlyn listened intently.

"And so that is where my love and knowledge of herbs comes from. I guess you could say it is in my blood."

"I wondered why your door was such a bright blue, and it's nice to have an explanation," Caitlyn said. "Do you plan to sell your herbs?"

"Yes, some, and Teddy'll help. He's going to need a job out of high school, and this will be the thing. We'll work together."

"Don't you think he'll want to go to college or a technical school?" Caitlyn asked.

"No! Anyway, the decision's made. He'll assist me in the business," Darcy stated.

A beep from Caitlyn's phone intruded into the space. Caitlyn looked down at the display and read: *"Meet me at Tony's at noon. E."*

Caitlyn slipped the phone back into her pocket and smiled at Darcy.

"It's been nice talking with you and learning about your folkway culture. I'm glad you're keeping it alive for another generation, and I do hope the wee folk are kind to you."

Used to sarcasm, Darcy was caught off guard by Caitlyn's sincerity.

"Sure, thanks. Maybe we'll run into each other again sometime," Darcy said.

"I'd like that," Caitlyn said.

~ THIRTY-SIX ~

Ethan listened as Fred Brown, a former colleague from downstate explained how two big oil service companies were drilling test holes around the state to see if there was oil, and if so, was there enough oil to invest in full scale well drilling.

"What do you mean by oil service companies?" Ethan asked.

"Let me explain. The oil companies aren't setting up rigs for hydraulic fracturing. They can't be bothered with that side of the business. There are oilfield service firms doing the fracturing, and then when they have something to sell, the oil companies step in and negotiate."

Fred went on to explain the fracturing process and how there was now evidence the process was polluting groundwater.

"From what I've been able to gather, they're driving around in unmarked trucks and in remote areas, not even getting the permission of the landowners and disregarding what the county's regs might state. They're staying under the radar as much as they can, and that in itself makes me suspicious," Fred explained.

"What would it mean for a community should they find enough oil to set up drilling fields?" Ethan asked.

"For the landowner it could mean a lot of money. They may be set for life. For the rest of the community it may mean devastation. Property values will plummet as the rigs are erected and the oilmen move into town taking over lodging facilities. Dirt, grime, bars. The town would be transformed. Yea, some would make money. Those who have rooms to let, restaurants, and of course the banks doing the financing. Unfortunately, the houses of ill repute will follow. As far as the general public, their quality of life will be gone as will property values. Any atmosphere the town developed over the years. Hell, forget tourism. I know your area, as well as ours, is big on that."

"Do you think home rule will be overturned in the senate?"

"It probably will. There's enough money and power to overturn the law. In fact, I heard there was a test hole planned for your town as soon as the new law is passed. Very hush, hush," Fred stated.

"I'm sorry to hear it. It would be impossible to stop the process if someone sells out. I'll mention this to the mayor, though I don't know if there is anything the town can do, maybe zoning or something like that, to stop this kind of thing. It would be a shame to see this beautiful community destroyed."

"Not to change the subject, Ethan, but did you hear Senator Smith is back in the hospital?"

"Yes, I did. Too bad. He's been a good senator for the state. I wonder what will happen if he can't finish his term?"

"The governor will appoint someone. I hear there's a certain amount of jockeying going on already. You know, the usual politics. But for someone with the wrong agenda, or a personal one, there's a lot of power in the senate. As much destruction can be done as good, especially with these oilmen nosing around. It's a worrisome thing. Well, good talkin' to ya, Ethan. Gotta get going," Fred said.

"Yea, you too, Fred. And thanks for the information on the oil companies."

Hanging up the phone, Ethan was left with a lot to think about. There was someone in the community, maybe more than one, vying for the attention of the oil companies to drill on their land. A get rich quick scheme. He hoped there was no oil to be found in this area. It was too beautiful to be spoiled by rigs. And apparently the vultures were starting to circle around poor Senator Smith. He wondered who those players were and what personal agendas they hoped to fill.

~

He didn't have long to ponder on what he could do if anything about the oil service companies scoping out the Riverview area. Maddie knocked at his door and then quietly let herself in. She must have noticed he was off the phone.

"Sheriff, there's a woman out there who wants to see you."

Ethan gave Maddie an inquiring look.

"So, who is this 'woman' and what does she want?" Ethan asked. "Maddie, I'm meeting someone for lunch. I don't have much time. Can't you handle it?"

"She said to tell you her name is Jennie."

Ethan's chest constricted. It couldn't be. It's been years since Jennie walked out and without a word since. He had wanted her to come back, but she made it clear she wanted a different life, one in which she didn't live in fear.

These thoughts passed through his head in milliseconds as Maddie stood there wondering what to do.

It could be another woman named Jennie. It could be someone with information on Todd Tilton's murder.

"Show this lady in," Ethan instructed. He girded himself for the worst, hoping for the best.

Jennie Ewing walked through the door. She was as beautiful as Ethan remembered his bride to be. Her clear complexion was framed by long blond hair, the wispy tendrils trimmed to perfectly frame her face. Her figure had not suffered either. She was dressed in black slacks accentuating her slim hips, topped by a light blue sweater that perfectly matched her eyes. Ethan took a deep breath and slowly rose.

"Hello, Ethan," Jennie said.

"What a surprise, Jennie. What brings you to Riverview?" Ethan asked.

"I inquired around in the old neighborhood and was told you took a job up here. I never thought you were a small town guy. I was downstate visiting friends during my school spring vacation and thought I would stop in and see you. I didn't plan on having to drive four hours. But, it's a quaint little town, what I've seen of it," Jennie said.

She walked around the small office, touching the back of the two chairs, desk and file cabinet, her expression exhibiting disapproval.

"They could have at least given you an office with a window." Jennie stated.

Ethan ignored the put-down, and instead responded to her first comment.

"It's a nice town and I'm quite enjoying my time here. But, Jennie, I'm in the middle of a difficult case right now, so I don't have a lot of time. And, I don't believe you came here to step back into our marriage, so why are you here?" Ethan asked.

Jennie sat down and gently brushed lint from her slacks with her meticulously manicured hands. She looked around the office, and then at Ethan.

"I wanted to make sure you were o.k. I'm sorry about what I did to you, and I know I can't make up for my actions. I enjoy my new life. I'm teaching, and have made a lot of good friends. I don't want a divorce, Ethan. Jim and I have gone our separate ways. We didn't have the same attraction, the same spiritual connection you and I have. So, in a nutshell, I was hoping you would come to Wisconsin and we could start over," Jennie said.

Before Ethan could respond, Jennie continued.

"Ethan, you know I love you. I've always loved you. But I hate what you do. I hated every minute you were at work. Each day I didn't know if you'd return. I dreaded the phone call that thank god never came; I dreaded the doorbell. I jumped anytime someone came to my door at school. I knew any day someone could show up telling me you were killed in the line of duty. It seems like anyone is allowed to own a gun and the violence is escalating. What's wrong with our world, Ethan?"

He didn't have an answer, and he understood her concerns. He knew she had lived in fear, but he was driven to bring stability and justice to his small piece of the world. Being a police officer was the way he chose to do that. Danger was inherent in his job. Every police officer knew their life could change in a second. It was part of the territory. Yes, there should be some firearm governance. Not everyone should have that right, and therein is the problem. The two sides of this issue seem incapable of sitting down and coming up with common sense legislation. He didn't understand why the issue was so polarized when he knew everyone wanted a safer culture. He knew money, which equates to power, wins out every time. He also knew he was powerless to make a difference in that arena, but he could continue to do his part to protect those on his turf.

"Jennie, you never understood my passion. I was not about to take a desk job. That's not who I am. I know you were unhappy in New York, but I loved my career, and I now know I can't have both. I never thought of myself as a small town cop either, but I have a life here now. I'm getting to know and care about the people who live here. The area's natural beauty is making this a popular tourist area, and I enjoy talking to those folks as well."

Ethan waited to see if anything he said was making an impression. She had tilted her head, as she used to do, when she actually listened to him, so he was hopeful she was beginning to understand the depth of his emotions.

Because he thought she was listening, and just maybe finally understanding him, he decided to continue.

"Jennie, I've been able to make it without you. And as far as not getting a divorce, I'll think about it. You may not want one, but neither of us can get on with our lives if we're still married."

Jennie started to argue. He raised his hand to stop her knowing this was not the right time or place for this conversation.

"Could we meet this evening? I could show you the place I'm renting, and we can work out how to proceed?" Ethan suggested.

Jennie's sudden appearance into his life was more than he could handle right now. He had to compartmentalize.

"I have to get back to the city by tonight to catch my flight," Jennie said. "I'm sorry, Ethan. I wish things could be different."

He couldn't take anymore. She was still able to keep him on an emotional rollercoaster. He reached for his hat and said, "Okay, then, Jennie, if you'll excuse me, I have a meeting. Have a safe trip back."

Ethan stood by the open door waiting for his wife to leave.

Jennie sat for a moment longer before rising. She wasn't going to let Ethan get the upper hand. She walked over to him and said,

"It was good to see you, Ethan. You're doing well for yourself and I hope it continues. Good luck with the case."

She handed him a card.

"Here's where you can reach me if you decide you want to talk. Goodbye, Ethan," Jennie leaned over and gave him a kiss on the cheek.

"Goodbye Jennie," Ethan said as he stood aside to let her pass.

Maddie watched this scenario and had a million questions she was afraid to ask.

~ THIRTY-SEVEN ~

Thursday Noon

Caitlyn pulled into the parking lot of Tony's Tavern a few minutes before noon. She didn't see Ethan's car, he could be delayed for any number of reasons, so she decided to go in and study the menu. The tavern was dark, mostly because of the dark wood paneling covering the walls. The wood floor was a dark pine. The booths were illuminated by amber hurricane lamps that provided a subtle, even romantic ambiance.

Tony, if that was indeed the owner's name, had decorated the interior so men coming in from a day of hunting or fishing, as well as college students, locals and wine trail customers would feel right at home. She marveled at the skill in which his interior designer accomplished this feat.

She seated herself and ordered water to start. The lunch menu was extensive for a small restaurant, but again, Tony was trying to please a varied clientele. She decided on a chicken salad wrap with side green salad.

Ethan popped his head in the door and looked around before spotting Caitlyn in a back booth.

"Thanks for coming," Caitlyn said. She detected a change in Ethan, an additional stress she hadn't noticed before. Maybe this case was getting to him.

"I thought it was me who suggested lunch?" Ethan said with a smile.

"You know what I mean. I sent you a text earlier asking to talk. I know you have a lot to do, but things happened recently I wanted to share with you because they might connect to why Todd was murdered," Caitlyn said.

"I'm all ears, and besides, I do get a lunch break," Ethan stated.

"I talked with my father this morning. Or what might be considered a conversation. He is consulting for the oil company though he disavows any knowledge of the fracking in New York. I don't believe him. I think he's up to his eyeballs in this business."

"Can I get your order please?" Their smiling waitress appeared and was ready to do her job.

Ethan was anxious to hear what else Caitlyn had to say, so he quickly scanned the menu looking for the easiest thing to order.

"Quarter pound hamburger, medium well, fries, and ice tea, unsweetened," Ethan said.

"And you, ma'am?"

"Chicken salad wrap, small green salad and the water is fine for me," Caitlyn responded.

Once the waitress left, Ethan said, "Okay, finish."

"I found something else when I was telling you about Todd's journal. Apparently the students started a secret club called, 'Clean Water Forever.' What do you think it means?" Caitlyn asked.

"That's interesting, but I can't see where a bunch of high school kids are going to be much of a threat to a large oil company and it has nothing to do with water," Ethan stated. "Tom is going through Todd's journal and noting any relevant information."

"My friend Abbie thinks Uncle Jerry and my father are involved in pushing the fracking operations in New York State. I've tried to talk with both Jerry and Dad, but haven't gotten anywhere. They seem to dance around the issue before changing the subject altogether. And, Dad knows one of my clients is The Outdoor Foundation. I never talk about my clients to anyone," Caitlyn said with fingers crossed under the table.

I'm not comfortable telling Ethan about possible pillow talk with Nick.

"I think you might be too sensitive. Your father is in the oil business. It is *their* business to know the competition, and as more of the environmental groups are getting better organized, they can be classified as a sort of competition, or at least a threat to be watched. It could be as simple as someone from The Outdoor Foundation mentioned you produced their annual reports," Ethan said.

144

"I'm not sensitive and stop treating me like a child, Ethan. I've lived with my father for thirty-one years and I know what he's like and what he's capable of. He doesn't care about anything other than his career and making money. If putting more money in his pocket means destroying the environment, well, to him, it's a necessary consequence," Caitlyn said as she slapped her hand down hard on the table.

The food arrived while silence reigned. Both thought about what to say next that wouldn't destroy their lunch and their relationship. They needed to turn the heat down. Ethan needed to cool off. Jennie's unannounced visit had him in emotional turmoil.

He took a bite of his hamburger, and then dipped a fry into a pool of ketchup.

"O.k. so now we suspect Todd, several of his friends, this Teddy person whose mother states has no relationship with Todd, though we know from the school interviews it's not true, and your father and uncle might all be connected through the fracking business, though they deny it. We have to connect the dots between these folks, and what is gained by Todd's death?" Ethan said.

"Another interesting situation. I was out for a walk with Summit and saw Darcy Risley hurrying towards the woods. I followed, curious as to where she was headed at such a pace. Did you know there's an old cemetery back there? She goes there to practice Appalachian Folk Magick handed down from her grandmother."

"You've got to be kidding," Ethan said.

"No, and don't make fun. She's serious about it, and you know the saying that there is much more that we don't know than we do know," Caitlyn said.

"Speak for yourself," Ethan said with a smile. "And boy this hamburger is really good. I love Tony's cooking."

"So there really is a Tony?" Caitlyn said.

"Yea, nice guy, but he stays in the back and his wife, Evie, runs the front."

The all too familiar beep of Ethan's phone halted the conversation.

"Excuse me a minute," Ethan said as he drew the phone from his belt clip. He read the screen, then swiped his finger across the phone. "It's my deputy. I need to read the text."

Caitlyn watched as Ethan's expressions went through a number of variations. Her curiosity was aroused.

Ethan placed the phone back in its holder.

"Apparently the Tilton's neighbor, Mr. Jones, is more than he seems. There was something about the guy that didn't sit right with me, and so I asked Deputy Snow to do some inquiries. Apparently, Mr. Jones works on the drilling sites by day, doing farm chores for the Tiltons evenings. Although he comes from a wealthy family, he is intent on making his own way. He owns quite a bit of land bequeathed to him, and his house sits on that land. So, if individual county control over drilling is overturned, Mr. Jones could come into a lot of money by renting his land to the oil companies. There appears to be a vein on his property that runs off the Utica Shale formation."

"It would give him a motive to get rid of Todd, if he found out about the vandalism, or if he was afraid Todd might influence his father, who is connected in both the banking and political world . . ." Caitlyn left the rest unsaid.

"Correct. I guess I need to go back and have another talk with Mr. Jones," Ethan said.

"We need to get back to the school and talk with Todd's nighttime companions and Denny Mathews," Caitlyn added.

"Let's meet at 2:30 at the school, so we catch them at the end of their day. They can choose to talk with us or be late for whatever athletic practice they attend. I suspect the coach knows more than he's telling. Maybe others at the school as well. Secrets are hard to keep in that kind of environment."

Ethan waved the waitress over and requested the check.

"My treat today."

As they left the tavern, Caitlyn stopped. It was time to fess up.

"Ah, Ethan, one more thing I forgot to mention."

Ethan turned, wondering what other important information she had forgotten to convey.

"Yes?"

Caitlyn hesitated, her face getting red.

Ethan waited, wondering what she had to tell him that caused her such discomfort.

"It may be that my boyfriend, Nick, is involved."

~ THIRTY-EIGHT ~

Thursday Night in China

The reception at the Beijing Hilton was everything it promised to be. The décor was tastefully done, the food delicious and plentiful. As the waiters circulated with trays of hors d'oeuvres and glasses of champagne, Nick looked around for a likely target.

"Mr. Lu, I'm Nick Spaulding, here at the conference representing the U.S. government. I'm enjoying the sessions so far, especially yours on the future of energy in China. I know your environment has suffered by the fast economic growth. I know many countries, ours included, have relocated their heavy polluting industries to China," Nick said.

"You're correct, Mr. Spaulding. China hoped by opening our borders and through various reform movements foreign technology would come. But instead, we get your low-tech, labor intensive jobs. It's changing, however. Our central government is working with some NGOs, and looking at more renewable forms of energy. We hope to eliminate our coal fired industries, and become less dependent on foreign oil," Mr. Lu stated.

"Yes, but productivity is the key to growth and will China be able to sustain it?" Nick said. "What if you could get oil from the U.S. at a much lower rate than what you are paying for Middle East oil?"

"It might be a consideration, but we need to know the exact terms. As you know, China holds a lot of U.S. debt now, so we are in a good bargaining position. Is that what your government wants?" Mr. Lu responded.

"That might be the case, Mr. Lu, but let's not get ahead of ourselves. The oil companies would have to be brought on board. It might take time," Nick said.

Why is he acting nervous? Is someone watching us?

"Excuse, me, Mr. Spaulding, but there's someone I need to speak with," Mr. Lu said as he scurried off.

"Certainly, Mr. Lu, it's been a pleasure talking to you," Nick replied to Mr. Lu's back.

~

In his hotel room, Nick pulled off his tux as quickly as he could. It was suffocating. He jumped in a hot shower to rid himself of the clinging smoke that filled the reception hall. He needed time to clear his head before he composed emails to the senator and to the oil company. Although government salaries were generous as were benefits, the extra money coming from this "consulting" job was providing him with a nice nest egg. As long as the senator didn't find out what he was doing, he would be fine.

Nick checked his watch, 10:00 p.m. making it 9:00 a.m. in DC. Perfect timing for filing a report. Sitting at the small desk, Nick opened his laptop and started composing. He'd include information from his conversation with Mr. Lu regarding China's willingness to purchase oil from the U.S. instead of the Middle East, but the price would be tough to negotiate, and would the energy companies be willing to sell at an agreed upon price if it was much lower than they could get elsewhere? He worded his report carefully so there would be no mistake in interpretation. This was critical information the senator would need as he drafted his energy bill.

The report finished, he closed his computer. It was government issue, so he dare not use it for personal reasons. He picked up his personal cell phone and tapped out a quick text to his contact at the oil company.

China agreeable to US oil; price negotiations crucial.

They would know what it meant.

His work done, Nick sat back and composed a different kind of text to Caitlyn.

~ THIRTY-NINE ~

Thursday afternoon in Riverview
Caitlyn had an hour before she needed to be at the school. Since she was close to the stores in Renwick, it was the perfect opportunity to stroll the city streets and look in shop windows. She had had enough family time and didn't relish returning to her aunt and uncle's house. In fact, if it wasn't for spending time with Ethan and working on the investigation, she would be back in DC.

Except for The Outdoor Foundation, her clients seemed to understand her circumstances, and said their work could wait until her return, though she knew it wasn't good business. Instant gratification was good when it came to clients, and Caitlyn always prided herself on turning work around quickly. The reason The Outdoor Foundation was insistent was the fact they were preparing for their annual board meeting as well as for a formal presentation at the upcoming UN summit on climate change. It was important stuff and she took pride in playing a small part.

She found a convenient parking spot right on main street. She put two quarters in the meter noting the time. She wondered if the store selling local crafts was still in business. She would walk in that direction and see if she could find it after all these years.

As she walked, she noted a couple of people conversing outside the Methodist Church, though most who exited the side door scurried away. She didn't want to intrude, so she crossed to the other side of the street. Curiosity got the better of her so as she passed the church she glanced over.

Was that her aunt? And nearby was it Mac Risley? She had only seen him from a distance, but she was sure it was him. What kind of gathering was this? Then it hit her.

Oh my god, could this be an AA meeting?

The way people were scattering gave that impression. She didn't want to be seen by her aunt, and thankfully the craft store was only two doors away. She hurried and entered the store as quickly as she could.

Caitlyn browsed the store, her heart rate returning to normal. She would not mention to Myra what she had witnessed. That was a very private affair and Caitlyn would keep the confidence. But she was glad Myra was getting help and support. She wondered if that was where she was last Friday afternoon, and if so, did she tell Ethan in confidence. Caitlyn would never know.

Browsing the store, she loved all the unique creations in wood, metal and fabric. She especially liked the bowls made of different woods, sanded to a smooth finish. She wished she could buy one of each. She came upon a section of fragrant sachets. She picked up one sachet labeled lavender and took a deep breath. The immediate calming effect was amazing. She took two to the counter.

"I love these. Do you know who makes them?" Caitlyn asked the clerk.

"I think some lady in Riverview," replied the clerk.

"Could it be Darcy Risley?" Caitlyn asked.

"I'm not sure, I work the counter. The owner is not here right now, but the name sounds familiar."

"Does she supply anything else?" Caitlyn asked.

"I think she supplies some of the bulk teas. You can find them along the back counter."

"Thanks. I'll check them out and be back another time. I have an appointment I mustn't be late for."

By the time Caitlyn left the store, the sidewalk in front of the church was empty. Caitlyn walked back to her car, noting she still had twenty minutes left on her meter. Maybe a quick stop in the Home Dairy for a milk shake would be the thing. Before she could talk herself out of the idea, and the calories it would provide, she pushed open the door and went straight to the counter.

As she crossed the threshold, Caitlyn was transported back in time. The Home Dairy was a local landmark. The tin ceiling was original to the old building. The owners kept as much of the

151

original décor as they could. She knew the restaurant, which served cafeteria style, operated a state of the art kitchen, but from a diner's point of view, they were transported back into the early twentieth century.

Caitlyn loved this type of restaurant and was glad it remained the same. She walked past the salads, hot foods, and desserts to order her chocolate shake. As she waited she looked around at the other diners, few this time of day. Then she spotted Mac.

Opportunity has presented itself, she thought.

She paid for her shake, picked up a napkin and straw and walked over to Mac's table.

"May I join you?" Caitlyn asked.

Mac Risley did not look pleased, but he was polite enough to nod his approval.

"Mr. Risley, I'm Caitlyn Jamison, Todd Tilton's cousin. I'm staying with my aunt and uncle for a few days while they sort things out. Darcy and I have talked a bit, but I haven't had the opportunity to visit with you."

Mac remained silent giving Caitlyn only an occasional glance before resuming his gaze out the window.

Caitlyn struggled with what she could talk about that wouldn't drive him away.

"Your wife showed me her herb gardens the other day and her plans to sell more. In fact, I purchased some of her lavender sachets at the craft store down the block. You must be proud of her."

"You don't know anything," Mac said under his breath.

"What do you mean?" Caitlyn responded, feeling like she had been stabbed.

She took a long sip of her shake to give them both time to compose. She could see he was steaming inside and ready to explode. She couldn't let it happen, but she was at a loss as to the root of his anger.

"I mean you don't know her. She's controlling, especially where Teddy's concerned. She's ruining our family. I'm not allowed to do much of anything except plow the fields, cut firewood, bring in enough money for us to live. I'm not an important part of our family."

Caitlyn could see this man was being torn apart and depressed. How different a viewpoint from her talks with Darcy. This conversation was shedding additional light on the family dynamics. She wondered if they knew about Teddy's nighttime excursions to the oil fields, and more importantly, how did Teddy accomplish these getaways without his parents' knowledge. Something else to talk with Teddy about this afternoon.

Mac started talking, "I'm convinced she does something to Teddy to make him sick. I've tried to get the school to do something, but they won't. Mothers seem to have all the rights. I talk to the doctors, and they can't prove anything. She's cunning and good at covering up. No one's able to catch her in the act. In the meantime our son has spent his entire life without a quality of life. He's dependent on her and it is exactly what she wants. The only reason I stay around is so I can keep an eye on things and hopefully someday, somehow, be able to rescue Teddy from his mother."

"Are you saying you think your wife has a mental illness?" Caitlyn asked.

"I don't know. I started drinking about five years ago to escape my home life situation. Then I realized I needed to stay sober for Teddy's sake. A few months ago I hit bottom, and knew I had to change. I started going to AA. That's where I was before I came here for a late lunch."

"I'm glad you felt you could tell me. I'll keep everything you said in confidence. I wish you well. I have to get back to Riverview for a meeting, but I'm glad we had a chance to talk," Caitlyn said.

"Yea, see you around," Mac said.

When Caitlyn dropped her empty milk shake container into the trash, Mac still sat, coffee cup in hand, staring out the window.

~ FORTY ~

Caitlyn pulled into the school parking lot minutes after Ethan arrived. She saw his car and parked as close as she could. He was just finishing a phone call, so they got out and walked towards the front entrance together. They rang the bell, announced who they were, and the door buzzed open.

Ethan told the school secretary they needed to talk with Denny, Susan and Teddy again.

"We'll need to talk with Coach Kollner," Ethan said.

The secretary invited them to be seated while she went into the principal's office for approval.

Principal Stewart came out of his office and introduced himself. "I'm sorry I wasn't here on Monday. I was away at a conference and was shocked when I received the call about Todd Tilton. He was one of our star pupils, both in the classroom and on the basketball court. Superintendent Boynton said you interviewed several students on Monday, so is there a specific reason you are focusing on these three now?"

"We can't discuss an ongoing investigation, Mr. Stewart, but we can say these three seem to be closest to Todd and we thought they might have a little more information to share," Ethan said.

This explanation seemed to satisfy the principal, so he nodded and asked his secretary to request the three students come to the office.

"I have a small conference room off my office you are welcome to use. I wonder if it would be appropriate to alert their parents of these interviews."

"You do what you deem necessary, sir," Ethan said.

~

The three students sat around the conference table. They each exhibited their nervousness in different ways. Denny leaned back in his chair, appearing smug and in control, picking at his fingernails; Teddy stared at his feet, his hands fidgeting, and Susan chewed gum and twirled her long blond hair. Ethan let them stew.

"O.k. folks. You three seem to have a close connection with Todd in a number of ways. We want straight honest answers or I will haul each of you into the station for further questioning, and the experience won't be pleasant. As of now, your parents and peers don't know you are being questioned, but if we have to bring you to the station, everyone will know," Ethan explained.

"I don't know what you're talking about, Sheriff," Denny said. "I didn't do anything to Todd."

"Let me explain further," Ethan said. "Todd and a few of his buddies were involved in activities having to do with the oil drilling equipment in the next county. I want to know what you know about those nightly excursions."

"I don't know nuthin'," Denny said.

Ethan turned to Teddy. "Teddy, tell me about your involvement. I know you were out with Todd on occasion."

Teddy turned red and asked to use the restroom.

"Not until you tell me about the excursions."

Teddy continued to stare at his feet until he couldn't stand the silence any longer.

"O.k. Todd and I went out a coupla times. We made a pack to do what we could to save the environment. One way to discourage them was to do enough destruction to the equipment so maybe the rigs would go away. We didn't do too much, put sugar in the gas tanks and stuff like that."

"How lame," Denny said. "You guys are freakin' fruitcakes."

"Enough!" Ethan said. "Anything said in this room is to go no farther. Do you understand?"

"Yea, yea, no one would believe me anyway," Denny said as he leaned back further in his chair, chewing the end of his pencil.

Ethan turned his attention back to Teddy.

"Did your parents find out about your nighttime excursions?"

"I think so," Teddy responded. "All of a sudden they wouldn't let me go to anywhere at night. And I haven't been feeling very well, so I didn't really care."

That answered one question, so Ethan turned his attention to Susan.

"Susan, what part did you play in this escapade?" Ethan asked.

Susan remained silent, tears forming in her eyes.

"I drove them. You see I'm seventeen, and have my night license. Todd wanted me to be the driver. I didn't want to be involved at first, but if you knew Todd, he was persuasive. We met after school, down by the lake. There's a summer house down there, with a barn. The people aren't there yet. We tried the doors, but they were locked. The barn was open, so we sat on hay bales and talked. It was quiet there. When you sit by the lake you understand how important it is to save the environment. Does that make sense?"

Ethan agreed, but he couldn't show that agreement.

"Go on."

Susan sighed. She put her head in her hands to catch her breath and, Ethan suspected, to get her emotions under control.

"We contacted a couple kids from a neighboring school to meet us there. Sometimes they did; other times they didn't bother to show up. It was tricky, getting out of the house without our parents knowing. I would have lost driving privileges if my parents found out. It was a big risk for me. Friday afternoon Todd said he had bigger plans and he would tell us over the weekend. He said he was doing some research. But then he was killed," Susan said as she wiped her eyes and blew her nose. "I hope it wasn't because of what we did."

Ethan watched the three students, giving them some time to assimilate what transpired. Caitlyn sat near the door quietly taking notes. She, too, was listening carefully and noticing their reactions.

Denny continued his smug expression, though a shadow had appeared across his face indicating he really didn't know what Todd, Teddy and Susan were up to. Ethan suspected he was wondering why he wasn't included in their save the environment clique.

"I know there were more involved in these nighttime excursions," Ethan stated. "Who else was there?"

Susan and Teddy looked at each other wondering who should speak and how much should be said.

Ethan waited knowing what was going through their minds. These youngsters had made a pact. It was important for them to honor that pact. These two students were at a crossroads. They knew a serious crime was committed on one of their own and the sheriff was serious about arresting them if they didn't share what they knew.

Susan spoke first.

"Like I explained, we were getting quite a following. Todd was a natural leader. He recruited several kids from this school, and a bunch from the next district. I can give you the names of the kids from this school, but I don't know the others. The weekend Todd was killed we were to gather and make some grand plans. We were going to make a difference," Susan sobbed.

"Write down all the names you know," Ethan instructed. He slid paper and pen towards Susan.

Ethan then turned to Teddy.

"Do you know the names of the other kids?"

"No. Todd never introduced us. When we met nobody said their name. Todd said it was better that way," Teddy responded.

With Susan's list in hand, Ethan waited a bit and then knew he had gotten as much out of Susan and Teddy as possible.

"We'll talk again later," Ethan said, dismissing the students.

Ethan and Caitlyn waited in the conference room for the coach to appear, and when he didn't within fifteen minutes, Ethan went to the office to see what was holding him up.

"I asked to see Coach Kollner as soon as we were finished with the students. We're done with those interviews, and I asked Denny to let you know. Could you please ask the coach to join us in the conference room?" Ethan asked as he started towards the office door.

"Sheriff Ewing, I told the coach you needed to talk with him, but he told me he had an appointment and would have to leave. Can you catch him another time?"

"I guess we will have to," Ethan responded. The coach's behavior was getting to be a little erratic. Looking at his watch, Ethan realized they wouldn't have had much time to talk with the coach anyway. He had a meeting to attend.

Caitlyn was waiting in the conference room when Ethan appeared at the door.

"Our coach has taken a runner," Ethan said. "Or maybe he really did have an appointment. Guess we'll have to catch up with him later."

As Ethan and Caitlyn walked toward the exit, he said, "Got to hurry. Have a meeting with the state police in a few minutes."

"That's fine. I wanted to visit the town clerk anyway, and this might be a good time to catch her," Caitlyn said.

~ FORTY-ONE ~

The Riverview town clerk's office was located a block from the sheriff's office. Caitlyn parked halfway between. Before entering she studied the building. Like the sheriff's office, the town government found use for another one of its stately Main Street homes. Not many families wanted to live on the busy main street where more and more shops were located. Instead of tearing down the lovely old homes to make room for utilitarian facilities to house government offices, the forefathers of Riverview had preserved the homes while making them useful.

Caitlyn slowly walked up the front steps, and noted the handicap ramp off to the side. She admired the large floor to ceiling windows over which sheer curtains hung giving the appearance of a home instead of a town office. The wide veranda held two white rocking chairs, which furthered a welcoming impression. The front door opened to reveal a center hall staircase flanked by rooms on either side. Looking to her right, she saw the sign that designated the town clerk's office. The office directly opposite was labeled probate. Caitlyn walked into the clerk's office and noted the clerk's name was Penny Mitchell.

The town clerk looked up as soon as Caitlyn entered.

"Good afternoon. How may I help you?"

"I'm Caitlyn Jamison. I was wondering if I could look at your land records."

"Certainly. What property are you interested in?"

"I believe it is under the name of Tilton," Caitlyn said.

Caitlyn wasn't sure how her request would be received. This was a small town, and she didn't know if the clerk had a close relationship with her uncle, and if so, would word get back to him about her researching his property. Once again she had not controlled her impulsive nature, and now thought about what the consequences might be.

Penny got up from behind her desk and introduced herself. "I'm Penny Mitchell, by the way. Come on through the gate and I'll show you where the land records are and how to use the index."

"It's nice to meet you, Penny. Thanks for your help," Caitlyn said.

Penny showed Caitlyn the sliding shelves housing Riverview's large heavy books containing land records, and the bookcase covering most of one wall where the name indexes were kept.

"You first look up the name in the index, and it will tell you in which book or books the deed is recorded. If you need help, ask," Penny said.

Caitlyn walked over to the wall of index books and scanned the letters until she arrived at the T's. Those were so plentiful she scanned several books until she found the one containing names starting with Ti. She pulled the book off the shelf and took it to the slanted reading counter where she could open it and find the volume number of the property location she needed. Her finger scrolled down the list stopping at the name Tilton. A few more lines down she found Tilton, Jerrold and Myra. The various properties he acquired surrounding the house were shown with dates purchased and previous owners. Caitlyn was only interested in the woods containing the cemetery. After several tries, she finally found the book recording the information she needed.

Caitlyn read the entry carefully.

The cemetery she stumbled upon was from the 1700s. There were no burials there after the mid-1800s, but it was still sacred ground and, according to state law, couldn't be developed. Why wasn't the cemetery mentioned in the latest land transaction record?

"Penny, can you explain something?" Caitlyn asked.

Penny walked back into the research area and leaned over the book.

"You see the latest transaction on this property? And then go back on this same tract of land and the cemetery shows up. How come it's not recorded in this latest version?"

Caitlyn stepped out of the way so Penny could study the records in question. She went back and forth between pages. After a few minutes she stepped back.

"I don't have the answer. It should be there. This transaction was recorded before I got here, and I know the previous town clerk was not the most accurate, and how do I say this, except to tell the truth, but we found he was not always ethical. We've found some similar situations. We've been correcting them as they are found, but it's a slow process," Penny said.

Caitlyn could see Penny was uncomfortable with the conversation. She was in an awkward position.

"I understand," Caitlyn said. "I've been to this cemetery. It's a lovely spot. I'm worried my uncle might sell this property. Surveyors were there last week. If he has the survey prepared so the cemetery doesn't show, then the land could be developed and the cemetery demolished. I think it is against the law, isn't it?" Caitlyn said.

"That is exactly right," Penny said. "Now that I know about this recording error, I'll keep an eye out for anyone looking up the land record and make them aware of the mistake in the recent recording. I'll make sure if the land is transferred it has the cemetery listed. We have procedures in place to take care of these kinds of things. You have no idea what people try to get away with," Penny said. "Makes my job interesting sometimes."

"No doubt," Caitlyn said. "Thanks for your help."

"Any time. Oh, and another thing that might be of interest to you. My husband, Doug, is the town historian, so if you need any further information he might be able to help," Penny said.

"Thanks. I'd love to meet him, but probably not this trip. I have to get back to DC soon. Is your husband retired?" Caitlyn asked.

"Not yet, but in the next couple of months. He's a real history buff, so when the previous historian gave up the post, he took it. He's into genealogy, so he's in the process of documenting the original families in this area," Penny explained.

"If I want to get in touch I'll try nights or weekends when he is home from work. I'm glad someone like your husband is taking an interest and keeping good records. Sounds like you two make a great team," Caitlyn said.

Penny smiled and nodded. They said their goodbyes and Caitlyn thanked Penny again for her help with the land records.

As Caitlyn left the clerk's office, she pulled out her phone to check emails, only to find it was not turned on.

Wow, a whole day without checking the phone.

She sat on the steps waiting for the phone to wake up. When it finally did, she heard a familiar chirp. There was a text from Nick.

~ FORTY-TWO ~

The sheriff's office was busy when Caitlyn arrived. Maddie was at the switchboard. Deputy Tom Snow's expression was serious as he talked on his desk phone. The atmosphere was tense.

Has there been a break in the case? Her heart skipped a beat.

She took a seat along the wall and waited until someone realized she was there.

Ethan walked out of his office, the first to spot her. His face lit up at her presence, before quickly changing expression as he turned to his deputy and gave further instructions.

"Come in, Caitlyn," Ethan said, waving her into his office.

Caitlyn complied with his instruction, careful not to say anything until the door was securely closed.

"What's going on?" Caitlyn asked.

"There's been an attempted robbery at the bank," Ethan replied.

"Oh my god, Uncle Jerry's bank?" Caitlyn asked. She turned, her instincts telling her she should run to the bank.

"Yes, but don't be concerned, everyone is fine. No money was taken. An alert teller rang the silent alarm, so we were on our way before any money was taken and before anyone got hurt. The robber sensed the alarm was triggered, so he grabbed his bag and fled. Unfortunately, by the time we arrived, he was out of sight, but the tellers and the one customer there gave us a good description. Plus, the bank has CCTV, so we should be in good shape. We've put out a BOLO. The state police have taken over, so the guy should be caught soon," Ethan said.

Caitlyn sat down with a thud.

Why were all these bad things happening to her family?

163

"Do you want to talk about the murder case, or should I come back later?" Caitlyn asked. "And do you think the attempted robbery has anything to do with Todd's murder?"

"Yes, I do want to talk about the case, and no, I don't believe the attempted robbery has anything to do with Todd. Although I don't believe in coincidence, I think this is just a coincidence."

Caitlyn thought about that and wasn't so sure she agreed with him.

"The case. Tell me what you've learned," Ethan said.

"I found this letter . . .," Caitlyn said.

"Letter? Do you have it with you?" Ethan asked, his frustration reaching a whole new level.

"I was searching for some staples the other day and I knew Uncle Jerry would have some in his desk. So in my search, I pulled out one of his desk drawers and it wouldn't go back in. I had to figure out what was making it stick. When I reached in the back of the drawer, I found this crumpled up letter. I pulled it out and quickly stashed it in my pocket, because I heard Uncle Jerry coming through the front door. He'd be really angry if he found me in his office, and I didn't want to upset him further, so I stuffed the letter and made a quick escape," Caitlyn explained.

"Did you by chance read this letter and is it by chance related to the murder of your cousin, and do you have it with you?" Ethan asked, his voice rising. He paced back and forth behind his desk to keep his frustration in check. He glanced at his watch, noting it was getting late. Caitlyn blushed with embarrassment.

"I didn't get a chance to read it right away. In fact, just before I came here did I remember. I didn't think it would have anything to do with the case. I just thought it was an old piece of mail. Once I had a chance to really look at it, I realized it's on oil company letterhead, which makes it pretty clear Uncle Jerry is working with the oil company in some capacity. As for the other stuff, I am a bit confused."

Ethan snatched the letter from her hand.

Giving him time to review the contents, Caitlyn continued.

"Apparently Uncle Jerry is being groomed for some political office and to help sway legislation that would open New York State to fracking. The letter mentions senators by name, and the amount of money being paid for their votes. I assume Jerry would receive this same amount of money if he votes the 'right' way."

Ethan read through the letter dated 5 January.

Dear Jerry:

Our outside consultant has made contact with the target and is confident of obtaining needed information. The corresponding plan is in place and the land is being prepared. You are to carry on with your tasks at hand and await further instruction.

The letter was signed by an oil company executive vice president.

"Do you realize how damaging this letter would be if it got out?" Ethan said.

"I do," Caitlyn said. "It's why I struggled with the decision to show it to you. I'm sorry, Ethan, but this involves my family. Can we stop this before it goes too far?"

Ethan read the letter over again trying to put the pieces together.

"How do we find out who the outside consultant is or who the target is?" Caitlyn asked.

Oh god, could the consultant be Nick and the target be me?

Her thoughts went back to that holiday gathering she had attended. The woman who invited her worked as a government contractor. Caitlyn had designed posters for some of their events.

It's possible she knows Nick and set up their meeting. It wasn't a chance meeting after all. But why her? Ah, her father worked for the oil company and is now a consultant. The pieces were starting to fall into place. Uncle Jerry was involved just as she expected.

"Caitlyn, are you with us?" Ethan asked.

"Yes, I mean, sorry. I was just thinking."

"Thinking about what?"

"Oh, nothing."

Ethan leaned across his desk and put his hand over hers.

"Caitlyn, this letter says they, whoever they are, have already gone too far. The wheels have been set in motion. I don't know what 'corresponding plan' they're talking about, but our first responsibility is to stop the kids from vandalizing the drilling sites. Then we find out if your uncle's involvement with the oil companies and Todd's involvement with the environmental group and the vandalism are connected."

Caitlyn nodded in agreement, wiping the tears from her cheeks.

"Okay, so what's the plan?"

"Since I have a meeting with the state police at their office in Renwick tonight, I'll assign Deputy Snow to keep an eye on the drilling site this evening. We have a reciprocal agreement with the next county, so he has authority to be there. He's not going to be happy about a late night assignment, but we have to protect these kids. I hope they have enough sense to cease their activities, but Todd's death may have given them reason to be even more aggressive in their activities. At this evening's meeting I'll ask for help with the oil company connection."

"I drove by the site one day after I talked with Abbie. It's just over the county line and easy to find," Caitlyn said.

"Yes, there's a pull off less than a quarter mile from there. Tom can park there and keep watch."

"Sounds like a good plan. It's imperative we stop these youngsters before something really bad happens. In the meantime, I've work to do, so I had better get back. See you tomorrow," Caitlyn said.

Caitlyn picked up her purse and hurriedly left the office.

~

Ethan had just turned back to the report on the attempted robbery when a young man pushed his way into the office.

Maddie came running in after.

"Sheriff, I told him you were not to be disturbed." Maddie said, yanking the arm of the intruder.

Ethan recognized the eager young reporter, Robbie Robinson.

166

"It's okay, Maddie, I'll give him a few minutes."

As the sheriff and his dispatcher were coming to the conclusion that he could stay, Robbie was able to utilize his upside down reading skill to make mental note of the contents of the letter on the sheriff's desk. Very curious that it was on oil company letterhead, and the words that jumped out at him were consultant and target. This story was getting weirder by the minute.

"What do you want Mr. Robinson?" Ethan asked.

"I'm wondering how the murder case is coming," Robbie said.

"I don't think I have much more to add than what Maddie told you the other day. We interviewed students and staff at the school, and we have interviewed neighbors. We're running down a few more leads that I can't discuss right now," Ethan explained.

"Anything to do with oil companies or fracking?" Robbie asked.

Ethan's back muscles tightened.

"Why would you ask that?"

"Just asking, that's all." Robbie said. "What do you have on the attempted bank robbery today?

"One man, dressed in black, with hoodie and stocking over his face. We have CCTV footage that we'll be releasing to the press soon. The state police are on the lookout. I don't think it will be long before this inexperienced man will be caught. Now, if you don't mind, I have a murder investigation to work on," Ethan said.

Robbie nodded, closed his notebook and left the sheriff's office with a smirk on his face.

~ FORTY-THREE ~

Using the philosophy it's easier to ask forgiveness than permission, Caitlyn decided to drive to the well drilling site herself that night. She thought she had a better chance than Deputy Snow of talking the kids out of their planned actions.

She arrived at the pull-off at seven fifty. There were few cars on the road at this time of night, and it was already dark. She fought off a sense of foreboding, telling herself Deputy Snow would arrive soon. If the youngsters showed up, she and Tom would present a united front in talking them out of whatever mischief they had planned for the evening.

Car lights approached. She slid down in her seat so she was eye level with the bottom of the window. As the car went by, she noticed it carried three or four teenagers. She slid up in her seat to see if the car went straight through or if it was going to stop at the drilling site. The car slowed, pulled off to the right and went into the weeds. So, that's where they hide their car.

Where was Deputy Snow? She checked her watch. Eight fifteen. He should be here.

Caitlyn watched as the youngsters ran across the road to the fenced in area. She wondered how they were planning to breach the secure gate. She watched as one of the young men pulled something out of his pocket and opened the gate. The group walked in, not bothering to shut the gate behind them. They each carried a bag.

Caitlyn couldn't wait for the deputy any longer. She'd stop the teenagers before they did something they'd regret, something that might possibly create a criminal record to haunt them for the rest of their lives.

She couldn't risk being seen or heard, so she opted to quietly jog to the gate, and since they didn't close it securely, she was able to slide in without making a sound. Once inside she looked around.

There wasn't much of a moon, and only the drilling rig had a light on it, not the surrounding areas. Where did the kids go?

She walked slowly, sticking close to one of the structures so she wouldn't be seen. She heard a noise to her right. She peered around the construction trailer and saw the teenagers gathered around one of the big earth moving machines. She suspected they were going to pour sugar in the gas tank, a quick way to bring the machine to a halt. She didn't know what other mischief they planned, and she didn't know if they'd gotten their hands on explosives. She had to stop them.

As Caitlyn stepped away from the trailer, she felt a presence behind her. Before she could turn, an arm went around her neck, making it difficult for her to breathe.

"I don't mean any . . ."

Before she could explain a foul smelling rag was jammed into her mouth and tied tightly at the back of her head. She was shoved inside the small metal building and the assailant, she assumed to be a man, because of his smell and strength, pushed her up against the wall. As he held her against the wall, he tied her arms behind her back secured with a rope of some kind. Another rag, this one oily, was pulled across her eyes and tied behind her head. Whoever it was, was strong and fast. She struggled but it was no use.

She heard her assailant leave as the door was securely shut. She could tell the structure was small. She moved around to ascertain how small. She quickly hit the sides confirming her first impression.

With her mouth covered, she struggled to breathe through her nose. The stench of the rag challenged her gag reflex. She would choke on her own vomit if she couldn't get herself under control. The next problem was with her eyes covered and knowing she was in a tight enclosed space, her latent claustrophobia kicked in.

I have to get out of here, she though as her heart raced and she started to shake.

Her breathing became more rapid as she fought her phobia. Her insides felt like they might explode as her anxiety heightened. She had to keep herself under control or she would be out of control. She *could not* let that happen.

Mind over matter, breathe, slow and steady.

Voices. She heard voices and strained to understand what was being said. Whoever tied her up and threw her into this confined space was now after the youngsters. Where in hell was Tom Snow? He was supposed to be here keeping the teens safe.

A gunshot rattled the sides of the metal building, the resulting vibration hurt her ears. Chills ran down her spine. She had never been so frightened. What had they gotten themselves into? They were going up against powerful people, a powerful company that wouldn't tolerate vandalism.

And what use was she? Here she was, herself incapable of saving them. Tears formed flooding her eyes from the frustration and anger of the situation.

Quiet reined outside. Caitlyn rested her head against the cold metal wall of her prison. She had to remain calm and in control of her mind and body.

Was she going to be the next gunshot victim? She listened for the sound of footsteps coming for her while she continued to fight the claustrophobia. She concentrated on any sound to help identify what was going on outside. After the gunshot everything was quiet. Too quiet.

She continued to struggle with the rope binding her hands. She slid down the wall to a sitting position, her bound hands touching the dirt floor. She moved along the wall hoping to find a jagged piece of metal in which to cut the ropes, but to no avail.

She pushed against the wall to rub the rag tied tight around her head. Nothing was working. Her legs tingled from the cold radiating from the dirt floor. She shimmied her way back up the wall. She pushed against the metal to make a sound, but with her hands tied so tightly, anything she tried didn't accomplish her goal. Her only hope was that Deputy Snow would arrive soon, see her car and come looking for her. She hoped she was still alive, as she didn't know what he would be up against when he showed up at the drilling site.

She waited and listened.

~

Tom Snow was not happy with the nighttime assignment. He had promised his girlfriend a night out with dinner and a movie. He hated calling her to take a rain check on their evening. Something he did way too often. She knew his position as a police officer meant interruptions in their plans, and he hoped she didn't get discouraged with their relationship.

He was halfway to the drilling site when his radio blared. Jeff, the evening dispatcher, reported a three car accident with fatalities, on the main road. Ambulances were dispatched, but police presence was needed immediately for forensic aid and traffic control. Sheriff Ewing was unavailable, so Deputy Snow was requested at the scene.

Tom made a U-turn, flicked on his siren and lights, and headed for the main road. When he arrived at the accident scene, he saw it was as bad as Jeff indicated. The ambulance with its screaming sirens arrived and the paramedics raced to the injured.

He went into action, setting out traffic cones and flares he carried in his trunk, directing traffic and assisting the medical personnel. The wrecker arrived to tow the cars away as the ambulance drove off.

When all was clear and the road swept clean of metal and glass, he got back into his car and headed for the county line.

~

Deputy Tom Snow arrived at the pull off Ethan described. There was a familiar car parked there.

Now where have I seen that car before?

He got out and peered in the windows. It then came to him. Caitlyn Jamison drove a rental car like this. He checked the plates and sure enough it was a rental.

What in the hell is her car doing here?

He straightened up and looked around. Where could she have gone? His internal alarm went off as the most obvious possibility hit him.

171

Oh, no, has she gone to the site?

He felt the weapon at his side, assuring himself it was still there. He didn't know what he was up against, but he needed to quickly find out. Tom jumped back in his car and drove to the site where he parked just outside the gate.

How did she get through the gate, if indeed she was inside?

Tom had a bad feeling about this situation and wished Ethan was there to provide instruction. He looked around, listened, and then walked to the gate and gave it a push. It swung open.

Once inside he stopped again, listening. Silence. Then he detected a dull thump. He walked cautiously towards the construction trailer, stopping every few seconds to listen. The thumping sound was closer. He kept walking. With his back pressed hard against the trailer, and gun in hand, he slowly turned his head to survey the site. He saw the well and drilling rig, some out buildings, and a couple of serious looking earth moving machines.

The dull thumping sound continued, and appeared to come from one of the small outbuildings. Then he heard a loud thump. With hand on his gun, he jogged over to the metal building he assumed was some sort of storage shed. He pulled the door open, positioned his firearm and turned on his flashlight to blind whoever might be hiding there.

"What the hell?" Tom whispered as his flashlight illuminated a bound and gagged Caitlyn.

He knelt down and untied the blindfold and gag that went around Caitlyn's head.

Caitlyn shook her head as the rags were removed.

"Arggh. The smell and taste is awful," was all she could say as she was freed from her bondage. She tried to spit the awful taste away.

Tom noticed her hands were shaking.

"What happened? Tom whispered.

Caitlyn couldn't answer immediately. Her whole body shook as she acclimated her mind to the relief she felt. Were they out of danger? She didn't think so. Whoever fired the shots might still be

172

on the property. She and Tom and maybe the youngsters could be in grave danger.

"I saw a car drive by with some kids in it. I watched as it slowed down at the gate. Someone had a key of some sort. When you didn't come, I thought I'd better get in there and stop them. I thought they might listen to me. As I was going to find them, someone grabbed me from behind. He bound my wrists, and stuffed the gag in my mouth. I couldn't move and could hardly breathe. The awful oily rag was tied over my eyes. I was thrown into this metal building. I couldn't see and couldn't even hear much with the rag over my ears, so I felt around with my feet. I realized the space was really small. I couldn't move my hands so I was getting claustrophobic. And then I heard a gunshot. And where the hell have you been?"

"There was an accident I had to cover, but I came here as soon as I could. I didn't see anyone when I came in, but I'll look around. You stay here. Hopefully what you heard was only a warning shot to make the kids run," Tom said.

Tom and Caitlyn slipped out of the metal shed and Caitlyn could see it was no more than that. She wondered how it withstood any kind of wind. She watched Tom survey the area and seeing no one he slowly walked to the bulldozer where Caitlyn had last seen the teenagers.

Nothing there.

Tom returned to where Caitlyn stood.

"We should get you back to your car," Tom said.

"Wait. What's that?" Caitlyn asked as she pointed to a dark spot past the bulldozer.

They walked towards the fence line, and as they got closer, they noticed a lump on the ground, and they both tensed.

Not one of the kids, Caitlyn thought. *Please, no.*

Caitlyn started to run, but Tom caught her and pulled her back.

"Wait here," Tom instructed.

Caitlyn started to argue, but decided speed was of the essence, so she kept quiet. This was getting to be too much. If one of the youngsters was hurt, or killed, she would never forgive herself.

There should have been another way to stop them from coming here this evening. She heard Tom talking into the clip on his shoulder.

"What is it?" Caitlyn asked.

Tom was too intent on his conversation to pay attention to her.

"Tom, what, who is it?" Caitlyn shouted, tugging at his arm. She ran to stand by his side, frightened at what she would see.

Tom finished his conversation, grabbed her arm so she couldn't go any further and said, "It's Clyde Jones. He's been shot. Shot right in the heart. I've called it in. Backup'll be here soon. I want you to stay put until we get this sorted out."

Caitlyn was stunned. What was Clyde Jones doing at the drilling site tonight? Why was he shot? Nothing made sense. She felt dizzy.

"Where are the teenagers? They were here. I saw them. What happened to them?" Caitlyn demanded.

Tom ignored her demands. He looked around and found an empty crate.

"Sit."

~

Ethan was the first to arrive. Officers from Sampson County arrived soon after. Tom met Ethan at the gate and filled him in on what he thought had transpired.

He knew Ethan would be anxious about Caitlyn's involvement and did his best to defuse Ethan's anxiety and temper before he got to her. Tom knew his boss's feelings for Caitlyn, and he knew Ethan was walking on thin ground allowing Caitlyn to be involved with the investigation of her cousin's murder. Tom had too much respect for his new boss to report this transgression, therefore putting himself in jeopardy of a reprimand or worse. Now there were two murders to deal with, making that situation even more tenuous.

Ethan hurried to where Caitlyn was sitting. She was staring at the ground, probably in shock. Ethan put a hand on her shoulder.

174

Caitlyn looked up, then got up and went into his arms. She let her emotions take control and sobbed.

Ethan hesitated only a moment before he allowed Caitlyn into his embrace, letting her cry. He barely heard her questions through the sobs, but understood enough to know she was scared and worried about the youngsters.

"On my way from Renwick I instructed Jeff to call the families to check on the kids. Just as I arrived here, Jeff confirmed Susan and Teddy are safe. Susan provided the names of the two other young men with them. I've asked the state police for assistance in tracking them down. They weren't at home, but I'm sure they'll show up."

I sure hope so, he thought.

"The state police will interview each of the kids to see what went down. We'll investigate Clyde's murder assisting the Sampson police."

With Caitlyn calmed, Ethan helped her sit back down on the crate so he could talk to the medical examiner before the body was taken away.

~

"Pretty simple," said the examiner. "Gunshot wound to the head. Since this happened in Sampson County, we'll be doing the autopsy. I'll keep you in the loop, since I know our counties have reciprocal agreements."

"Thanks, Doc. I look forward to your report."

"We'll gather what evidence we can, and work closely with your office," the medical examiner explained.

When Ethan finished with the medical examiner, he walked back to where Caitlyn was sitting.

"Let's go," Ethan said.

He drove her to her car.

"Are you sure you're able to drive?"

"Yes. Now that I know the kids are safe, I feel better, but I need to get a shower and clean my mouth out. Oh, god, how disgusting," she said as she continued to spit out the oily substance. "I can't imagine how many germs have invaded my body through that filthy rag."

Caitlyn explained how she came to be at the drilling site.

"When will you learn this is serious business?" Ethan asked. "We're dealing with one or more ruthless individuals. I think we should end our collaboration. I can't trust you to use common sense."

"No, please. I will use common sense. I want to continue working with you," Caitlyn exclaimed. "I want to find Todd's killer."

He could see she was fighting back tears in her attempt to appear strong. Ethan's heart tugged at her plea. He didn't want her to know the terror he felt when he received the call from Tom about the shooting at the drilling site and how he had found Caitlyn.

His way of dealing with his emotions was to bring the conversation back to the business at hand.

"Let's discuss this situation tomorrow when we're both more clear headed. I'll come back here in the morning to talk with the foreman and workmen," Ethan stated has he helped Caitlyn into her car.

As he watched her drive off, he talked into this clip, "Follow her to the house, just in case."

~ FORTY-FOUR ~

Friday morning

When Caitlyn entered the kitchen for her morning coffee, Myra was sitting at the table reading the paper.

"You were out kind of late last night," Myra stated.

Caitlyn waited for her coffee to finish brewing before she responded.

"Sheriff Ewing and I were talking about the case. I like being able to do something to bring justice for Todd."

"You and the sheriff seem to be spending a lot of time together. Is there anything more going on?"

"Absolutely not, Aunt Myra, how can you think such a thing? I have a boyfriend in DC, well, actually he's in China now, but we've been seeing quite a lot of each other lately. The relationship with Ethan, I mean Sheriff Ewing, and I is purely professional."

"Well, then, what have you and the good sheriff learned about Todd's murder? Is he any closer to identifying the person?"

Caitlyn noticed a slight tremor in her aunt's hands. The stress of not knowing, of being in limbo was weighing heavily on her. And maybe the tremor was from alcohol withdrawal. That was a battle to be fought every day.

Caitlyn sighed. "Unfortunately, no. But he has leads he's following. And he's investigating the attempted bank robbery. Is Uncle Jerry all right?" Caitlyn asked.

"Oh yes. The attempted robbery has caused quite a bit of excitement at the bank, and since no money was taken and no one was hurt, they're all chattering about it," Myra stated. "We just didn't need this on top of . . ." Myra couldn't finish the sentence.

"So what needs to be done here?" Caitlyn asked changing the subject. "Are there any more thank you notes to write?"

177

"Thankfully, no. I think those are done. Actually Jerry helped with the last batch. It was nice to have him home and engaged in something not work related. I don't know what he is going to do now. He has political aspirations, and I believe sits on some kind of energy board, but before Todd died, Jerry was starting to have second thoughts," Myra stated.

"Second thoughts about what?" Caitlyn asked.

"Well, Todd argued the environment was most important, and any energy exploration should keep that foremost in their plans. He and Jerry had many heated discussions about all this energy versus environment stuff over the last few months. So much so I tuned it out. Sometimes Todd would get so mad and frustrated with his father that he would go to his room and slam the door so hard the house would shake. I hated those nights. Everyone went to bed angry. Then, all of a sudden I noticed, actually in the last two or three weeks, that Jerry started to listen more and argue less. I took his silence to mean he was *actually* listening to Todd and willing to understand another point of view. Quite a change for Jerry."

"Well, that is interesting. Thanks for telling me, Aunt Myra. It shows another side of Uncle Jerry, doesn't it?" Caitlyn said.

She and Myra laughed at the visualization of a new Jerry. It was good to laugh. There hadn't been much to laugh about in this house lately.

"Has Uncle Jerry left for work already?"

Caitlyn didn't see evidence of his breakfast dishes on the counter. Nor did she hear the shower running.

"Jerry went to Albany," Myra responded.

"Albany? Does it have to do with the attempted robbery yesterday?" Caitlyn asked.

"No, no. One of his vice presidents is handling that. Jerry received a call last evening, and all he said was he was needed in Albany. He never tells me much. I've gotten used to it, so I don't even ask anymore. Political business I assume."

This was an interesting development. Caitlyn wondered if her father was involved as well. She and Ethan had not talked further about the letter, and what he decided to do with the information.

178

There was something else on her mind and with Jerry away this was as good a time as any to broach the subject with her aunt.

"Another thing I wanted to talk to you about, Aunt Myra."

Myra inclined her head wondering what was bothering Caitlyn. Her silence encouraged Caitlyn to continue.

"I need to know why you and Mom aren't speaking. I think it's tragic when two sisters who should be close aren't. There has to be a way to patch up whatever happened," Caitlyn said.

Myra continued to sip her coffee, willing her hands to be still, and carefully chose her words. After a few minutes she began.

"As you know, Caitlyn, your mother and I are about the same age. But she was into all sorts of activities and I was more of the stay at home type. I resented the fact she was so active and popular. Then she was off to college, married and moved away while I stayed at home with our parents. Boring, I'll tell you."

Myra paused, her attention going to her coffee. She swirled the brown liquid around without spilling a drop. Caitlyn waited giving her aunt time to pull up the painful memories.

"It started out with little things. Because she lived away I kept her out of the loop as far as family things. It became a game, but it was only a game. When she and your father moved to Riverview because of his job, we got together socially and things seemed to be right again."

Myra paused.

"We had some pretty wild parties. We were young then and that was the thing to do. We were beyond the wife swapping days, but things like that still went on."

Myra paused, looked at Caitlyn to get a sign that she should continue. Maybe this was more than Caitlyn wanted or needed to know.

Caitlyn held her coffee cup tight, bracing herself for information she might regret knowing. She nodded indicating Myra should continue.

"We thought we had to keep up or compete with the other couples. It was sort of like 'keeping up with the Joneses' And then I did a stupid thing. One evening during one of our wild parties, I made a pass at your father, a very suggestive pass. Remember, to me it was all a game. I was young and naïve, and I might add, just a little drunk. Your mother was furious. She didn't understand I had had too many Margaritas, and my actions really didn't mean anything. But it was too late. Your mother stormed off and the divide has only widened over the years."

Myra paused again.

Caitlyn was sure her aunt was thinking about all those lost years. Lost because of a foolish act brought on by too much alcohol.

"Communication stopped, they moved away shortly after that. Your dad was transferred, or maybe he asked to be, anyway, the void between us grew as each year passed. Silly, isn't it? Do I want things to change? Of course I do. I'm sorry for what I did. I miss my sister. Does she want to talk? I haven't seen anything indicating she wants a closer relationship."

Caitlyn processed what her aunt had shared. Little things began to add up. One small thing built on another and eventually was blown out of proportion. Caitlyn would have to go to Florida and have a serious talk with her mother. It was going to take real effort on her mother's part to put the past aside. What a mess her family was.

"Thanks for telling me this, Aunt Myra. I know it was difficult and how hurtful it was to share this with me. It's difficult to admit someone close to you doesn't like you, or doesn't want anything to do with you. I'll have a talk with Mom and see what she has to say. Maybe we can make things better," Caitlyn said.

"That would be wonderful, Caitlyn. But I wonder if too many years have gone by to undo all the built-up hurt?" Myra said.

"We'll see, won't we?" Caitlyn said.

"Now, I better get up to my room and do some work. My clients can reach me anywhere, and they have been. I'll put in a couple of hours of work to keep them happy until I am back in DC.

~

Caitlyn's phone was ringing when she entered her room. Hoping for another call from Nick, she ran to the dresser.

"Hello."

"Caitlyn, it's Dad."

Trying not to let her disappointment show, she replied, "Oh, hi Dad. What are you up to today? And where are you?"

Caitlyn tried to sound light and funny, like where in the world is Waldo, hoping her father would fall for the ploy. He did not.

"I've something to explain to you. It'd be much easier to do in person, but since I can't be there I'll do my best by phone."

Caitlyn sat back against her pillows and waited for what she knew was going to be some kind of lecture.

"I heard about the situation last night at the drilling site. I learned you were there, and one of the oil service company employees was killed. Am I correct so far?"

Caitlyn hated it when her father knew what she was up to.

"Yes."

"Caitlyn, this is a dangerous situation you have gotten yourself into. It's not a game. It's serious business. *Listen to me.* The company I work for or any other oil company doesn't do hydraulic fracturing. It's done by oil service companies, and I know for a fact that several are working in New York. Their employees are sometimes, how shall I put this, not the most ethical. The fact that one of the employees was murdered last night on the site is very disturbing. I've been on a conference call with the vice presidents this morning. Until the circumstances surrounding the cause of death are determined, the company isn't going to make a statement. And so, when you think Uncle Jerry and I are in 'cahoots' as you call it, we are actually consultants, but that's it."

"The oil companies have the money and the power. They could stop the methods used by the, what did you call them, service firms, and do more research on environmental effects," Caitlyn retorted.

"We're doing that, Caitlyn, but in the real world, energy is in higher demand as each year passes. Third world countries are now demanding energy. We not only have to keep up with demand here in the states, we have to compete on the world market. Don't see us as the bad guys, Caitlyn. We're trying to make the world better by supplying enough energy."

It was hard to argue with her father when he made sense. But it was not her style to let go. Before she could come up with a retort, Herb added, "Stay away from the sites. This is serious business. Will you promise me?"

There was no way she was going to let her father know all of what happened last night. She learned her lesson, so this was an easy response. "Yes, Dad, I promise."

"Great. Then finish up there and get back to Washington. I'm sure your clients want you back at work."

"Right, Dad. I will."

"Bye, honey, talk to you soon."

"Bye, Dad."

Caitlyn hit 'end' and stared at the phone.

She now understood there were several layers involved with the production of oil and natural gas, which added more suspects in Todd's murder. If either the oil company or the service firm found out about Todd's environmental activism, and Jerry, with one foot in Albany, was starting to have second thoughts, they might choose to eliminate the cause. What bothered her was the comment Harriett the cafeteria lady said when she overheard the boys mentioning water. What was that about? She sent a text off to Ethan, and then readied herself for work, assuming she could get Summit off her computer.

~ FORTY-FIVE ~

The sudden jolt woke him. He was disoriented, so it took a few seconds to achieve full consciousness from the deep sleep that had overtaken him. As his mind acclimated to reality, Nick knew the plane had touched down at Reagan International and he was back in DC. He was exhausted from his stint in China, evidenced by the fact he slept so deeply on the last leg of the journey.

For the past ten days adrenalin had kept him going day and night. Balancing two employers tested his mettle; his government employer and the unauthorized consultant position that could possibly put his career in jeopardy.

Was it worth it? Greed made people make bad decisions, and now he was having second thoughts about some of his decisions.

As soon as he filed the next report, he was going to get out of his contract with the oil company. He hoped it would not jeopardize his relationship with Caitlyn.

Nick grabbed his bag from the overhead compartment and slowly made his way off the plane. He would head right to Capital Hill. There was no time to stop by his apartment to freshen up. That would have to wait. The text from his boss instructed Nick to attend a meeting in, he looked at his watch, half an hour.

The family in front of him was taking their time retrieving their carryon luggage from the overhead compartment. It might go faster if their attention was on what they were doing instead of their cell phones.

Come on, he thought.

He jockeyed back and forth hoping they would get the hint.

Damn tourists.

He finally made it past, bumping the husband with his bag.

"Excuse me," Nick said, as he rushed past. "I'm late for an important meeting."

Nick knew the jerk didn't have a clue as to how important the meeting really was.

Finally out of the airport, Nick jumped into the first waiting taxi and gave the address. He was on his way.

~

Caitlyn needed a break from working on an advertising brochure. How many ways can one describe the latest washing machine? She was giving it her best, because the Washington area Whirlpool account was lucrative.

She checked her email, answered the important ones, and then surfed the web. This was her form of relaxation. She surfed her favorite sites, and checked the news headlines. Nothing good was happening in the world if you read the headlines. It was a shame the news media favored violence; a sad statement about our society. Caitlyn wished things were different.

If wishes were horses... she remembered her mother saying.

Caitlyn decided to read some small town newspapers, gleaning current trends she might be able to use in her work. Her search brought her to a small town in the Catskills. A short article caught her attention. She leaned into her laptop to read the words. The article described drilling in some remote areas the reporter didn't think was oil-related. The reporter, Matt Miller, suggested the rigs might be searching for water. What if, he wrote, someone wanted to capture the veins of water into a holding area, and then sell water to municipalities such as New York City? The entity would become wealthy to say nothing of the power they would hold.

What an intriguing idea, thought Caitlyn.

She wondered about the oil service companies with rigs roaming New York, and the push to open the state to uncontrolled drilling. It would benefit those drilling for water as well as oil and natural gas assuming this reporter's research and hypothesis were correct.

Things began to come together in her head—Uncle Jerry's abrupt departure for Albany, his political ambitions, his drive for money and power. It would give the legislators more incentive to open the state to drilling if there was water involved.

She would send Matt Miller a note. She clicked on the "contact" icon and sent off an email.

In the meantime, she would get back to describing the features of the newest Whirlpool washer and dryer.

~

Caitlyn was deep into developing text for her animal rights group client when there was a soft knock at the door.

"Come in," she called, not wanting to lose her train of thought. She was in her creative groove and any disturbance could knock her out.

"Caitlyn, there's someone here to see you," Myra said, barely poking her head through the door.

Damn, thought Caitlyn. *I'm going to lose the passion I built up for this section.*

"Who is it? Caitlyn asked angrily.

"He's the tenant neighbor, Risley, I think," Myra said.

Caitlyn couldn't believe her aunt didn't know who their renters and neighbors were.

"Okay, I'll be right down." Caitlyn said doing her best to control her frustration at the interruption.

Mac Risley was standing in the front hall as close to the door as he could. Hat in hand, he kept worrying the brim with his fingers.

"Hi Mac, what can I do for you?" Caitlyn asked. She decided not to take her anger out on him. He had no idea her train of thought was disrupted, and there must be a good reason why he was at her door.

"Oh, come on in the living room and sit down." She noticed Mac's nervousness and knew something was wrong.

Mac remained standing in the hallway. Being in the Tilton's big house made him nervous.

"Teddy's sick again. Darcy's taken him to the hospital. I think she's done something to him. She loves being in the medical setting

185

and 'assisting' the doctors. No one will listen to me," Mac said, wiping a tear he quickly brushed away, embarrassed at his emotions.

"Since our conversation the other day, I thought I could talk to you," Mac said.

"Of course, Mac, and as I said, anything you tell me will remain confidential," Caitlyn responded.

"We've got to do something to stop her. She's sick; I know it. She's going to do a lot of harm to Teddy if she isn't stopped," Mac pleaded.

"Okay, let me see what I can do. Would you like me to go to the hospital and talk with her?" Caitlyn asked.

"No! I mean, no, thanks. It would set her off and she might leave with Teddy. If you could just get someone to listen . . ." Mac said as he broke down in tears. He wiped his tears with his sleeve. "No one will listen to me."

"I'm listening, Mac. I hear you and I'll do what I can to rectify this situation. I sensed there was something going on that was not to Teddy's benefit. I'll research to see what we can find out and then we can make a plan," Caitlyn said.

"Thanks, ma'am. Whatever you can do to help I'd appreciate. I'm at wits end," Mac said. He continued to wipe away tears.

Mac nodded to Caitlyn, turned and walked out the door.

As she watched Mac walk to his pickup truck, she wondered why her aunt didn't know his name. Didn't she see them both outside the church? Maybe it was because whatever was said in those meetings, even names and faces were to be kept in the strictest confidence. Myra was keeping that confidence. Good for her.

~

"What was that about?" Myra asked.

"Mr. Risley is concerned about his son's health. I told him I would do some research to see what might be done to help him," Caitlyn responded.

186

She wasn't going to tell her aunt the real issue, since she promised Mac confidentiality. Now she had another issue to research along with keeping her clients happy. Why did time sensitive client demands come on top of each other at the most inconvenient time? One of the questions of life.

~

When Caitlyn returned to her computer, she found an email from Matt Miller.

Well, he's right on top of things.

Very excited to read his reply, she read the email before she'd research Teddy's various medical conditions, and before getting back into the creative groove for Save Our Friends, the animal rights client.

Clicking on Matt's email, Caitlyn read:

Ms. Jamison: Thanks for your interest in my article on drilling in the Catskills. An anonymous source told me a small group of legislators, backed by Wall Street bankers, hired a drilling service firm to explore the areas just north of the city looking for water. If they find rich veins of water, properties will be bought up, reservoirs dug and filled with water, diverting the water away from the city reservoirs already in place. Some of this work has already been done, deep in wooded areas where no one will notice. It's been said the next war will be fought over water. I'm not sure about that, but I do know water is necessary for life, and if this consortium can capture the water supply for New York City and surrounding areas in the Hudson Valley and Western Connecticut, they'll be multi-millionaires overnight. There is legislation coming up to open New York to drilling. No more home rule. Those seats are being filled with those who will vote for it. The major opponent is Senator Smith, but it's unknown how much longer his supporters can keep the hole plugged.

The disclaimer here is that I haven't gotten verification on any of this, but I'm following some leads.

Caitlyn felt a cold sweat coming on.

Is Uncle Jerry involved with this? Not oil drilling but water drilling? Is he dealing on both sides? Is it why he was listening to Todd more, because of the conservation, environmental concerns impacting water quality? How, if anything, does any of this have to do with Todd's death?

She needed to think this through before calling Ethan. She didn't want to send him on a wild goose chase.

Now two murders, a robbery, and possible fraud faced them.

~ FORTY-SIX ~

It was a hell of a day. No progress had been made on the attempted bank robbery, even with the state police on the case. Ethan asked Deputy Snow to review the CCT tapes once again to see if they missed something during the first few viewings. Any detail might be the clue they needed to identify this would-be robber.

More pressing were the murders of Todd Tilton and Clyde Jones.

Ethan grabbed a cup of coffee before settling down at his desk to review the case file notes. There had to be some detail they missed.

A knock on the door disturbed his concentration.

"Come in!" He yelled.

Robbie Robinson entered with a spring in his step.

Ethan was starting to dislike Robbie's cheerful attitude.

"What can I do for you?" Ethan asked.

"I have information Jerry Tilton received a letter mentioning a land deal. With hydraulic fracturing in the state coming up for a vote soon, would this letter have anything to do with that? And, how would this effect the residents of Riverview?" Robbie asked, his notebook ready.

The question took Ethan by surprise. How did Robbie know about the letter?

He looked down at his desk and then remembered. The day Caitlyn brought in the letter, Robbie had barged into the office. The letter was still on the desk. He must have seen it.

"I don't have the information you are looking for," Ethan responded.

"But sheriff," Robbie exclaimed.

"No buts. I don't have any information, and now if you don't mind, I need get back to my investigation."

"I guess I'll have to go to another source then," Robbie replied.

"I guess you will," Ethan said. "Please close the door after you."

~

Anna Jones drove to Sampson to identify her brother's body before returning to Riverview to talk with Sheriff Ewing. When Anna walked into his office, Ethan noted this sixty year old woman wore little makeup, but then her skin didn't require any. She also wore her graying hair with pride. Anna Jones was a classy lady.

Ethan stood, shook Anna's hand, then motioned for her to have a seat.

"Can I get you some coffee or tea?"

"No thanks, sheriff. I'm fine. Let's just get this over with." Anna replied.

"What can you tell me about your brother? I had a brief discussion with him about the murder of Todd Tilton, but I didn't have the opportunity to get to know him, I'm sorry to say," Ethan said.

Anna sat for a minute collecting her thoughts.

"Sheriff, we're a family of some standing in this community. I don't mean to sound egotistic; I'm just stating a fact."

Ethan continued to be amazed at the stature of this woman. She was not self-important. He could tell she spoke from the heart.

"In our family there were four children, two boys and two girls. Three of the four went on to make a mark in the world, if you count wealth and community standing a 'mark.' After attending prestigious universities, my brother is a doctor and my sister is a lawyer. I became a university professor, and married an engineer. I decided to keep my maiden name for professional reasons."

Anna paused, deciding how best to describe her brother.

"Clyde didn't march to our tune; he forged a different path. In a way I admire his courage to make it on his own. He was a real trial for our parents, but they didn't give up on him. They gave Clyde the old farmhouse, just up the road from the Tilton's. He didn't even want that, but after some time I think his practical self realized he needed a roof over his head. Because of his behavior, Father cut Clyde out of the will. The three of us siblings didn't feel comfortable about the situation. We discussed it and agreed we'd give Clyde a percentage of our inheritance. Clyde refused. We set up an account in the local bank in his name so if he changed his mind, the money would be there for him. I'm co-signer on the account, and as far as I know, the money hasn't been touched."

Anna stopped her recitation, staring into space. Ethan thought she was probably pulling up memories from long ago. Some of the memories would be painful. He knew to stay silent so as to not interrupt her train of thought. She'd continue when she was ready.

"A few months ago, maybe almost a year now, Clyde took a job with the oil drilling service company. I tried to talk him out of it, but he insisted. Clyde was pig-headed and did only what he wanted to do. I now wonder . . ."

"Wonder what?" Ethan asked. He knew he should stay silent to let her continue, but his curiosity got the better of him. "Wonder what," he repeated.

Anna paused wondering how much she should share with this newcomer.

"Did the police go through his belongings?" Anna asked.

"Yes, we did a search, but only looking for information that might have tied him to the murder of Todd Tilton. We found nothing," Ethan explained. "Why do you ask?"

Anna sighed at the thought her brother could be a murder suspect. She let a tear run down her cheek before gently wiping it away.

"I was going through his house early this morning looking for the financial papers. I found letters from an organization called The Outdoor Foundation. Your people probably thought they were just a solicitation that we all get from time to time. Apparently The Outdoor Foundation is an environmental group working to stop the hydraulic fracturing in our state. I was quite surprised to see these letters in my brother's possession, since I didn't think he cared anything about the environment. Or anything else for that matter."

Anna paused again. Ethan was getting impatient. He wanted her to get to the point.

She continued, "The letters indicated he was actually giving them information on hydraulic fracturing in this area and even down in the Catskills. My brother was a spy! Can you imagine that? I saw something about drilling for water. I can't imagine what it's about, but The Outdoor Foundation is quite concerned about this secret drilling activity."

Anna looked at Ethan. He could tell she was spent. Too much had hit her in a small amount of time, and he knew he wouldn't get more information from her. At least for now.

"Thank you, Ms. Jones. I appreciate your coming in and sharing the information with me. It helps to make sense of what happened at the site last night. Please accept my condolences to you and your family."

~

After Anna Jones left his office, Ethan thought about what Todd and Clyde had in common. Both lived on the same road, both had connections to oil drilling. And now there was an added wrinkle of this environmental foundation Clyde apparently was working for, or at the very least sharing information.

A thought occurred—could it have been Clyde who put Caitlyn in the shed? Did he want to keep her safe because he knew there was an armed guard on premises? Was he able to warn the youngsters in time that may have saved their lives as well? This put a whole new light on the situation.

The tiepin found at the Tilton crime scene still bothered him. He kept it in his desk instead of returning it to the secure evidence locker. Not very professional, but there was something about the pin he needed to figure out, and having it nearby to twirl around in his fingers helped him think.

It came to him. The aerie number on the pin was from an Elks Club located in the south. The Risley's were from the south. Mac might have belonged to such a club. Ethan would ask Mac, and he could double check by contacting the club. He picked up the phone and dialed.

"Hello. Mac here."

"Mr. Risley. This is Sheriff Ewing."

Ethan felt the tension through the phone lines.

"I wonder if you ever belonged to an Elks Club? Maybe before you moved here?"

There was silence on the line, like Mac was trying to figure out the best response. Ethan waited.

"Yea, as a matter of fact I did. Why? It was a long time ago."

"I found an Elks tiepin the other day and I thought maybe it belonged to you. Did you ever have one?"

"Not in a long time. When we moved a lot of stuff got misplaced. You know how it is. You pack it and then can't find it when you unpack. Darcy used to wear a lot of my stuff. She thought it was fashionable to wear men's jewelry, so I lost a lot of stuff that way. She isn't the most careful person with things. But like I said, I haven't seen the pin in a while and I didn't care since I'm no longer involved with the group."

"Thanks for the information, Mr. Risley. It's possible this isn't your pin, so I'll keep searching for the owner. That's all for now. Have a good day," Ethan said as he hung up the phone.

Wow. He knew this pin was a critical piece of evidence. It might put one of the Risley's at the crime scene. Ethan knew the pin was not in the grass very long or it would've shown signs of wear and rust developing on the metal parts. There was none.

So, which Risley was at the Tilton's last Friday afternoon?

~

Caitlyn recaptured her creative groove and finished the Save our Friends marketing piece. She saved it to her computer's desktop as well as backing it up on a thumb drive. She'd let it sit for a few hours and then review. She could always find ways to tweak her work if she let it sit. Her canine assistant Summit was looking at her with those soulful eyes. She suspected he wanted to go out for a walk, but she had promised Mac she would work on Teddy's situation.

"We'll go for a w-a-l-k in a while," Caitlyn said, careful to spell out the operative word, as Summit knew the word well and if verbalized, he would not be willing to wait.

Caitlyn clicked on Firefox to search a variety of medical conditions, and then those in combination with each other. She was surprised at what she found.

Munchausen by Proxy was a mental condition where the caregiver, most often the mother, causes symptoms making the child ill. Symptoms faked or real were listed. The caregiver has an insatiable need for control and enjoys interaction with medical professionals. From this interaction the person has a higher self-esteem and feeling of power. The caregiver will do whatever is necessary to keep control.

After reading through the MedlinePlus information, as well as a number of other medical sites, Caitlyn sat back and thought about Darcy. Caitlyn liked Darcy. She was an interesting person, and Caitlyn enjoyed learning about the herb garden and her folk magick practices. Caitlyn didn't want to believe Darcy would intentionally hurt her son. But here it was, in front of her, a roadmap of Darcy's actions, and there is no accounting for what goes on with mental illness.

A chill went through her body. If she accused Darcy of this disease, and was wrong, irreparable damage would result with their relationship. But what did she really care? She was going back to Washington soon to never return.

For some reason she did care. She cared about Darcy, Mac and Teddy, and the fact Mac confided in her had forged a special relationship between them.

What a mess.

~ FORTY-SEVEN~

Nick was exhausted from his stint in China and the long trip back. No layover in Hawaii to refresh. Time was of the essence in presenting the intelligence he acquired in his ten days away. Although the meeting with his boss seemed to last forever, he returned to his small office with a list of items to be written up. The senator needed to know every detail of his conversations and observations, who he talked with and when.

He was glad he took meticulous notes and his memory for detail was sharp.

Back at his desk what he really wanted to do was contact Caitlyn. She must be frantic not hearing from him much over the past two weeks. With his boss's to-do list in front of him, he pulled out his cell and touched her number. He didn't know whether she was in Arlington or still in New York with her aunt and uncle.

"This is Caitlyn. Please leave your name and number and I'll get right back to you."

Damn. Why doesn't she pick up? Is her phone off or did she check the caller ID and decide she didn't want to speak with him.

He wouldn't have the answer until he had the chance to talk to her. If she didn't call back today, he would go to her apartment. If she wasn't there, he would hop a plane to New York. That was easier said than done. He had no idea the name of her aunt and uncle, and he had only a short time before leaving on his next assignment. But he was not going anywhere until he squared things with Caitlyn.

~

Caitlyn returned from her walk with Summit. They went further than usual today, but on their return they ventured through the fields into the woods.

Would Darcy be there and what would Caitlyn say to her? The cemetery was deserted to Caitlyn's relief.

All the information she found this morning was swimming around in her head and she didn't know exactly what to do with it. With all the new privacy laws there was no one in the medical community with which she could discuss the situation. Should she tell Ethan? Did it have anything to do with Todd's death? How would it? Darcy's illness seemed to be contained to their family, as sad as that situation was.

Being alone in the cemetery gave her a chance to look around. Some of the stones were crumbling, and some were flat on the ground with weeds encroaching upon them. Caitlyn took her foot and gently pushed aside the grass. The name on the stone was Jones. She bet it was an ancestor of Clyde's. Old cemeteries always intrigued her, but today she could not get caught up in the stories they told. Her clients waited for her to finish their projects so they could get on with business.

Reluctantly she turned to head back.

"Come on Summit. I know you want to stay and sniff all the new smells, but duty calls."

The little dog seemed to understand, although she knew he was disappointed.

"Don't worry, we'll be back," Caitlyn told him.

~

Nick tried Caitlyn's number again.

Damn-it, where was she? He was getting angry that she wasn't answering.

"Hello." A distracted voice answered.

"Caitlyn, is that you? It's Nick."

"Nick!" Caitlyn screamed. "Where are you? I haven't heard anything from you in so long. I was so worried."

"I'm back in DC, but have another assignment next week. I have to see you."

"Nick, I'm still in Riverview. There's so much going on here. We need to talk. Can you come up for the weekend? I'm sure my aunt and uncle won't mind if you stay here."

"I'll try. Will let you know as soon as I can make arrangements," Nick said.

"Can't wait, Nick. I really need your advice about some things," Caitlyn said.

Nick felt their relationship was getting out of control. If he wanted to keep control he would have to go to New York.

"I'll do my best to fly up in the morning," Nick said.

"Okay. Got to go. Client on the line," Caitlyn said.

~

It wasn't a client, but Abbie's husband, Tim.

"How's Abbie?" Caitlyn asked.

"Holding her own," Tim replied. "She wanted me to call you for a couple of reasons. First, have you found anything out about the drilling? And second, Abbie wondered if we could hire you to develop a brochure for the winery. She told me how creative you are."

"She flatters me, and yes, I would love to develop a brochure for you. What fun. I'll come up early next week and get background information and take some pictures," Caitlyn said.

"That would be great. Thanks a lot. We think we're going to have a banner year ahead. The vines to the south of us are doing great, making up for the ones struggling on the north side," Tim said.

"As far as the hydraulic fracturing goes, I confirmed my dad is consulting with the oil company. He told me it is not the oil companies drilling, but oil *service* companies. When they find oil, they negotiate with the oil companies selling out to the highest bidder. You probably heard about the murder at the site the other night."

197

"Yes, we did. What a tragedy," Tim said.

Caitlyn didn't tell Tim she was in the middle of that fiasco.

"One of my clients is an environmental organization, and so when doing some web research I learned about drilling concerns and water rights. I'm trying to find out more about the situation, though I know that is not something you are concerned about now. You have enough on your plate caring for Abbie and keeping the winery going."

"You got it. Thanks again for your help, Caitlyn. I'll tell Abbie you're willing to create a brochure, and we look forward to working with you," Tim said.

~ FORTY-EIGHT ~

Saturday Morning
Caitlyn drove to the airport to pick up Nick from his early morning flight. She had asked her aunt if they could entertain a houseguest for a couple days. Since Jerry was still in Albany, god knows doing what, Myra was only too happy to have another young person in the house. It kept her mind off the loss of her son, and wondering what her husband was up to.

On their way back to Riverview, Caitlyn filled Nick in on the week's events. Was it only a week? It seemed like a lifetime. She waited until they reached the Tilton's driveway to tell him about her involvement with solving Todd's murder. It wasn't a surprise that Nick was disturbed by her news. It was evident he didn't know her well enough to understand her passion for justice.

She knew she would have to introduce Nick to Ethan, and she didn't now how she felt about that. She'd been able to keep her two worlds separate and now they were colliding. Her feelings for both men were strong and confusing. Caitlyn couldn't let emotions cloud the most important issue, finding Todd's murderer.

As they entered the front door of the house, Myra came running from the kitchen.

Ignoring Nick, Myra yelled, "Caitlyn, Senator Smith died. Jerry called. They're appointing him, appointing Jerry, to fill Senator Smith's seat!"

Caitlyn watched Myra pace back and forth.

Is she happy about this appointment or not? New beginnings and all that? Her body language says she's conflicted.

"Calm down, Aunt Myra," Caitlyn said, as she led her aunt to the living room. "Now, tell me what Uncle Jerry said. Oh, Aunt Myra, this is Nick."

Myra nodded to Nick, and put out her hand.

199

"I'm sorry to be so rude. It's just so many things happened this week. I'm a bit flustered. Not myself at all. It's nice to have you here, Nick. I have your room ready, and please, do stay as long as you wish."

"Thank you, Mrs. Tilton. I hope I'm not a bother to you," Nick replied, taking Myra's outstretched hand.

"Absolutely not. I'm so glad Caitlyn is here helping me. Otherwise I think I'd go insane," Myra said.

"Aunt Myra, tell me what Uncle Jerry said."

"Apparently Senator Smith died a few days ago, but they kept it quiet until they, the senators, could get their ducks in order, so to speak. It's why Jerry was called to Albany. They've been prepping him for months, unbeknownst to me, for the position. And now the time is right. Though I guess it is wrong for Senator Smith. Oh, here I go again, rattling on."

"You're fine, Aunt Myra. So now what? Aren't they supposed to have the vote on hydraulic fracturing soon?" Caitlyn asked.

"I've no idea about any of that political stuff," Myra said with a frown.

"We have to get in touch with him. He has to know the damage it would cause the state if the bill is passed," Caitlyn said.

Nick remained silent. Although he had hooked up with her to learn about The Outdoor Foundation's plans, he never realized Caitlyn was passionate about the environment. He could tell from her voice and body language she definitely was concerned. He wondered when this happened. They certainly never talked about environmental issues. Now he really was in a bind. He couldn't let her find out his role in feeding the oil company information about potential foreign markets, or that his boss was drafting an energy bill that would promote hydraulic fracturing in a number of states.

Nick felt Caitlyn's eyes on him.

Did she suspect? He wondered.

Is he part of this? She wondered. She had to be careful.

"Nick, I'll explain all of this to you later, but right now I have to make a call," Caitlyn said. "Let me show you to your room."

~

When Caitlyn returned to the kitchen she found Nick and Myra in an animated conversation. Nick was regaling her aunt with stories of his travel. Caitlyn watched them a minute before entering. She hated to interrupt the flow. But she promised to meet Ethan at Tony's for lunch. She dreaded what Ethan and Nick would think when she introduced them to each other, and she dreaded facing her feelings when the two men in her life came face to face.

~

When Ethan saw Caitlyn enter Tony's Tavern his heart beat faster. His feelings caught him by surprise. He was still a married man. But he couldn't help it. Over the past week he and Caitlyn had developed a special bond, one not unusual for two people working towards a common goal, but this bond went beyond that. It was deeply emotional, at least for him. Within seconds those feelings dissipated as he noticed the man following closely behind her, with a possessive hand on her shoulder. Could this be the boyfriend she mentioned?

"Ethan, this is Nick Spaulding," Caitlyn said as they arrived at the table. She wanted to get introductions over as soon as she could. She was a nervous wreck.

"Nick, this is Ethan, otherwise known as Sheriff Ewing." Caitlyn tried to sound as light hearted as possible. It wasn't working.

The men eyed each other as Nick and Caitlyn slipped into the opposite side of the both. Both men uttered a "nice to meet you."

God, this is awkward, thought Caitlyn.

Handing Nick a menu, Caitlyn said, "Let's order, then we can share information. Nick, I hear the burgers and fries here are phenomenal."

She winked at Ethan hoping Nick wouldn't see the silent communication.

The waitress took their order and after a few minutes of small talk, and Nick telling Ethan a little about himself, Caitlyn decided it was time to get down to business.

"So, what have you found out?" Caitlyn asked.

Ethan twirled the straw around his glass of water before responding. He needed to decide how much to tell her with a big unknown, Nick, sitting at the table. Ethan knew Caitlyn understood the importance of confidentiality, but Ethan didn't know Nick, so he chose his words carefully.

"We've learned more about Clyde Jones. It seems he wasn't such a bad guy after all. Just different. I think it was he who pulled you into the storage unit. He wanted you out of danger since he knew armed guards were securing the location. He figured out a way to keep you safe, even though it was over the top. But that is how his sister described him, and with his Vietnam background, I can see him taking extra precautions."

"Oh, my god!" Caitlyn gasped. "I don't believe it. I have him to thank for saving my life?"

Nick looked at Caitlyn. "What the hell is this all about?"

"I'll explain later, Nick. For now, just be quiet," Caitlyn instructed.

She couldn't believe she was talking to him this way, but she had changed in the last week. She lived in a different world, a world in which violence erupted at any time, any place. And because of the events of the last few days she had become a much stronger, and maybe even wiser person.

"Apparently Clyde was rushing towards the kids to get them out of there when he was shot. The guards didn't know Clyde was an employee. Thinking he was an intruder, they shot first, asked questions later. Not professionals by any standards, and trigger happy. They'll be arrested and charged with Clyde's murder. Clyde's actions not only saved you, but saved the lives of the kids. He was able to scare them off in time," Ethan explained.

"If the oil service company was aware of the young environmentalists, and knew the leader was Todd Tilton, the thugs they hired to protect the site might have paid Todd a visit to

202

persuade him to stay away. From what we now know about Todd, he would have blown them off. That action might have gotten him killed."

Ethan took a breath and gathered his thoughts. He looked at Nick and said, "I don't know anything about you, Mr. Spaulding, but what I am sharing with you and Caitlyn is to remain strictly confidential. Do I have your word?"

Nick nodded, and then said, "Yes, of course."

Caitlyn tapped Ethan's leg under the table signaling for him to be cautious.

Ethan gave a slight nod.

Nick kept glancing at Caitlyn with dismay. She was not the same woman he knew in DC.

What's happened that changed her?

Nick suddenly realized Ethan was including him in the conversation.

"I talked with one of my downstate colleagues about fracking in his area," Ethan said.

Nick shifted in his seat, hoping Ethan or Caitlyn wouldn't notice his sudden unease.

Caitlyn did.

"There're rumors something is happening in the Catskills regarding drilling for water. Apparently a group of Wall Street investors want to capture the water supply to sell to the city of New York. Water will be diverted from the reservoirs the city uses now. Those reservoirs will draw down and the city will be in dire need to find enough water. The 'conglomerate' will sell water to the city at rates to realize a quick return on their investment. Once they have a monopoly on the water supply, they'll be able to charge whatever they want. It seems the future is now, and environmental agencies, with their limited funding and limited staff, are scrambling to find where they are drilling."

Caitlyn listened, nodded, and then said, "I just read an article about this. I emailed the author, so I suspect maybe it's more than rumor. Uncle Jerry has just been appointed to Senator Smith's seat. Wasn't Senator Smith against fracking?"

"Yes, I think he was, and he carried a lot of weight with the junior senators. His leadership stalled the change in home rule," Ethan responded. "With Senator Smith gone and your uncle in, home rule is jeopardized and the state might open to hydraulic fracturing for oil as well as for water. That's another group who might have wanted Todd dead if he was persuading his father otherwise."

"And he was," Caitlyn said. "Aunt Myra told me they used to have loud arguments about the pros and cons of fracking, but lately, the arguments weren't so loud. Uncle Jerry was listening more and talking less. Maybe, just maybe, he started thinking about what fracking was doing to the environment, and maybe it was becoming more important than his greed."

Nick took this in with great interest. This information might be of interest to Senator McConnell. So much for "confidentiality." All's fair . . . as the saying goes. Then he wondered, *Is the good senator involved with this group planning to capture the New York City water supply? How far did senator's tentacles reach, and if so, why wasn't I included?*

"Nick, are you with us?" Caitlyn asked.

"Yea, sure," said Nick as he was jolted back into the conversation.

Have I been duped by my own boss? Nick continued to wonder.

Caitlyn didn't know what was going on with Nick. All of a sudden he was absent from their discussion. She couldn't worry about him now. She decided it was time to share her information.

"I've found out some disturbing information about the Risley family," Caitlyn began.

"I have as well," Ethan said, "but you first."

"Mac confided in me his concerns about Darcy and Teddy. I did some research. There's a mental disorder called Munchausen by Proxy. It's when a caregiver, often a mother, intentionally makes another person, mainly a child, ill. It's a little known disease and difficult to diagnose. Medical professionals have to follow clues, such as careful review of a child's medical records. If the family moves, as did the Risley's, most likely that review will not happen. Mac has tried to get the doctors and the school to look into the issue, with no result. They mostly take the side of the mother. And the disease is not well known. The school, especially, is reluctant to get involved in something like this."

Caitlyn paused to let the information sink in. She looked from Ethan to Nick. Both were listening and, she supposed, trying to come up with an opposing point of view.

"The current laws all favor the mother," Ethan said. "This is such a rare occurrence I doubt many school officials are aware of it, and if medical records aren't shared, doctors wouldn't want the liability."

"Now that Teddy's reaching a certain age, I suspect Darcy is desperate to keep him under her control. It's not so easy anymore. I think his developing friendship with Todd was worrisome for Darcy, if she knew. And I think she did," Caitlyn said.

Caitlyn took a breath. Her thoughts had spilled out as she spoke.

"That's all very interesting, Caitlyn," Ethan said. "I would never have come up with the scenario. You remember the pin I found at the scene?"

Caitlyn nodded. "Yea, I guess."

"I did some research of my own and found it's from an Elks club in the south, an area from which the Risley's came. I asked Mac if he ever belonged. He had, but lost his pin. Then he admitted his wife often wore his pin. She thought it was fashionable. She seldom returned the items belonging to him, so he hasn't seen the pin in a long time."

At this point Nick spoke for the first time.

"Do you think one of them murdered Todd? I mean, isn't that a drastic measure? If they didn't like their son's interaction with Todd, they could have moved." Nick stated, obviously having no understanding of the family's circumstances.

"It's not that easy, Nick. The Risley's rent from the Tilton's. It was a hard winter. They didn't have enough wood to heat their house, so they had to purchase fuel oil. I think they're living hand to mouth. And jobs are hard to come by, especially for someone like Mac," Ethan explained.

"From my research, someone suffering from Munchausen by Proxy would go to any length to reach their goal. To me, that includes murder. We can't assume whomever killed Todd intended to do so. It might have been an accident," Caitlyn said.

"How do you explain the hay bales that knocked you over?" Ethan asked.

Again Nick took a sidelong glance at Caitlyn.

"I think there're some things we need to discuss," Nick said, his temper starting to show. He didn't like the fact she was keeping things from him and he didn't like what he saw of the developing relationship between Caitlyn and Ethan.

"Later!" Caitlyn replied. She moved what remained of her lunch around her plate.

Silence reigned as they finished their lunch, and digested their food as well as the information presented.

Caitlyn finally broke the silence.

"I'm devastated by all this. I like Darcy and Mac. They have their troubles, but they're trying to make it. And Teddy, he's just a kid. If she's making him sick, how awful."

"I know," said Ethan. "The downside to police work. Too often we only see the bad side of life."

Nick was relieved to get away from the discussion of oil drilling.

"It wouldn't be easy for a kid, such as Teddy, and probably impossible for his mother. She's facing loss if Teddy breaks away from her," Ethan observed.

Caitlyn noticed Nick had become more attentive to the conversation when they stopped talking about fracking.

"We still have too many scenarios for Todd's murder. One is the oil service company and another is to check out the environmental groups in case they wanted to get back at Jerry Tilton for some reason. We have the Risley family, and possibly a jealousy factor of one or more of the kids," Ethan said.

"Don't forget the other scenario. We haven't had a chance to talk again with the coach. He has a close relationship with the boys and I suspect he knows more than he is saying. So, what do you want me to do?" Caitlyn said.

"I think you have a houseguest to entertain," Ethan said, nodding at Nick.

"Nick is only staying the weekend. He has to get back to work on Monday," Caitlyn said. "But this afternoon we're going to see Abbie and Tim. I want to show Nick the winery, and Abbie might have more information on what's going on with the drilling. I'll ask if the winery group has any information on what's happening in the Catskills," Caitlyn said.

The conversation was winding down and each had somewhere else to be. Nick offered to pick up the tab. Ethan put down a tip, and they left Tony's, each with their own assignment.

~ FORTY-NINE ~

Saturday Afternoon

The drive to the winery was tense. As soon as they were in the car, Nick started grilling Caitlyn about her involvement with fracking and her relationship with Ethan. Before responding, Caitlyn thought about how much she was willing to tell him.

He'd be furious if he knew every detail of her night at the drilling site. On the other hand, the more she shared with him, the more he might be able to help. She decided to fudge the truth a bit. And she decided to ignore his question about Ethan. It was none of his damn business, and she didn't know the answer herself.

Nick seemed satisfied with her explanation of what happened at the site, though clearly not happy. And he didn't press the question about her relationship with the sheriff.

"You can't be putting yourself in such danger, Caitlyn," Nick said.

"I know that now, Nick, but I didn't know the service company had such thugs, and I only wanted to get those kids out of there," Caitlyn responded. Her hands gripped the steering wheel. She didn't want to get into a fight.

She hated being treated like a child. Between her parents and Nick, she about had enough.

"Caitlyn, the business of energy, no matter what form it takes, is serious business. It means big money, make or break for big companies. They'll do whatever it takes to protect their interests, and of course they're going to secure their drilling sites any way they can," Nick replied.

"I learned my lesson. I'll be more careful next time. You know, it just started out with my taking notes for the sheriff. Just sitting in the back of the room, jotting down what was said and observing body language. Then I started connecting with those kids. And they are just kids. They have that youthful passion for changing the world. I commend that. And it's why I felt the need to talk some sense into them. Oh, we're here! Look at that view, Nick. Isn't it stunning?" Caitlyn said, happy to change the subject.

Abbie and Tim were at the door when Caitlyn pulled into the parking lot. Caitlyn noticed Abbie wore a wig covering her baldness due to the chemo treatments. She must have felt it necessary to make a good impression on Nick. Abbie had explained that "chemo heads" sometimes make for awkward moments for those not accustomed to the sight.

Caitlyn introduced Nick, and then stood back while Abbie and Tim took over the tour.

The winery tour over, they adjourned to a window table while Tim opened a bottle of their new variety.

"I would like your honest opinion on this," Tim said as he poured the four glasses.

Each person swished the wine around the glass before sniffing the aroma. They took their lead from Tim as he took a small sip. He held the wine in his mouth allowing his taste buds to do their job.

"I think it's great," Caitlyn said. She was not a wine connoisseur, so she knew her opinion would carry no weight whatsoever.

Nick, on the other hand, made all the right gestures. He observed the wine's color at different angles. He carefully swirled the wine around the glass.

When she gave him a questioning look he said with a smile, "I'm looking for 'tears.'"

"What's that?" Caitlyn asked.

Abbie and Tim remained silent, letting Nick impress Caitlyn with his knowledge.

"If the wine produces 'legs' or 'tears,' down the sides of the glass, it has good alcohol content and for me, a full body taste," Nick explained. "Now, I'll sniff the wine. Watch as I hover over the glass. Some people poke their nose right down into the glass, and when I see that I say, 'wine connoisseur wanna-be.' It takes training to identify the various fragrances, and I'm first to admit I'm an amateur and not familiar with the New York State varietals. But it's fun to try."

Finishing the wine lesson, he said, "And now for the best part, enjoyment of the wine."

Nick took a small sip, swished it around in his mouth, and then swallowed.

Several tense seconds passed before he said, "Lovely. Just lovely."

Tim and Abbie breathed a sigh of relief. Nick put on quite a show, and they enjoyed listening to him describe the experience and Caitlyn's expressions as she listened, though it didn't get past them that he was a bit of a show-off.

"Thank you. I'm so glad you like it. We worked hard nurturing these vines, and we hope they'll produce a good product for us," Tim said. "Although we remain concerned about ground water contamination from the drilling that is occurring north of us."

"Did we hear your uncle was nominated to fill Senator Smith's seat?" Abbie asked.

"Yes. That's correct. It came as quite a shock. My aunt is in a tizzy. And we don't know what it means for the vote coming before the senate allowing hydraulic fracturing throughout the state," Caitlyn said as she stood and faced Nick giving him the sign they needed to go.

"I hope you can talk some sense into him," Abbie said. She then turned to Nick.

"I know you're not from this area, so I'm not sure how much you know about our fight to keep our environment and ground water safe."

Nick nodded doing his best to put on a concerned face and said, "Caitlyn has been filling me in."

Caitlyn noticed the slight catch in his voice.

What was that about? Or was she becoming overly sensitive about Nick's reactions?

"It's time for us to get back to Riverview. I don't want to leave Aunt Myra alone too long," Caitlyn said. She gave Abbie a big hug hoping she'd have the opportunity to see her again soon.

Today Abbie looked good, but Caitlyn knew the chemo treatments took so much out of her, and there was no guarantee. Pushing those thoughts aside, they said their goodbyes and Caitlyn said she looked forward to her next visit.

~ FIFTY ~

Saturday
Albany, NY

Jerry Tilton was up at the crack of dawn. He was grateful for the coffee maker in his hotel suite as he had to get quickly up-to-speed on pending legislation, decide on staff, and get to know the movers and shakers in the Albany scene. The morning hours disappeared without notice as he diligently plowed through the piles of paper.

As noontime approached he remembered his wife back in Riverview. He had barely given her a thought as he faced his new legislative responsibilities. His excitement over finally reaching his goal was almost overwhelming.

He wondered how she would adapt to the political realm. If she didn't like it she could always stay in Riverview and he would have a pied-à-terre in Albany. It might actually be the better solution so he wouldn't be tied to domestic responsibilities. He made a note to call her this afternoon to check in.

He assumed Caitlyn was still there, which would keep Myra off his back for a while. But Caitlyn would return to DC soon, and then Myra would be his responsibility. He'd worry about that later.

A loud knock at the door brought him out of his reverie. Who could it be? Housekeeping? He got up to answer.

Two men, dressed in shirts and ties stood before him.

"Mr. Tilton, we're from Senator Harrison's office. He's on his way up to have a chat with you. May we come in to check your room before he arrives?"

Jerry was taken aback. What in the hell was this about?

"Let me see some ID."

"Of course. Excuse us. We should have shown you our credentials first."

The two men took out their wallets and flashed IDs identifying them with a well-known security company.

"I guess it's okay," Jerry said tentatively. "I'm the only one here. And don't touch anything,"

He followed them in and watched as they used special equipment to check the suite, closets, and bathroom.

"All checks out, Mr. Tilton. We'll tell Senator Harrison he can come up now. Enjoy your chat."

Jerry shut the door and leaned against it. This situation was unsettling. They were searching for listening devices. He wondered if all new state senators were treated this way.

A loud knock made him jump away from the door. He took a deep breath and turned the knob.

"Jerry Tilton," Senator Harrison said in his loud booming voice.

The senator entered holding out his hand for a hardy shake. Following the senator was one of his staff, who entered with one hand out, the other pulling a medium sized suitcase.

"James Ross, Senator Harrison's aide. Nice to meet you."

Jerry smiled and led the senator and his aide into the room. He suddenly felt way out of his league. What was he doing here? The grooming he was promised didn't happen due to Senator Smith's sudden death. Jerry was supposed to work his way into this position, but instead here he was, in Albany, meeting with a senior senator.

"So, how do you like the accommodations?" Senator Harrison asked, looking around the hotel suite.

"Very nice. Thank you," Jerry responded. He didn't know what else he was expected to say. "Please sit down. What can I do for you?"

Senator Harrison looked around and chose a comfortable chair with ottoman on which he propped his feet while surveying his surroundings.

"Jerry, may I call you Jerry?"

"Yes, of course," Jerry replied.

"When a new senator comes on board, we like to have a little chat to orient them to their new position and responsibilities. You

213

are about to step into a very important position. Senator Smith has been around a long time. During his time he made many friends and many enemies. He has a large following, and you need to quickly connect with his following and bring them under your wing, which now is our wing," Senator Harrison explained with a chuckle.

"Yes, of course," Jerry said. "I spent the last few days reviewing all the upcoming legislation, as well as recent legislation trying to get up to speed as quickly as possible."

"Good, good. But there's one issue overriding all the rest," Senator Harrison said.

He paused, letting the message sink in. He wanted Jerry's full attention, and the silence would accomplish that.

"Go on," Jerry said.

"There's critical legislation waiting to be voted on. I know you're aware of the fracking legislation to overturn home rule. Senator Smith and his junior senators were threatening to vote against it. Their vote would drive hydraulic fracturing right out of the state."

Senator Harrison paused again. He waited until Jerry gave the nod that he understood.

"There's a group of senators, and you are now one, working with an influential Wall Street group that wants to drill for water, not oil. That cannot be accomplished if fracking is voted down. So, no matter what you think about fracking for oil or natural gas, we need this process in order to find the water veins."

Senator Harrison stopped once more. He had given Jerry a lot of confidential information to digest in a short time. It was of utmost importance that Jerry comprehend and agree to the whole picture.

"I guess I'll need to study the issue more before I decide the best path," Jerry said.

"Damn it, Jerry, you don't understand! Your appointment to the senate seat is contingent on your complying with our demands. *You* are a player now. That means *you* play by our rules. *You* do as we say," Senator Harrison yelled.

James Ross stirred in his seat. The situation was getting tense. He didn't want the senator to start threatening, so it was his cue to step in and defuse.

"Mr. Tilton, I'm happy to meet with you early next week and walk you through the legislation. It's quite simple, actually. The drilling service company has been employed to take great care of the environment. Having a privately held water supply will ensure that the residents of New York City and surrounding towns will continue to have a safe and steady water supply well into the future. This is a good thing."

Jerry looked from one to the other. Senator Harrison had cooled down and was leaning back in his chair again with the fellow well-met smile on his face. Jerry decided he best play along for now.

"Sure, thanks Jim. I'm happy to meet with you and find out the details of this bill," Jerry said. "It sounds intriguing."

Satisfied, Senator Harrison rose, nodded to his aide, shook Jerry's hand, and left the room. Jerry watched as James Ross scurried to pick up his notepad, turned, and pointed to the suitcase he brought into the room.

"I'm leaving this material for you to review. It goes without saying this material and what was said in this room today is in the strictest confidence. You are not to say a word to anyone. When you leave the room, all material is to be returned to the suitcase and locked. Here's the key. Pull the case into the closet and cover with some of your clothes. Do you understand?"

Jerry nodded.

James Ross left the room, hurrying, Jerry suspected, to catch up with the senator.

Jerry shut and locked the door behind them. The meeting had shaken him. He now realized the two men from Albany that had come to the bank were actually talking about drilling for water, not oil. Was he a fool not to know about this before now?

The first twinge of fear traveled up his spine. He had worked his way up to this position to be in control, not to be controlled.

He didn't know anyone he could trust enough to talk to.

Have I backed myself into a corner?

~ FIFTY-ONE ~

Sunday

Caitlyn awoke with a start from a bad dream, nightmare really, one so vivid it startled her to wakefulness. She sat up dangling her legs over the side of the bed as she tried to capture the essence of the dream before it evaporated into the recesses of her mind.

Nick was in the dream and he was in danger. She couldn't retrieve all the details, but those she could she mulled over. She tried to figure out where dreams, good and bad, came from. She always thought it was something that happened during the day that planted the seed. She couldn't remember any particular incident or even a word to bring on such a horrible sweat.

Did this dream have to do with their relationship?

She jumped into the shower, washing away her anxiety, and dressed quickly without drying her hair. She was afraid Nick was already downstairs and he might feel awkward if he was alone or with Aunt Myra this early in the morning.

When Caitlyn walked into the kitchen with Summit at her heels, she realized how wrong she was. Nick and Myra were sitting at the kitchen table, both with hands circling their coffee cups laughing over something. They seemed to have a natural bond.

"Good morning, sleepy head," Nick said.

"Good morning. I don't know what got into me. I don't normally sleep this late," Caitlyn said. "I'm glad you're up and around though, because I want to take you to the lake before you catch your plane back to DC."

"I'd like that," Nick said. "I've heard many good things about the Finger Lakes, and I was hoping to get a chance to poke my toe into the water even though I know it'll be cold this time of year."

"That's right," Caitlyn said. "Come back in September when it's the warmest."

The two finished a quick breakfast and set off for the lake. Once in the car, Caitlyn shared some of her local history knowledge, especially about the Great Spirit and the first settlers that landed on the point. They arrived at the lake just as she finished her Chamber of Commerce monologue.

Since it was before Memorial Day, the men in green weren't at the gate taking admission. The park was wide open to them with only a few dog walkers in sight.

Caitlyn parked the car next to the bathhouse, a building constructed in the 1930s. A short walk brought them to the edge of the lake.

Caitlyn immediately knelt down, her fingers searching through the small pebbles lining the shore. She found one to her liking, turned sideways, leaned down and tossed it onto the water. The stone skipped along the surface four or five times before it sunk from sight.

She repeated this several times while Nick watched. He then knelt down and let his fingers search for just the right stone.

"It has to be thin and flat. A flat surface to skim along the water and thin so there is little weight," Caitlyn instructed. "When you get just the right one, hold it between your thumb and index finger, twist your wrist back like so, crouch down so you are as close to the water's surface as you can get and then keep your wrist level as you flick the stone out over the water."

Nick tried several times before he got the hang of it, but once he did, he delighted in watching the stones skip across the surface. They counted the skips their stones made, each hoping to outdo the other. When they tired of the game, they walked to a nearby bench and sat down.

"This is lovely, Caitlyn," Nick said. He was looking south down the lake, unable to see the southern end as there were several land points preventing the eight mile view.

"You seem to like it here," Nick said. "This area suits you well. Would you ever consider moving back?"

This comment caught Caitlyn by surprise. The thought never crossed her mind.

In a way, Nick was perceptive. She did feel at home here. She loved the lake, the hills, and now that she had reconnected with Abbie, Caitlyn loved the fact this area was an up and coming wine country destination.

"The idea is new to me, so I don't know how to answer," Caitlyn said. "I thought I had a life in Washington."

She paused, letting the sun warm her face. She dreaded the possibility of ruining this lovely day together, but the charade had gone on long enough. She was having nightmares about their relationship. *How silly was that?*

She took a deep breath and said, "Which brings me to what I wanted to talk with you about."

Nick became uncomfortable. He knew what was coming and he knew it was time to be as honest as he could with her. He had to come up with a story to cover his deceit.

"Nick, I need to know exactly what you do and who you work for. I know Washington is full of secrets, but if we're going to have any kind of relationship, we can't have secrets," Caitlyn stated. "Our relationship, if we have one, has to be based on trust. And right now I don't trust much of anything you have told me about your life. Can you prove me wrong?"

There was silence as Nick pondered exactly how much he would share with her and how she would react. He took some comfort in the fact Caitlyn indicated their relationship might have a future.

She watched him stare out across the water. She sensed his inner struggle, and the tightness around his mouth and of his shoulders was starting to frighten her.

"Caitlyn, I never meant to deceive you," Nick started to explain, but stopped knowing his tone was too stern.

"You have to understand. I was caught up in circumstances I thought were right, but now I realize were far from right. I work for a US senator. I'm sent overseas to gather information. That much is true. I did, however, meet you under deceitful terms. I was asked to get to know you so I could gather information about the environmental foundation you work for. I know it was wrong, and I

218

ask your forgiveness. I'm not going to work for this group any longer, because I value our relationship more than the money it'll bring in."

"It was my Uncle Jerry who put you up to it, wasn't it?" Caitlyn said.

"No. But it was someone from the oil company who knew about you and that The Outdoor Foundation was one of your clients," Nick explained. "Washington's a small town. Not much remains confidential. People talk at cocktail parties, art shows, wherever they gather. Information is shared and all you need to do is ask the right question. And believe me, people in the Washington scene are skilled at asking the right questions."

Caitlyn sat, stunned by his response. Her emotions were running in every direction. Trust was the basis of any relationship and Nick had violated that trust from the start. Her heart hurt, and she turned to Nick carefully surveying every feature of his face.

Could she ever trust this man again? She didn't have the answer. Not yet. Her emotions were in turmoil. Caitlyn rose and said, "Let's go. We need to get back to the house to pick up your bags before we head to the airport."

~

Jerry Tilton woke at four a.m. and gave up trying to get back to sleep. He had tossed and turned most of the night knowing there was a pile of documents to go through. He staggered into the bathroom and was horrified at his reflection. Was the stress of this position taking its toll before he even arrived on the senate floor?

He made a cup of coffee and then settled down to read. The meeting with Senator Harrison and the aide disturbed him greatly. He didn't think it would be like this. He knew fitting into the political scene was not going to be easy, but he didn't think he would be treated so poorly. He was not stupid. He wasn't going to be pushed around.

He pulled out the briefing materials James Ross left for him to study. The first softbound document was labeled "Avalon Study."

He read through carefully learning about how the small Catskill town of Avalon was chosen for the reservoir. Project "partners," officials within the town government were approached, paid to look the other way, and when permits were needed, they were to be granted without question. The report provided the geographic layout of the town, the demographics, and government structure. The residents of Avalon were sold a bill of goods. They were told they would reap the benefits from tourism dollars for those coming to hike, kayak, and enjoy the area.

Further reading of the report stated that *at some point* residents would receive compensation from water sold when the reservoir was used. What the residents didn't know was that they were responsible for the millions of dollars it was going to cost to build the dam, and Jerry saw in the numbers that use of the reservoir would not provide payments for many years down the road.

Someone's done their homework thoroughly.

Jerry saw this plan was going to make the Wall Street bankers and a certain group of congressmen a lot of money. If he played along, he, too, would be raking it in. Just what he had worked for all his life—money and the power that came with it. It was now at his fingertips. All he needed to do was gather Senator Smith's followers and convince them hydraulic fracturing was the best avenue for the state.

He grabbed a pencil and paper and started jotting down talking points.

An hour had passed before he knew it.

He got up to stretch his legs. He needed time to think about this project. He sat back down, eager to find out more. As he dug deeper into the report, he was shocked to see this small town of citizens, mostly blue collar workers, were being taken in by the Wall Street financiers. A reservoir was planned like none other in the United States. As he read further into the report not only was the mayor being paid off, but so were the county commissioners. When taxes to pay for the dam became an issue, Wall Street firms would come in with interest swap agreements and refinance schemes keeping the people of Avalon poor for the rest of their lives, as well as the lives of their children and grandchildren. All the time a few town "leaders" were paid millions of dollars to "do nothing."

"My god," Jerry exclaimed. *This is the same scam run on the residents of Jefferson County, Alabama in 1996 and culminating with an FBI investigation in 2002. After paying a few fines, the Wall Street bankers came out of that scam just fine. Now they've found another victim. Another rural community will be crushed under the weight of financial ruin.*

Jerry got up and paced, wiping the sweat from his brow. He went over to the window and turned the A/C on high. He couldn't breathe.

Making money is a good thing; ruining a whole town population, a whole region, was another. How could he, one individual, stop this madness?

He continued to pace, trying to get his heart rate down. He remembered reading about the Jefferson County situation. It was all over the national news, for a brief time. At the time he thought the plan was a stroke of genius, though clearly unethical. That didn't seem to bother him then. What changed?

Clearly the death of his only child was a life-altering event. But there was something more, something inside him that was changing his view from gaining power and money to the bigger picture of quality of life. This change was making him uncomfortable. For the first time in his life he didn't know which road to travel.

~

Several hours passed as Jerry paced and talked to himself. Finally he knew the road to take. Although he was in favor of fracking for oil and gas, this particular legislation had to be voted down in order to stop the "Avalon Plan." A new energy plan for New York had to be developed.

He would notify Senator Smith's supporters to say he was going to take the same stance as the senator. Every vote would be needed to vote down this fracking bill.

He would then point their attention to the town of Avalon and see what financial assistance the town needed to recoup what was spent on this large cement hole that he hoped would not be the future reservoir for New York City. Jerry planned to track down those town leaders who were paid off and make sure they were prosecuted. He knew he didn't have a prayer of getting any of the Wall Street firms indicted, but hopefully their latest scam would be brought to light. It might slow them down for a few years before they tried again.

His breathing finally under control, he sat down to read through the rest of the documents. He had to be fully apprised of the details so he could plan his counter attack.

~ FIFTY-TWO ~

Monday Morning
The early morning songbirds woke Caitlyn, a wake up call she didn't mind at all.

She had a lot on her mind. Nick flew back to DC yesterday and she wondered about the phone call he received from his boss just before boarding. Nick's expression and body language while on the phone told her the news wasn't good. When she asked about the call, he passed it off as another committee meeting to attend, but she sensed it was something more. More secrets. She pondered what to do with the information he shared at the lake.

And then there was her cousin's murder. Ethan was following up on the oil service company and environmental groups. He was going to track down the coach. Ethan had a hunch he wanted to follow up on, and she had no desire to be in the coach's presence again.

Then there was Denny Mathews. Both she and Ethan knew there was more to Denny and his overly competitive nature. They had to decide how to approach him and get more information about his relationship with Todd.

She offered to have another talk with Darcy Risley. Mostly because she was bothered about the situation with Teddy. She really liked Darcy, but abuse couldn't be tolerated. If Caitlyn couldn't talk Darcy into getting help, the authorities would have to be brought in, and it was something Caitlyn would like to avoid. She'd walk over there this morning, hoping to catch Darcy out in her garden. Caitlyn wanted to persuade Darcy to get the mental health help she needed.

How do I approach her about that sensitive subject?

Jumping ahead in her thinking, after that situation was handed over to the proper authorities, it would be time she returned to

Washington. Her clients were patient, but there was a limit and she couldn't afford to lose any of them. Since her uncle was expected back in Riverview today, Myra wouldn't be alone. What was going to happen with them? Would Myra survive the Albany political scene or would she end up staying in Riverview? Neither seemed a good alternative, so maybe Myra would set off on her own. Caitlyn wished her mom and Myra would connect again. Myra needed a family support system; she needed her sister.

And what to do about Ethan? As much as Caitlyn wanted to get back to her own life, she had to admit there was a special bond between them. Well, maybe more than a bond. There was something deeper, a feeling she found herself pushing against. She and Ethan lived in different worlds, and she suspected he would never consider relocating to Washington. She didn't think she wanted to live in a rural area again. Or did she?

Nick's comment yesterday about it being her natural environment hit a nerve.

Too many problems to solve. If she kept thinking about them all she would never get out of bed. She would get dressed and walk over to the Risley's. If she could convince Darcy to get help that would be one problem off Caitlyn's plate.

~ FIFTY-THREE ~

Wind-driven spring rain hit the hotel room's windows when Jerry Tilton woke from his first good night's sleep since coming to Albany. He had worked his way through the reports left by Senator Harrison's aide, and Jerry had used the rest of Sunday to develop a way to bring their plan down.

He was appalled the men he thought he knew, the men he dreamed would be his colleagues, were actually a part of this scheme. It was not for the benefit of Avalon or the City of New York, but to fill the pockets of a few, and make financial firms buckets of money while destroying a beautiful area of the state.

The first thing Jerry needed to do was identify people he could trust. It wouldn't be easy. He would be careful and approach one person at a time to feel them out.

All Sunday afternoon and evening he sketched out ways to identify the right people, what words to say that wouldn't set off alarms should he approach the wrong people. It would be difficult being a newcomer, but he could work it to his advantage. People would know he was feeling his way around and may share more than they normally would.

Before he could make his first call his cell phone rang.

Without checking caller ID he responded, "Tilton here."

"Jerry, Jim Ross. How're ya doing this mornin'?"

Jerry hated this guy already. The fake southern drawl grated on Jerry's nerves, and Jim's association with Senator Harrison made him even more disagreeable. Ross's cheery energetic voice at this early hour was more than Jerry could take. He remembered his manners and replied, "Fine, thanks, how about you?"

"Doin' great! It's a beautiful day when it rains, don't you think?" Jim said. Before Jerry could respond Jim continued, "The Senator wanted me to check in with you to make sure you have everything you need. He wanted to find out if you read over the materials we left on Saturday."

"I don't need anything, and yes, I did read over the materials carefully. In fact, I spent all day yesterday going over them and making notes."

"Great, great. We knew you'd be a team player," James said. "So, if you need anything else, just give me a call. I think you said you were going back to Riverview soon. We'll let you know when your confirmation comes through. So, stay in touch and have a safe trip back."

Jerry rung off and put his head back on the pillow. For the hundredth time since Saturday he wondered what was he into? Was he in too deep to dig himself out? He had to make a decision soon. A group of junior senators waited for his leadership. He needed to get to them before they could be swayed over to the other side.

Jerry closed his eyes and Todd's face appeared. He was startled, then relaxed. As he closed his eyes he heard Todd's voice and passionate pleas about the environment. There were so many unknowns, but it made sense to stop toxic chemicals being injected into the earth. And was this plan to monopolize the drinking water for New York City a wise move? What if rates went so high people couldn't afford it? All because bankers and senators wanted to make even more money? There would be no way he could stop the momentum, and unfortunately, this was part and parcel to the hydraulic fracturing legislation.

Late last evening he called Senator Smith's aide and arranged an early morning meeting. Jerry requested the presence of a trusted elected official from the Southern Tier. The aide, Marty Dent, and whoever he trusted to attend this meeting were due in under an hour, so Jerry decided he had better get out of bed, shower and be ready for them when they arrived.

The knock on the door was promptly at ten o'clock. The two men standing there were Marty Dent, Senator Smith's aide and Jonathan Hart, a county commissioner who had carefully researched the issues surrounding hydraulic fracturing in the southern tier of New York.

Jerry welcomed the men into his suite and offered them coffee. Once seated, Jerry explained his conundrum. Marty was sympathetic though relieved Senator Smith's replacement was not going to undo all the work that had been done.

"This is how it works," Marty explained. "What we call 'landmen' drive around locating residents who hold the largest tracts of land. Mostly they're farmers or their descendants who are told if they sell the mineral rights, they could get rich. What's not to like? Many signed away their mineral rights without completely understanding what it would mean. Much of this happened in 2008 as the economy tanked, and then many more after. Some attorneys and business people saw the danger, and started giving presentations to caution landowners."

"I heard about these while in Riverview. With my lack of knowledge at the time I didn't think much of those meetings. I thought they were just scare tactics. I know now those meetings were an important public service," Jerry said.

Jonathan Hart decided to jump in.

"Hydraulic fracturing for oil and gas is a complex business and what the landowners didn't realize was the state's permit guidelines for this sort of thing are outdated. Some landowners got together and developed their own contracts, but it didn't solve the real problem, which was what would full scale hydraulic fracturing do to the environment?"

"That's right," Marty said. "At one of the meetings someone asked what emergency plans were in place to handle if a spill, fire, or explosion happened on site. Were the emergency responders prepared? There wasn't a good answer. In fact, there was no answer, because emergency responders weren't trained. The answer they gave was there was little chance of any 'accident.'"

Jerry listened and made notes as the two men talked. He had read enough about the environmental impacts of hydraulic fracturing, the unknowns, the risk of disaster at a rig where small town responders were not prepared nor did they have the equipment to handle such an emergency. He brushed it off, as did the State Division of Mineral Resources personnel, as unlikely to happen. The benefits outweighed the risks as far as he was concerned. But at the time he was viewing this issue from the other side of the table. He now knew there were real concerns and solid research behind these concerns.

Marty continued, "You probably heard about the water well explosion in Dimock, PA. Following that incident people in environmental research firms started uncovering data held by the DEC and found hundreds of files reporting spills, well contamination, explosions and methane seepage. You know, the DEC is the Department of Environmental Conservation."

"Yes, yes, I know, please continue," Jerry said impatiently.

"Well, once these complaints were known, more county agency files were researched and they discovered even more complaints."

"I assume you have this information in report form?" Jerry asked.

"We do. And I brought you a copy," Marty said.

He reached into his briefcase and pulled out a bound edition. He placed it on the coffee table.

"This is what we are up against. Money and power. Not an unusual pair and as the saying goes, the root of all evil. But we are making progress in educating the public. We hoped the recent drop in gas and oil prices would prompt the rigs to pull out. But it didn't happen, so we have to keep up the fight."

Jerry nodded. He was starting to understand.

"Thanks for your time and efforts. I'll read through this information and get back to you. In the meantime, I want you, Marty, to stay on as my aide. Are you willing to take on the task?"

"Senator Harrison will not be pleased. He dislikes me, and anyone else who worked with Senator Smith," Marty responded. "Are you sure you want to burn that bridge so soon?"

"You're right, of course. But I need your knowledge, experience and contacts. I want you to keep working, so let's do it under the table. If anyone asks, tell them I asked you to clean out the senator's office so I can move in," Jerry said.

"Sounds good," Marty said.

"Thank you both again. Keep up the good work and I'll be in touch," Jerry said as he led them to the door.

Jerry closed the door behind the men. He now better understood both sides of the issue and it was up to him to make the monumental decision. He felt the weight of the world on his shoulders.

He was resolved to set his own affairs right. When he returned to Riverview he would contact the survey company and make sure the old cemetery was included. He would then take the new survey to the town clerk and make sure it replaced the older version. He didn't want anyone to know he paid Riverview's former town clerk to leave the old cemetery off the land record. At the time he planned to lease his property to the oil company. They wouldn't have considered it if the survey showed the cemetery. They had promised to pay a hefty sum. At least that was what was promised a few years ago. Since he was still on the board, he assumed the promise still held. But would it?

Didn't matter now. Everything had changed and Jerry had to figure out a way to save himself and his career.

As he leaned against the door with eyes closed he again felt Todd's presence. It was a comforting feeling he didn't want to end. As he opened his eyes the presence dissipated. Jerry looked up and whispered, "I'm going to do the right thing, Todd. Thank you for your wise counsel. I'm so sorry I didn't accept it and tell you before."

He wept.

~ FIFTY-FOUR ~

Caitlyn debated whether Summit should accompany her on her walk to the Risley's. It would be good for him to get out to stretch his little legs, but if the conversation turned serious, she didn't need the distraction of a dog.

"Sorry, SumBum, but you have to stay in today," Caitlyn said as she saw the little dog waiting at the front door.

His tail wagged in anticipation as he watched her put on shoes and coat and knew what it meant. When he realized she was going without him, he put on his disappointment face, turned, and ran to the living room window where he could watch her go. When she was out of sight, he walked into the sunroom to curl up in his favorite fleece bed to mope.

Caitlyn rehearsed how to start the conversation with Darcy. She had to frame her words just right to get Darcy to admit to the Munchausen by Proxy. When that happened the challenge would be to get Darcy to accept help. Teddy had to be released from the abuse, and maybe Darcy and Mac's marriage would be saved in the process.

Caitlyn reached the bright blue door remembering it's meaning. Keeping the evil spirits at bay. Apparently it didn't do its job for Teddy. At her knock, Darcy opened the door.

"What do you want now?" Darcy asked.

"We need to talk," Caitlyn responded as she pushed herself into the house.

Darcy reluctantly let Caitlyn push by.

"Talk about what?" Darcy said, her face red with anger. She was getting tired of Caitlyn popping over whenever she felt like it.

"You might want to talk to me here instead of with Sheriff Ewing at the police station," Caitlyn responded. "We have reason to believe you are abusing your son."

"What in the hell are you talking about?" Darcy yelled, turning even redder. She glared at Caitlyn. "I'm a responsible mother! How dare you accuse me of abuse?"

Once again Caitlyn realized she had spoken before thinking, putting Darcy on the defensive.

Stupid!

She had to continue, but more calmly in order to get control of the situation. She took a breath and smiled.

"Because we talked with Teddy and he told us of his constant illness. I did some research, talked with doctors and the school officials about his repeated absences. Teddy appears to be suffering from a condition called Munchausen by Proxy."

"Mun, what? Never heard of it," Darcy said, turning away from Caitlyn.

"Few have," responded Caitlyn to Darcy's back and keeping her voice under control. "I think your situation fits the description."

In response Darcy walked around the table to stand by the kitchen sink. She looked out onto the back yard. Tension rippled down her back.

Caitlyn knew she'd hit a nerve. This was the moment of truth. There *was* something going on here. Darcy's stress was mounting. Caitlyn had to think of something to calm things down.

"I'd love a cup of your special blend tea, Darcy. Let's have a cup and we can just talk. Okay?" Caitlyn said.

Darcy turned, a smile replacing the frown on her face. The tension suddenly lifted, and Caitlyn was pleased that she was able to turn this situation around so quickly.

"Yea, okay. I'll put the kettle on," Darcy said.

An awkward silence reigned while they waited for the water to boil. In the meantime, Darcy set out two mugs; Caitlyn's had a crack. She understood the message. Darcy then went to the cupboard to the right of the sink where she kept her canisters of tea and herbal potions. The canister she chose had a pretty leaf pattern.

Once the tea was poured and Caitlyn had taken a few sips, she continued her questioning. She hated to break this moment of peace, but she had to get to the bottom of this.

"Darcy, were you upset by Teddy's friendship with Todd? Did you know Teddy was part of the 'Save the Environment' group Todd formed? Did you know Teddy was sneaking out at night to vandalize the oil company's equipment?"

"Yes, I knew he was sneaking out and I knew who drew him out. He thought I didn't, but I did," Darcy said, anger rising. "Todd was taking my Teddy away from me. Teddy was starting to talk about college, having a career. Todd was filling Teddy's head with all sorts of silly notions. He wanted to hang out with Todd. Do you think I liked that? Absolutely not. I increased his herb potion so he didn't feel his best in order to keep him home more, with me. I hated Todd Tilton, and I went over to tell him to stay away from my son."

"When did you tell him, Darcy?"

Darcy turned her back to Caitlyn and continued to stare out the window to the tree line beyond. That was where Darcy found solace, in the woods, in the little abandoned cemetery. Darcy was mentally in the cemetery, performing her rituals. Rituals going back to a simpler time with her grandmother.

Caitlyn felt sorry for Darcy. Her world was coming apart, and Caitlyn was the one destroying it.

"I saw him come home from school." Darcy said softly. She began to slowly sway, grabbing hold of the counter.

Is she going catatonic on me? Caitlyn thought.

"I had to put a stop to the relationship. It was ruining our family. All I wanted was to ask him to leave Teddy alone. That's all. Simple. Don't bother us, and we won't bother you," Darcy explained.

"What was Todd's response?" Caitlyn asked softly.

"He laughed," Darcy responded.

Darcy remained silent for what seemed like a long time, but was probably only seconds. Caitlyn waited, holding her breath. She was on the cusp of something important and the slightest mistake, the slightest noise would ruin everything.

"He laughed," Darcy repeated.

Again, silence as Darcy continued to stare out the window.

232

"After he laughed at me, I got so angry. He had no right. He's some fancy rich kid. Always got what he wanted. Didn't work for what he got. And he was taking Teddy away from me, filling his head will all sorts of things. I wasn't going to stand for it. I begged him, and he only laughed and then turned back to his horse," Darcy said.

"Is that when you hit him?" Caitlyn asked. The question surprised her. She didn't know where it had come from, and she was shocked the conversation was going in this direction. She never suspected Darcy of violence. She was into subtler ways of control. She hoped she hadn't pushed Darcy too far.

Another moment of silence. Caitlyn felt her heart pounding.

"Yes. I picked up a shovel I saw leaning against the wall. All I wanted to do was to knock some sense into him. I didn't mean to hurt him. I mean hurt him bad like. Just hurt him a little. Give him a headache. A headache to make him think about what I said. I guess I'm stronger than I thought. And the shovel was sharper than I knew. As soon as the shovel hit him I knew it was more than I intended. I heard his head crack. At least I thought it did. And then the blood started," Darcy said. "I hate the sight of blood."

"Then what happened?" Caitlyn asked.

"He turned, looked at me with shock in his eyes. I'm sure he saw the shock in my eyes as well. He knew I didn't mean to hurt him so badly. He staggered towards the door at the back of the barn. I guess he wanted to get away from me and get to his house," Darcy said.

"And?" Caitlyn asked.

"I assumed he was going to the house and so I hit him again, just to slow him down to give me time to get away from there. I don't know what came over me. I was just so angry, and then so frightened. What would happen to me? What would happen to my family when Todd reported what I'd done? I watched him go down on the ground. I put the shovel up in the hayloft. Hid it under several bales and decided I would come back for it later. Bury it out in the old cemetery where no one would find it," Darcy said.

Caitlyn wondered how the police missed the shovel in the loft. She would talk with Ethan about this critical oversight.

Darcy turned around and looked at Caitlyn. Her eyes were dark with anger making Caitlyn more nervous.

She definitely was in over her head. If Darcy turned violent, she didn't know if she could handle the situation. She felt in her pocket for her phone. It wasn't there.

Damn. I left it on the front hall table as I was putting on my shoes, she thought.

Darcy continued. "The day I decided to retrieve the shovel you showed up in the barn. What in the hell were you doing there?"

Caitlyn saw no reason to respond. In fact, she was finding it difficult to form thoughts. She tried to keep her eye on Darcy, but even that was becoming more difficult.

"So it was you who pushed the hay bales over on top of me?" Caitlyn muttered.

"Yea. What else could I do? I didn't know what you were up to. If you decided to check out the loft, you would have caught me. I couldn't allow that. A few hay bales would distract you enough so I could escape. And I did," Darcy said gloating.

Caitlyn was at a loss as to what to do. Her phone was back at the house, so she couldn't call Ethan. She knew he was following up leads on Clyde's murder, so she didn't expect him to contact her anytime soon. She figured Darcy wouldn't be going anywhere, but could she take the chance? Caitlyn rose slowly from the chair. She was getting dizzy. Was it because she hadn't eaten enough today?

"Darcy, let me call the sheriff and you can explain how you didn't mean to kill Todd," Caitlyn suggested, her voice becoming slurred.

"You're not going to call anybody!" Darcy pronounced as she turned to face Caitlyn.

Caitlyn noticed Darcy's hands, previously hidden behind the kitchen table. In her right hand was a sharp knife. In her left she had a handgun that she placed on the table.

"Darcy, don't do anything stupid. Don't make matters worse," Caitlyn pleaded.

"How could they be worse? I killed a boy," Darcy started to weep as she moved closer to Caitlyn, effectively blocking any escape route. "Turn around."

"Please, Darcy, don't do anything stupid. We can talk this out," Caitlyn said.

Darcy was now so close Caitlyn could feel the knifepoint in her side. Darcy was putting pressure on it to the point Caitlyn felt it pierce her skin.

"Never mind. Put your hands behind your back," Darcy said.

Caitlyn felt the room start to spin. What was wrong? Then she knew.

There was something in the tea; Darcy poisoned my tea.

"I don't feel so well," Caitlyn stated.

"Shut up!" Darcy yelled.

Caitlyn did as she was told keeping her eye on the gun that was within Darcy's easy reach. Darcy tied Caitlyn's hands with what felt like a thin rope.

"It's too tight."

Darcy ignored her.

"There's the door. Start walking."

Caitlyn knew Darcy was taking her to the cemetery. There would be no escape unless she could find a moment when Darcy let her guard down. Could she do anything with her blurry vision, upset stomach and pounding head?

Caitlyn walked slowly around the table, hanging on to the edge, and then headed for the back door. Darcy followed close behind with the knife pressing against Caitlyn's back.

"You should know by now I'll do *anything* to protect my son. I've killed once, so it's no big thing. Isn't that what they say?" Darcy asked.

She's having a mental breakdown.

Caitlyn's pulse quickened as her fight or flight reaction took hold. Her anxiety was at an all time high, and there was nothing she could do to address it. Her options were limited. Her hands were tied, and a knife was at her back.

235

They walked in silence through the scrub brush to the tree line. Caitlyn stumbled often as they progressed, the brush scratching her skin. Once they reached the cemetery, Caitlyn knew there was little chance anyone would see or hear them. She was alone. How could she convince Darcy to change her mind?

Upon arrival at the cemetery the comfort previously felt there was gone. The disintegrating stones with weeds growing over them now took on a menacing appearance. Caitlyn thought about the history represented by the stones. Each had a story to tell. Each person represented life experiences between the dash representing birth and death. She wished she knew their stories, and now there was a good chance she would never have that opportunity.

"Sit over there," Darcy instructed.

"Darcy, let's talk about this," Caitlyn mumbled.

"Shut up! I'm through talking. You've threatened my family. I have to take action. You'll soon join your beloved cousin in the next world. I'll bury you among these nice folks. Didn't you tell me once how peaceful you thought it was?" Darcy said.

Caitlyn knew she couldn't overpower Darcy, not in her current condition and without the use of her hands. Besides, as soon as she got close enough, Darcy would stab her with the knife. At least she left the gun in the house.

Darcy pushed Caitlyn to the ground.

"I have a ritual to do," Darcy explained. "Be still. This won't take long."

~ FIFTY-FIVE~

Ethan hoped he wasn't arriving at the Tilton's too early. He knew Caitlyn was getting ready to return to Washington, and he needed to talk with her. He couldn't let her just walk out of his life.

He still hadn't found Todd's killer, but he was confident they were getting close. They were close to catching the men who shot Clyde. The men were on the run, but it wasn't going to be difficult for the state police to track them down.

Ethan knew Caitlyn couldn't stay in Riverview forever. His relationship with Jennie was unresolved, but he had reached a decision. If she wouldn't start the divorce proceeding, he would. He believed marriage was forever, but sometimes the union is not meant to be. Each person has a right to be happy and he was no exception. He had loved Jennie once, and maybe still did. But their lifestyles didn't mesh, and probably never would. It was time to end that chapter.

Ethan rang the bell and heard it resound through the house. No one came to the door, but he could hear the dog barking wildly. Caitlyn's car was in the drive, so he knew she had to be somewhere near.

As he turned to walk back to his car, the door was opened by a woman he didn't recognize.

Ethan turned and said, "Hello, I'm Sheriff Ewing. Is Caitlyn at home?"

"Nobody in the house," said the woman in broken English, obviously a housekeeper.

"This dog driving me crazy. He barking and scratching frantically at the door. The Mrs. going to have a fit when she see the damage." As an afterthought, she added in a whisper, "Like the day Todd was killed."

Summit continued to bark and jump up and down. Ethan knew this was not the dog's normal behavior. He knew enough about dogs that they could sense things humans could not.

Had he heard her correctly? Why hadn't the Tiltons called him when their housekeeper returned?

Ignoring the dog, Ethan focused on the woman and tried to assess how much she understood English.

"What's your name?" Ethan asked slowly hoping his enunciation was good enough for her to understand what he was asking.

"Rosita."

"So you were here in the house the day young Todd was murdered?" Ethan asked.

"Oh, yes. Just finishing, cleaning the upstairs. The dog barking and jumping around. The Mrs. wasn't home so I ignore him. I don't do dogs, or any animals. Am afraid. I finish work and left hoping he don't do damage. I don't write so well so I don't leave the Mrs. a note."

"I understand. Did you see anyone on the property before you left?" Ethan asked.

"I see Todd come home. He drive black car. He like to go to horse after school. I don't see him."

"Did you see anything else?" Ethan asked again.

"Men on the road with stick machines," Rosita said.

Ethan knew she saw the surveyors. He smiled. Their equipment did look like "stick" machines.

"And the lady," Rosita said as an afterthought.

"What lady?" Ethan asked a little more forcefully than he intended. He didn't mean to scare this woman and shut down the information she held, but he started to suspect Caitlyn might be in danger, especially if she had gone to confront Darcy on the Munchausen issue.

Rosita was startled by his reaction.

Ethan smiled, and said softly, "Can you tell me what lady you saw? It might help us find Todd's killer. It would make Mr. and Mrs. Tilton very happy if you help us."

Rosita continued to stare at Ethan deciding whether she could trust him. She knew the lady was not supposed to be on the property. The Mr. made that clear. Would she be in trouble if they found out she saw the lady walk into the barn and not told them?

"I don't know," Rosita said. "I might be in trouble with the Mrs. and lose job."

"I'll make sure you are not in trouble and don't lose your job. The Tiltons will praise you for your assistance," Ethan said reassuringly.

"It was lady from tenant house. She not supposed to be here Mr. said. Her husband works the fields, but he not to be on this property either. I saw her go into the barn after Todd come home that day. I finish work and left. I in hurry to catch bus to New York. I visit my sister. She had operation," Rosita said.

Ethan's heart stopped as he put it together. Darcy was on the property when Todd was murdered. Caitlyn's car was in the drive, but she wasn't in the house. The dog barking and acting frantic. This confirmed what he thought. She was with Darcy. Summit sensed Caitlyn was in trouble. Ethan quickly thanked Rosita and ran to his car with Summit at his heels.

"Okay, you can come," Ethan said as he lifted the dog and flung him into the passenger seat. Ethan flew out the Tilton's drive and drove the few yards up the road to the Risley tenant house. Once there, he and Summit raced to the front door. Ethan knocked, hearing nothing, tried the knob. It opened easily. They both rushed in. Summit sniffing everything, and then went to the back door, barking and scratching. Ethan noticed the gun on the table before he opened the door for the dog. Summit raced through the back yard and disappeared into the brush. Ethan ran after him, but couldn't keep up. He called to Summit, but there was no response.

Damn dog. Where is he?

He followed Summit's trail through the brush. The thorny branches snagged his pants and slowed him down. He was getting close to the old cemetery where he suspected Darcy and Caitlyn might be.

239

Ethan slowed down, not wanting to be heard. He stopped, listened.

Nothing.

He wondered where the dog was, and maybe Caitlyn wasn't with Darcy at all, but went for a walk by herself and the dog was mad about that. Ethan felt like a fool.

~

"Ouch!" Caitlyn cried when her arm hit a sharp rock after Darcy pushed her down. The offending rock dug into her arm, which now was bleeding.

Be still. Is that what she said?

Caitlyn's mind was in panic mode. Her head pounded, she was dizzy, and she wanted to vomit.

It's the tea.

She'd been so intent on choosing the right words to keep Darcy talking she didn't notice if Darcy had actually drank any of her tea. Caitlyn tried to shake off the dizziness. She had to think of something to save herself.

The rock. Caitlyn repositioned her hands so the rope that was tied tightly around her wrists was adjacent to the rock. She moved her arms slowly back and forth hoping to cut through her bonds. The motion was painful, but she had to try.

Darcy walked in circles on the other side of the cemetery. She recited something in a singsong way.

"Darcy, please. We can work through this," Caitlyn said softly, but loud enough for Darcy to hear. She didn't want to push Darcy too far as she still had the knife in her hand.

"Darcy, put the knife down. Let's talk about the problem. Maybe there's an easy solution."

Darcy turned around, her eyes wide, swinging the knife to and fro.

"I didn't mean to do it," Darcy cried.

"I know," replied Caitlyn.

She felt the rope start to loosen.

240

Darcy turned back to her ritual, ignoring Caitlyn.

The rope broke free. Caitlyn rubbed her hands together and quickly surveyed the rope burns on her wrists and the deep cut on her arm. She rose slowly and quietly. Stepping carefully, she approached Darcy from behind.

Caitlyn's left arm went around Darcy's throat, while her right hand hit Darcy's wrist with such force the knife was knocked to the ground. Darcy struggled, trying to twist out of Caitlyn's grip, but she held tight and continued to talk to Darcy, trying to calm her down, trying to bring her out of her trance.

Just as Darcy seemed to be calming down, Summit arrived, jumping around in front of Darcy, barking like a deranged animal. Darcy jerked back against Caitlyn, frightened of the barking, snarling dog.

"Don't let it bite me; get it away from me," Darcy screamed, kicking at the dog.

Caitlyn tightened her grip on Darcy as she took backward steps.

"Down, Summit. Back. Stay. Place." Nothing was working. Apparently Todd never trained this dog to the normal commands. Summit kept up his nasty snarls, nipping at Darcy's feet.

Summit's uncontrolled rage helped keep Darcy from her struggle to be free, and allowed Caitlyn to turn Darcy around to head back to the house.

That is when they came face to face with Ethan.

~

The dog's sudden barking from the area of the cemetery told Ethan that Caitlyn was probably there. As he rounded a stand of trees, he ran right into Darcy and Caitlyn, noting Caitlyn's tight hold around Darcy's neck.

Ethan's sudden presence seemed to bring Darcy fully out of her trance and back to reality.

"I'll not come with you," Darcy spat at Ethan.

"What do you mean, Darcy?" Ethan asked softly.

"I didn't mean to do it," Darcy said with a whimper. She started to shake as she now faced her worst nightmares, confinement, and separation from Teddy.

Before Ethan could respond, they heard someone coming through the brush. If it was Mac Risley with his gun, they might be in trouble.

Ethan hadn't felt it necessary to carry a firearm in this small town. He would have to rethink that decision. His only hope was to call 911.

He slowly rubbed his hand along his hip feeling for his phone hoping Darcy wouldn't notice. She did.

"What're you doing?" She said, her voice loud and strained.

He walked slowly towards Darcy intending to take her from Caitlyn.

"Just come with me and we can talk this over," Ethan said. Before he reached Darcy, she turned her head at the sound of someone approaching.

Ethan turned to see Deputy Snow at the other end of the cemetery. Ethan waved him back, but the distance was such Tom couldn't read the hand signals.

Tom approached cautiously, noting the situation.

Caitlyn loosened her grip as Ethan approached to take custody of Darcy. In that split second, Darcy twisted away from Caitlyn's grasp screaming, "I don't want to go to prison. I can't stand confined spaces. I couldn't stand to be locked up in a small cell, not able to get out whenever I wanted. I need air, and Teddy needs me."

Before Ethan could catch her, Darcy lunged for the knife. She waved it at Ethan and Caitlyn before she plunged the knife into her chest.

Ethan pulled his phone from its holster and dialed 911. He didn't know if Darcy was going to make it, but he'd do what he could to save her. He stayed with her, putting pressure on her wound until the paramedics arrived.

Tom took Caitlyn aside and examined the deep gash in her arm. He cleaned it the best he could and knew the paramedics would do the rest.

When the paramedics arrived and were attending to Darcy, Ethan rushed over to Caitlyn and Tom.

"Tom, how did you know where I was?" Ethan asked.

"Forensics came in on the evidence you collected at the murder scene. I wanted you to have it right away. Maddie said you had driven over to the Tilton's. I couldn't reach you on your cell, so I drove over. The housekeeper told me you were looking for Caitlyn and then you and the dog ran off. She watched you go through the fields behind the Risley's house. She thought it was strange you were chasing a dog. I remembered the old cemetery back in the woods and put two and two together."

"Thanks, Tom. You did the right thing, and it was good to have the extra support. I silenced my phone when I was talking with the housekeeper. Now I am doubly glad I did. I hope Darcy makes it, and in the meantime, we need to get Caitlyn to the hospital as well."

Caitlyn, with head in her hands, still feeling sick from the tea and the exertion, didn't argue.

~

When Ethan arrived at the hospital several hours later, Caitlyn was sitting on the edge of the bed. Her hair was tousled, and her complexion pale, but Ethan thought she looked great.

"The ER doctor hasn't been in to release me yet," Caitlyn said before Ethan had a chance to ask her how she was. "Aunt Myra brought me some clean clothes. I assured her I was okay and that everything was going to be fine. She's a wreck, of course. Poor Aunt Myra."

Ethan nodded, relief washing over him.

"And before you ask," she said, "I'm fine, just a lingering headache. They pumped my stomach, god what an awful procedure. The tea Darcy gave me was a deep sleep blend. I think she made that when she needed to keep Teddy under control. When she found out he was going out at night, she developed this brew to give him in the future. It would make him too sleepy to go out. I have a couple stitches for the cut on my arm. I didn't think it was that bad, but apparently the ER doctor had a different opinion. And then there are the antibiotics I have to take for a week in case of infection."

Caitlyn's diatribe was interrupted by the arrival of the emergency room doctor and the nurse who attended Caitlyn. After more poking and prodding, she was deemed fit for release, though with precautions.

Ethan suspected the ER staff was probably as relieved to release her as she was to be released. Caitlyn, in her present mood, would not be the best patient.

"Thank you both for all you did for me. I'm sorry if I was a bit curt with you," Caitlyn said as she slipped off the examining table.

The doctor and nurse both nodded. This was not their first patient in a hurry to escape emergency room confines.

As soon as Ethan and Caitlyn passed through the doors, he said, "So, what happened out there? What did Darcy tell you?"

"She said she was sorry. She didn't mean to hurt him," Caitlyn sobbed.

She wiped away the tears and looked at Ethan.

"Did you arrest her?" Caitlyn asked.

"Not yet. Darcy's in intensive care. She did some serious internal damage when she plunged that knife into her chest, and she isn't out of the woods yet," Ethan explained.

"Oh, I'm so sorry," Caitlyn said as she stumbled. "It's my fault. I never should have accused her of abuse."

"It's not your fault. Darcy is a disturbed woman. She desperately needs to control her environment and in order to do that she needs to control her son. We brought Teddy in so the lab could do some testing. Apparently, Teddy has been given large amounts of sage, a plant easily grown in any garden. As you know, it's used to flavor foods, most notably the delicious stuffing at Thanksgiving, but consuming large doses over a long period of time can be poisonous. It contains a chemical, thujone, that can cause seizures, damage to the liver and nervous system," Ethan explained.

"So I was right. She was suffering from Munchausen's by Proxy," Caitlyn said.

"Yea, I guess so," Ethan responded. "The mental health professionals have been alerted, and as soon as Darcy is out of ICU, they will talk with her."

Ethan helped Caitlyn into the passenger seat of his cruiser. When she was settled, he continued.

"The pin found at the scene came from a Elk's club in a town where the Risley's lived. Tom followed us to the cemetery to tell me this. Since Mac hadn't seen this pin in a long time, it meant that Darcy, not Mac or Teddy killed Todd. Darcy found out about the relationship between Todd and Teddy. She couldn't stand the thought of losing control of her son. Tom was coming to tell me that one of the small blood samples was positive for Darcy. Apparently when she visited Todd, she came straight from gardening and hadn't removed her gloves. That's why there were no fingerprints to be found, other than the family's. It was her bad luck that her gloves were worn and she had cut herself before visiting Todd. Just enough blood had soaked through."

"She kept saying she was sorry," Caitlyn said. "And she didn't mean to hurt him. I think she just went over to talk with Todd and when he blew her off, which I could see a teenage boy doing, she got mad and grabbed whatever was closest to take a swing at him. I believe her. She didn't mean to kill him," Caitlyn said.

"Besides her need to keep her son under her control, her life was complicated by the fact she practiced Appalachian Folk Magick. She believed the spirits wouldn't forgive her and she might be banished. She couldn't deal with that. I think she believed by sacrificing a human, you, it would be enough," Ethan explained.

"Oh, poor Darcy," Caitlyn said. "How are Mac and Teddy doing?"

"I don't know. I told Maddie to make sure there was someone from social services to help them through this," Ethan said. "Now, let me take you home."

~FIFTY-SIX~

Tuesday

It was time to leave Riverview. A lot happened over the past couple of weeks, and Caitlyn looked forward to getting back to her normal routine. But there was one more thing to accomplish and she would do it this morning.

Caitlyn parked her rental car in front of the sheriff's office and walked up the steps to the front door. She paused, took a breath, and turned the handle.

The familiar surroundings now took on a sinister feel. A police station, any police station, had a cold harsh atmosphere. She suspected it was because it was a place where people who did bad things were brought. She had been able to override those feelings when she was working closely with Ethan. Today was different.

She stood at the counter waiting for Maddie to finish her call.

"Caitlyn, you here to say goodbye to the sheriff? Sorry, but he's out at the moment," Maddie said.

Caitlyn cleared the lump from her throat.

"No. Actually I want to file a sexual harassment complaint."

~

Maddie made sure Ethan read Caitlyn's complaint as soon as he arrived back in the office.

"Why didn't she say anything before?" Ethan asked, his face red with anger. It hit him then. She had tried to bring this up when they were at the school, but he was too focused on the murder investigation to listen.

"These things are too painful, Sheriff. You see how long it took her to come to grips with the situation? It's not easy," Maddie replied.

"I'm going to the school to get to the bottom of this," Ethan said as he grabbed his keys and headed out the door.

~

Ethan was buzzed into the high school and immediately went to the superintendent's office where he explained the complaint he received.

"Since I am fairly new to this school, I haven't any knowledge of this type of behavior from Coach Kollner. Let's go talk with Mrs. Lowe. The kids tend to go to her when they have something bothering them. She has been here as long as the coach so maybe she knows something."

Upon entering her office, Ethan came right to the point. His harsh tone was used to get results. From the look on Mrs. Lowe's face, he was successful, especially with the superintendent looking on.

"Why, I didn't know, I don't have any idea," she stammered.

Ethan could tell she was lying, and so he went in for the kill.

"How many girls have come to you over the years, Mrs. Lowe? How many young women in this school have endured the 'attentions' of the coach?"

He watched as Mrs. Lowe began to shake, fumble with the papers on her desk. He suspected she was not used to having people talk to her that way. She looked to the superintendent to stop the verbal assault, but he stood his ground with arms crossed.

"I have nothing more to say," Mrs. Lowe declared. "How dare you come in here and accuse two dedicated school staff of such behaviors? You ought to lose your job. Her defiant look told Ethan everything he needed to know, and thankfully the superintendent wasn't going to interfere.

"You might not have anything more to say now, Mrs. Lowe, but I'll be back to talk with you either here or in my office," Ethan said.

Ethan and the superintendent left the office and walked down the hall. Halfway back Ethan turned and said, "I'd like to talk with Susan Doyle again."

"I thought Todd's murder was solved?"

"I want to ask her help with this issue," Ethan responded.

Superintendent Boynton hesitated, fear mounting as to what Pandora's box was being opened by this line of investigation.

"Are you sure it's appropriate?"

"I think this abuse is far reaching over a couple generations of students, and those going through this building now are not immune. I think Susan can help persuade others to come forward." Ethan said.

"Okay, then, I'll have her join you in the small conference room," Superintendent Boynton responded.

~

Ethan watched Susan Doyle walk into the room. He could tell she was wondering what trouble she was in now. He knew she had quit the environmental movement whose main goal was destruction, and found an organization that used positive steps to improve the environment.

What Ethan asked her was totally unexpected. She began to cry, and was embarrassed by her tears and what she felt. She never wanted anyone to know about what went on in the locker room, and in fact had been threatened if she told anyone.

"I need you to spread the word, quickly and quietly. Say I asked you to help. It doesn't implicate you at all. You are the conduit into the female student pipeline here. Do you understand? We need to stop this behavior now," Ethan explained.

"I don't know. I don't know if I can do it. I'm scared," Susan replied wiping the tears away. "What if he finds out I'm asking around? And I don't know if there is anyone else."

"I *know* there are others. In fact, the complaint we received at the station was from someone who graduated many years ago. We'll follow up with the graduates, but for now I'm confident you can do it. You're a strong person. You've proven that you stand up for what you believe in. Look at what you are accomplishing on behalf of the environment?" Ethan said.

"This is different. He threatened me," Susan said.

"His threats have no power over you anymore. He'll no longer be employed by the school, and in fact, will probably serve jail time. You do know that sexual harassment isn't about sex. It's about power. Power over another person. I think Coach Kollner picked the most popular girls, and possibly boys, to harass and threaten. He's on a power trip," Ethan explained. "We, and the adults in the school, are here to see that you and any others are protected. Susan, I once saw a sign that said, 'When good people fail to act, evil persists.' Do you want evil to persist in this school?"

"No, I guess not," Susan replied.

"O.k. then spread the word. I'm going to sit in this room for the next two hours. After that I can be reached on my cell, and on this card are my contact numbers. Everything said will remain confidential."

~ FIFTY-SEVEN ~

Jerry decided to spend another day in Albany. He wanted to see his new office, even though Senator Harrison made it clear Jerry was not to be seen in the legislative office area until he was confirmed. But curiosity won out, so here he was walking down the hallway in which his new office was located. When he reached the door, a sign indicating the office of Senator Smith was still in place. Jerry figured that would be removed within the next few days, after a respectful period of mourning was observed.

He noticed the door was open a crack, and wondered if Marty was working. He pushed the door open and peeked in. It was at that point he heard voices. Jerry slid into the room and closed the door behind him. He entered the outer office that held a desk, filing cabinet, and several comfortable looking chairs. All decorative items were removed, probably by the senator's wife, or maybe by Marty.

It was the tone of the voices coming from the inner office that disturbed him. He walked quietly to that door and peered in. The two "security" men who had searched his room for bugs before Senator Harrison's visit on Saturday had Marty Dent up against the wall.

"Make no mistake, Mr. Dent. If we find you in this office again, or even in this building, we won't hesitate to use a little more force. Do you understand?"

Marty nodded his head.

"Say it."

"Yes, I understand," Marty said.

"And if we catch you talking with Mr. Tilton, your life isn't going to be worth two cents. Is that understood?"

"Yes," Marty said in a whisper.

"We're watching you, Mr. Dent. And we're watching Tilton."

At that point the man backed away and let go of Marty's shirt. They seemed satisfied they had gotten Senator Harrison's message through. Jerry had to get out of there and quickly. If he was seen in the vicinity, he would be in big trouble and they might take revenge on Marty.

He walked quietly across the outer office and slipped back out the door. Gathering Senator Smith's supporters was going to be more difficult than he thought. He walked quickly down the hall until he spotted a men's room and slipped inside. He waited a good length of time before leaving. Taking a deep breath and praying no one was in the hall, he carefully opened the men's room door and peeked out. No one in sight, and as he walked by Senator Smith's office, the door was now shut tight.

~

Caitlyn watched the now familiar landscape disappear as the plane righted itself and headed south. Her seat belt was safely fastened and her seat was in its upright position. The dog carrier containing Summit was safely stowed under her seat until the plane reached altitude. As she put her head on the headrest she thought about all that happened in the last two weeks. A wave of emotions washed over her.

Before she left, Nick called to tell her the senator had learned about his off the books consulting. The senator was furious that Nick would jeopardize "his" energy bill by selling out to an oil company.

Nick was now out of a job, and probably would not be hired by anyone else in Washington. As he told her, Washington is a small town. He would be blackballed. He wasn't sure what he was going to do, and he surely didn't want to go back home.

Nick was good at what he did, and he loved to travel. He was now paying for a lack in judgment, and that is as it should be. But since their relationship began and continued under false pretenses, she knew she would never be able to trust him. She hated breaking up with him over the phone, but she would not lead him on. She made it clear their relationship was finished. She just hoped he would not keep calling.

Unsure about whether her relationship with Ethan would continue, and whether she wanted a long distance relationship, Caitlyn would concentrate on building her business and keep her clients happy. That would take up much of her time. Maybe she would take a long weekend and fly to Florida to visit her parents. There was a lot of relationship mending there to be done.

While packing she received a call from Abbie, who continued to fight her disease. A big part of that fight was mental attitude and Abbie was already thinking about this year's harvest and planning special events at the winery. They were going to have the best year ever, and develop some new blends.

Abbie shared ideas for the winery's new brochure. Caitlyn promised to work on that as soon as she got home, and she promised to return in the fall to taste their new vintage.

~ FIFTY-EIGHT ~

Late September

Caitlyn Jamison watched the cursor blink on the computer screen. A quick glance at the top right corner of the same screen showed the digits turn to 5:00 P.M. An empty bag of potato chips lay to her left with crumbs marking a trail from the bag to her keyboard.

It was hump day. The photos taken early this morning at the National Zoo had been downloaded and carefully placed within the annual report of her new client, World Environmental Group. She had acquired the World Environmental Group account upon recommendation of The Outdoor Foundation.

The fact it was her uncle who had continued Senator Smith's work to stop hydraulic fracturing in New York State had won her points with her new clients, and she hoped her creative talents also counted in those recommendations.

October was just around the corner and the smell of fall was in the air. Caitlyn couldn't believe the summer months were just a memory, although she looked forward to cooler nights. She could barely tolerate the hot muggy summers in DC.

She hadn't seen Nick over the summer, for which she was much relieved.

On the other hand, Ethan called often. Conversations were easy as they shared information about what was going on in their lives. He called when Darcy was released from the hospital. While there he had interviewed her and as soon as she was well enough he arrested her for the murder of Todd Tilton. That was supposed to bring closure, but in reality it didn't. Caitlyn liked the Risley's and still couldn't believe Darcy was capable of such an act.

Thoughts of Ethan brought Caitlyn to think about the few dates she had had over the summer. She had met a couple of nice guys at the local bar meet-up events, but none she cared to spend much time with.

What's wrong with me? Why can't I find just the right guy? Am I being too picky?

Caitlyn couldn't shut her thoughts off, so she tried to focus on the more positive things in her life.

Her mother finally called Myra, and according to her aunt, they had a good talk. Caitlyn hoped the sisters could mend their relationship and the two couples become a foursome again. The family would never be able to fill the void left by Todd's tragic death, nor the many years they were apart. There are some things that can't be fixed. Life goes on and each member of the family had to find their own way.

Uncle Jerry was an enigma. Caitlyn was shocked when she learned he had gathered Senator Smith's supporters and they rallied to defeat the hydraulic fracturing bill. News headlines across the country screamed that hydraulic fracturing was no longer allowed in New York State. Senator Harrison and his followers were stunned, as were the Wall Street bankers. She wondered what role Matt Miller played, if any, in the water reservoir scheme.

Caitlyn knew there had to be more to the story. Her uncle wouldn't change his stripes so drastically. There had to be some plan in the making that would allow for the oil companies to continue with their drilling activities. She'd have to wait for that plan to reveal itself. In the meantime, her uncle had his hands full mending the bridges he burned by voting the legislation down. She was certain it would be back up for a vote at some point.

There will be more to this story, she thought.

In the meantime, she was proud that her uncle and a group of junior legislators were in the process of helping the people of Avalon recoup their investment.

~

Caitlyn went through the process of closing down her computer for the day. She sighed. Her weekend calendar was blank.

She looked down at the little white dog sitting by her desk. The soulful eyes looked at her and she knew it was time for a walk and then dinner. She was so glad she had brought Summit back with her. Her days were never empty with him constantly by her side.

Caitlyn grabbed the retractable leash and headed for the door.

"Let's go little fellow," she said.

Her phone rang with a familiar chime and the now familiar area code appeared on the screen.

"This is Caitlyn," she said with a smile.

"Caitlyn, it's Ethan. We've got another murder and I was wondering . . ."

Acknowledgements

I am indebted to a number of people who made this book possible. First, I thank my sister, Michelle Jackson, who suggested years ago that I write about Munchausen's by Proxy.

I would be remiss if I didn't acknowledge my parents Ed and Carol Nunn for their decision to raise their family along the shores of Cayuga Lake in Upstate New York. This beautiful area lends itself as the perfect setting for any book.

A special thank you goes to my four first readers who helped me achieve a deeper level of writing: Cheryl Wicks, Andrea Zimmermann, Melissa Maki, and Marian Wood.

Where would we be without the support of writing groups? I thank my writing groups at the C.H. Booth Library, the Central Rappahannock Regional Library, and the Virginia Chapter of Sisters in Crime.

I am grateful to Richard Welch of Cayuga Images who graciously provided permission to use his photograph for the cover.

My friend and neighbor Suzette Young did a great job designing the cover. She shared her creativity, time and *patience* as I muddled through.

And Summit, who unbeknownst to me, inserted himself into the book making it even more special. Thank you little guy.

I wouldn't have gotten this far if it hadn't been for the love and support of my husband, Ray, and children Melissa and Brennen.

Made in the USA
Charleston, SC
22 November 2015